i want candy

By Kim Wong Keltner

I Want Candy
Buddha Baby
The Dim Sum of All Things

i want candy

Kim Wong Keltner

An Imprint of HarperCollinsPublishers

HarperCollins books may be purchased for educational, business, or sales promotional use. For information please write: Special Markets Department, HarperCollins Publishers, 10 East 53rd Street, New York, NY 10022.

FIRST EDITION

Interior text designed by Diahann Sturge

Library of Congress Cataloging-in-Publication Data
Keltner, Kim Wong.
   I want candy / Kim Wong Keltner.—1st ed.
   p. cm.
ISBN: 978-0-06-084798-2
1. Teenage girls—Fiction.   2. Chinese Americans—Fiction.
3. Chinese American families—Fiction.   I. Title.

PS3611.E48I3   2008
813'.6—dc22   2007020024

08 09 10 11 OV/RRD 10 9 8 7 6 5 4 3 2 1

i want candy

The Eggroll Girl

*N*one of the Judy Blume books had Chinese people in them. There was no *Are You There God, It's Me, Mei-Ling*, and I wouldn't have minded finding a book like that, especially because I'd just gotten my period for the first time two months before.

I'd been sitting at home on the couch, getting ready to write my social studies report, Small Mammals Who Call the Rainforest Home, when I felt a weird, hot sensation and then something gushed out of me and onto my underwear. Good thing the sofa cushions were covered in thick plastic. I held my hand over my crotch and ran to the bathroom, and after changing my underpants, I stuck a wad of toilet paper down there and went to get my mom. The restaurant was really busy, so while my mom crammed a to-go box full of *chow mein*, she explained to me matter-of-factly that under the bathroom sink upstairs were a belt and some pads.

A belt for what? Holding my crotch, I carefully walked back up the steps, went into the bathroom, dug around, and found the stuff. My mom eventually came upstairs and showed me how to put on the elastic belt and hook the hammock-like pad through the loops to keep it in place. I felt like a sumo wrestler. I asked about adhesive pads, but my mom said they were a waste of money because the belt thingy worked just as well, and furthermore, the nonadhesive pads were cheaper by five cents each, which over time, added up to big savings. As I got used to the feeling of the pad in my underwear, my dad yelled up, "What taking so long?"

Really loud, my mom yelled back, "Candace body just become ready for sex!"

It was 1983 and I was feeling my hand along the cool, clammy wall of fourteen-years-old. The wall, I knew, was only in my head, but it was the blockade between who I was—a fat, fucking dork—and who I wanted to be, the girl on the cover of *Candy-O*. I imagined Ric Ocasek from the Cars looking through the window of Eggroll Wonderland and seeing me toiling at the deep fryer, arranging six cream cheese-filled wontons on a plate with a side of red sauce. I was sure that only a rock star could save me from my ho-hum, chicken drumstick life.

I still liked to read Maurice Sendak's *Where the Wild Things Are*, but on the radio, Lou Reed beckoned, "Hey, Babe, take a walk on the wild side." Through my TV-glazed eyes I was checking out the world, and I was confused to find that the actress who was Jan Brady now played a hooker in a short fur coat. Another girl I once saw on *The Courtship of Eddie's Father* had become a young poisoner in *The Little Girl Who Lives Down the Lane*. What lane did I live on? Where *Sesame Street* met *The Streets of San Francisco*.

My whole life, I lived in Eggroll Wonderland. That was the name of the Chinese restaurant where my family worked. My parents dreamed of someday owning the place. But seriously, that was my idea of hell. An assortment of San Francisco's desperate, perverted freaks frequented the place, and I wondered why they all came here, and why they all liked Chinese food so much.

My dad was a cook, dishwasher, and busboy all rolled into one. He wore an apron stained with brown gravy, and he always had shrimp particles splattered on his shoes. When he came home to our apartment above the restaurant, he smelled of grease and beef. As for my mom, she was an expressionless waitress who shuffled back and forth in a daze, waiting on tables and running the take-out counter. She would bark over the microphone, talking to my dad back in the kitchen, telling him which things in the trays needed to be replenished. She yelled, "*Chow fun, Gai Lan Ngow Yook, Gah-lee Gai, Woh-tik . . .*" There were only two things she barked in English and they were always meant for me, either "crab Rangoon" or "eggroll." If it was a rush job, she added, "*Fai-dee, Bi Bi . . .*"

I was the *Bi Bi*, still a baby in my parents' eyes, even though I had a younger brother. For some reason, he never had to work in the restaurant, but I did. I'd been chopping bamboo shoots and water chestnuts since I was small, having learned to hold a cleaver before a pencil. Instead of playing with building blocks like regular kids, I used to stack wobbly cubes of tofu, and when my parents bought me a Fisher-Price stepstool it wasn't for fun, but so I could look over the stovetop. When I first started frying eggrolls, I think I was about five years old. As far as my parents were concerned, I was employable.

Ever since I could remember, I was the restaurant's eggroll girl. It was my job to toss the hand-rolled, cabbage-and-pork appetizers into the hot oil. I timed it just right so the wheat wrapper got to be like crispy paper, but not too brown. Plucking them out just in time, I arranged them on a plate with a ramekin of bright red sauce. I performed the identical task with the cream cheese-filled wontons called crab Rangoon.

But even though we were restaurant workers, we weren't poor. At least I didn't think we were. My dad always said it wasn't how much money you made, but how much you saved that counted. And my parents had saved a lot. Enough to send me and my little brother, Kenny, to private school, and enough to have a few nice things around the house, like the burlwood coffee table, some porcelain statues of Chinese gods, and tons of toys for Kenny that were constantly strewn about the living room, even though he never even played with them anymore.

Although I didn't get an allowance, I had saved a lot of money, too. Ever since I was a little kid, I knew I didn't want to work in a Chinese restaurant my entire life, or any part of my life, for that matter. I was dead serious about saving money for my imminent escape. Each Chinese New Year, adults gave me *lay-see* envelopes with bills inside—fives, tens, or twenties, depending on how well the people knew my family. The red envelopes came in pairs, and had pictures of children or fruit on them, or gold Chinese characters that signified words like "prosperity," or "good luck." I didn't give a Fig Newton about what the envelopes looked like. The important part was the money inside, and I was proud of having saved all my *lay-see* from the last three years.

But I had even been saving money before that, too. I stashed cash that I acquired from the tooth fairy, coins I found beneath the sofa cushions, even dimes and pennies that I fished out of the street gutter. I "borrowed" money from the ceramic chicken on my dad's nightstand, and when change came spitting down the chute at the checkout stand at Safeway, I scooped out the coins before my parents noticed.

Occasionally, I also slid the meager tips off the restaurant tables and told my mom that the cheapskates left nothing. I was certain I would need the money someday for my as-of-yet unplanned escape from Eggrollville, so I carefully hid my money, and rotated the secret hiding place from time to time in case my brother was ever snooping around for extra cash. My current savings were under the bed, wedged in the wheel-well of my Barbie Corvette.

Plus, I needed *cashish* for certain things I couldn't ask my parents to buy. Embarrassing things. Zit cream. Boxes of Kotex with Cathy Rigby spreading her legs on a balance beam. I was still too squeamish to try tampons even though my best friend, Ruby, said that once the cotton pony was in, it was like not having your period at all. Ruby also said a tampon went in the same hole where a guy stuck his Thing during sex. But I figured she was just a liar.

Anyway, I was walking home from school one day, heading back to Eggroll Wonderland. Working there was so automatic, I didn't even say hi to my mom, just went right in and started shelling a huge pile of peas. When I was done, I got up to clear away small dishes of hot mustard and sweet and sour sauce from the adjacent table. When the restaurant emptied out, I tromped through the kitchen, zigzagging through the pallets of onions and oranges in plastic netting. I passed the stacked cans of baby corn and button mushrooms, and ducked under the makeshift laundry line hanging with dried Chinese sausages. I headed up the back stairs that led to our apartment.

On the second floor, in the tidy, carpeted flat, I smelled Chinese food. The aroma of stale rice, soy sauce, and cooking oil was both comforting and sickening, and permeated every room. I passed the kitchen with its orange-and-yellow wallpaper and particle-board cabinets, and pausing by the aluminum-framed window, I parted the heavy drapes and stared briefly at the bus as it accelerated by, its lights illuminating the streaky rain that began to patter.

The San Francisco I lived in was primarily bordered by the route of the 19 Polk, which was the bus that took me most places I needed to go. It stopped right in front of Eggroll Wonderland, went all the way to Pier 39 in one direction, to the Main Library the other way, and in between was my school and Ruby's place.

Continuing down the dim hallway, I ducked into my little room. I sat on my twin bed with its rainbow sheets and stared at the wall. The unicorn-Pierrot motif was white-hot that year, and my room reflected the trend. I had a calendar, Pee-Chees, stationery, and blankets that depicted faeries, centaurs, and assorted diaphanously clothed man-beasts. From the wall, surveying my dioramas of fairyland creatures, were David Bowie from the *Young Americans* album cover and Adam Ant from *Kings of the Wild Frontier*. On my pillowcase, the Fiorucci angels hid their bloodshot peepers behind star-shaped sunglasses.

As I looked around my room, I had to admit I had a lot of stuffed animals. And thank god I did. More often than not, in the quiet darkness of wide-awake nights, Jemima Puddleduck and Señor Mouse were deployed to play hide-and-seek in my underpants. I had no words to explain why Mr. Ferrettface had permanently matted fur, but many mornings I awoke with his snout still cozily snug between my warm legs.

Sitting on my bed, I grabbed my beanbag frog, Big Mama, and held it against my cheek. The frog reminded me of my dead Auntie Melaura. She had been real pretty, and was even a runner-up for Miss Chinatown USA when I was little. But one afternoon she slipped and hurt her back while ice-skating at the Sutro Baths. Doctors put her on medication that ended up making her crazy. She wasn't her same self, but crying, swearing, and moaning all the time. She was no longer the favorite daughter, or the pretty auntie, just the crazy lady. She would sit in her bedroom for hours laughing to herself or writing letters addressed to my mom saying that Kenny and I were going to die. One time, she hid behind the bushes on the sidewalk and chased away the mailman with a meat cleaver. Another time she took off all of her clothes and walked around downtown. The police brought her home.

These were stories that I had heard whispered over the years. I wondered what really had happened, but no one in my family would say anything.

The only thing I did remember was from when I was about eight. Auntie Melaura pulled me inside a closet and plinked on the light switch.

"You love me?" she asked.

"Yeah," I said, hoping for some candy.

"Good girl," said my aunt. She pulled a hand-sewn, bean-bag frog as big as a catcher's mitt out of a plastic bag, and added, "I made this for you."

I held out my small hands and accepted the hefty frog. It was made of two fabrics—a fuzzy, cream-colored fur on top and the underbelly done in a silky-to-the-touch calico pattern. The frog's button-eyes were cheery in a way that Auntie Melaura's were not.

"Thanks," I said, enjoying the slippy feeling of the dried beans shifting within as I pulled the frog's arms and legs this way and that. Upending the soft, gigantic amphibian, I let all the beans drain from the hind legs and swung the frog around like a medieval weapon.

"And this is for good luck," Auntie Melaura said, taking off her gold chain with a jade pendant carved in the smooth shape of a curled-up rabbit. She slipped it over my neck, and as she popped it under my collar I could still feel her body's warmth in the jade as it came to rest against my flat chest.

I was at home later that same afternoon when the police came to the door. I remembered my mom screaming, and when I jumped off the couch and asked, "What's wrong?" my mother slapped me hard against my face and yelled, "Go to your room and stay there!"

Crying on my bed, I had hugged my beanbag frog. Nobody had specifically told me that Auntie Melaura was dead, or how it happened, but I'd figured it out from whispered conversations. After she'd given me Big Mama and the jade necklace, Auntie Melaura had driven to the Golden Gate Bridge, set her purse on the railing, and jumped off. The coast guard retrieved her body out of the bay near Baker Beach.

At the Cathay funeral parlor in Chinatown, I sat alone in the lobby on a chair upholstered with a pink, floral pattern. I wasn't allowed in the chapel room, and sat in that chair even while the funeral procession went out to the cemetery. Hours later, my parents picked me up and we drove home. Kenny was just a baby, and I remember him wailing in the car. My parents never talked about Auntie Melaura again, and nobody ever asked me where I'd gotten my jade necklace or my beanbag frog.

Now I reached up to my throat and touched my jade necklace, sort of a nervous habit. With my sleeve I gave a light dusting to my tape player, turntable, and radio, and took a second to rearrange my cassettes and records, then paused to check on my pet hamster, Twinkiechubs, who was sleeping. After unsuccessfully trying to wake her by tapping on the Habitrail wall, I went out to the hall. Opening the door that led to the restaurant kitchen, I took a few steps down, but hung back in the darkness of the stairwell, watching.

Through the kitchen door I could see my mother going about her tasks. Even though a few minutes ago the place was empty, now there were three tables with customers, and my mom was bringing them all glasses of water. Walking back and forth, she looked as if she could do it in her sleep, like a mouse who had learned to zigzag in a maze. My dad came into view, stopping in front of the row of gas burners to sauté something in a wok. Fire was flashing in the pan as he tossed the contents with chopsticks and smoked a cigarette with his free hand. His expression was somewhere between blank and pensive, the same as when he was changing television channels with the clicker.

Heading down the stairs, I stopped and stood at my dad's side, quietly observing as he lifted a huge portion of purple eggplant and pink shrimp into a stainless steel tray.

"You bring out," he said, mumbling with the cigarette in his mouth. He carried the empty wok over to a deep sink and blasted it with water, sending up a billow of steam.

I stared at the steaming mound of food. The dish was called General Tso's Eggplant, with red peppers and a sticky, sweet sauce. I had no idea who General Tso was, but I brought the tray out just the same, walking past the cash register to the front take-out counter. Lifting up an almost-empty tray of spareribs, I replaced it with the eggplant, making sure to check the level of hot water in the trough below which kept all the to-go stuff warm.

That done, I couldn't wait to get out of there. I scanned the restaurant and saw a group of people waiting for their check. Another table was occupied by someone sitting alone. I recognized him as a guy who worked at the copy place down the block. He looked like Martin Fry from ABC. I figured he must be on his lunch break.

Just then, my mom caught my eye, giving me a nod that signaled it was okay for me to go, but right before I stepped out the door, she yelled, "Wait! Order, eggroll!"

Ugh. I stopped in my tracks and ran back into the kitchen. The eggrolls, preassembled the night before, rested like miniature logs on a cookie sheet in the fridge. I grabbed three with my bare hand and trudged to my frying station. There was a skillet of oil waiting for me, and I turned on the gas until the bubbles formed. I gently dropped the eggrolls into the hot oil, and waited about two minutes, until they floated to the top. Fishing them out at the right moment with a mesh spoon, I deposited them onto a porcelain plate and placed a dish of sauce on the side. I did this roughly ten times a day, every day of the year, even on Christmas. With simple math I calculated that it was 3650 times per year. At three eggrolls per order, that meant I cooked more than ten thousand eggrolls each year. I didn't know how much longer I could stand it.

Fast out of the kitchen, I saw my mom nod, signaling that the eggrolls were for the Martin Fry guy. Without looking at his face, I delivered the appetizers, then wanted desperately to leave before anyone else ordered something I'd have to get. As I moved toward the door, the guy snickered, "Thanks, eggroll girl." The way he said it, I could tell I was somehow being put down. Not looking back, I ran out the door and hoped he'd choke to death.

A Big, Red Target
Painted on Her Ass

Walking to my best friend Ruby's house, I shuffled along the sidewalk, still thinking about my first period. I told myself it could have been worse. For instance, look what happened to Ruby.

It was two years before, on St. Patrick's Day. We didn't have to wear our uniforms since it was a holiday. As we were all lining up to buy our Shamrock Shakes that were specially delivered from McDonald's, Ruby walked up in her green shirt and white Jordache jeans to get hers, and she had this bright spot of blood leaking out onto the seam of her pants. It looked like a big, red target painted on her ass, and all these kids pointed at her butt and laughed. I ran across the schoolyard and whisked Ruby to the bathroom. Taking off my own sweater, I let Ruby tie it around her waist to hide The Spot. For the rest of the day she went around with the cardigan covering her butt, lying to everybody by saying that she sat on a red Magic Marker. But everyone knew the truth, even the boys. Really, I thought that was just about the worst thing that could happen to anybody.

"Hi, Cissy," I said, walking into her mom's shop, Empress Wu's Antiques. "Ruby here?"

"Yeah, upstairs."

Cissy was regluing kingfisher feathers onto a fancy headdress. There were Peking opera costumes and lots of hats, fans, and pretty fabrics all around the place. I liked hanging around and thought I might like Cissy even if she wasn't Ruby's mom. Actually, sometimes I wished that Cissy was my mom instead, and maybe then Ruby would be the one stuck frying eggrolls all day and night.

I went through the beaded curtain and headed down the hallway to the back of the store where rows of spider plants and dead ferns were lined up on either side of the runner. Ducking under another drape, I entered a huge kitchen, and went up the back stairs. At the end of another dark hallway with cupid heads on the cornices, I found Ruby in her room.

Like me, Ruby was still in her school uniform. With a huge set of earphones on her dainty head, she was dancing around with her eyes closed and her skinny arms flailing around. The music was cranked up so loud that, as I stood there, I could hear a tinny version of "Does Your Mother Know" by Abba blasting through the headphones.

Ruby and I had been best friends since fourth grade, and I couldn't believe we were already eighth-graders. For the last few years we'd been the *Say, Say, Oh Playmate* schoolyard champs, meaning we were faster than anyone at hand-clapping games, so much that no one even challenged us anymore. Even still, school could only be described as a major suck-a-thon. We couldn't wait to get out each day and watch Afterschool Specials on TV, or go to Pier 39 to check out the bulges on the high-divers who jack-knifed into the Plexiglass cubes. Ruby said one day when I wasn't there, one diver's dick flopped out, and I missed it. She said I was always missing good shit. Of course, instead of realizing that Ruby made herself feel better by putting me down, I just focused on the certainty that I was a total dip. I thanked God she let me be her friend.

"We're not like the other girls at school," Ruby had said the week before. Her comment had nothing to do with the fact that she and I were both Chinese. There were several other Chinese kids at school. She meant something different. "We're seekers," she said. "And jailbait to boot."

I wasn't exactly sure what she meant by that. Maybe it had something to do with the fact that late at night, in the darkness of my bedroom, I kissed my pillow and pretended it was Adam Ant while I shoved a stuffed animal between my legs. Pathetic, yeah, but it was better than frying eggrolls. And just as she'd never had to fry an eggroll, I was sure Ruby didn't have to rely on plush pals to get herself off, either. We didn't really talk about sex stuff, but I could tell something was going on with her. Maybe she'd even Done It.

I wasn't sure. As I watched her dancing around the room, I was too mortified to think anymore about whether or not my friend had Done It, so instead I thought about how different her house was from mine. Except for Kenny's toys all over the place, our apartment was superclean. My mom swept, mopped, and vacuumed constantly, whereas Ruby's carpets looked and smelled like they hadn't been vacuumed in a way long time. And furthermore, while I slept on a twin bed covered in clean, white cotton, Ruby slept on a queen-sized waterbed with black satin sheets. When the black sheets were in the wash (and that wasn't very often), Ruby just slept on the bare mattress, and lots of times just in her uniform clothes or whatever she happened to be wearing that day. I had never *not* changed into my Holly Hobbie nightgown before going to sleep, no matter how tired I was. Also, I always had clean underwear, and Ruby never seemed to. She bragged about how she saved on doing laundry by turning her undies inside out to wear them a second day, which I thought was just disgusting. Half the time she also wore her bathing suit or bikini bottoms instead of clean panties, which was also totally weird.

But still. Everything at Ruby's seemed free and bohemian, and I was jealous. As far as I could tell, Ruby never got grilled about getting straight A's, and she could eat Ding Dongs and Twinkies for dinner. However, I did suppose maybe one drawback was that Ruby's socks were always dirty and smelled like corn chips. Cissy never did Ruby's laundry or made her lunch because she was always either working in the boutique or going out late at night with some barfbag. Nonetheless, hands down, I would have much preferred to have Ruby's life and suffer that one small thing, Corn Chip Socks Syndrome.

Still dancing, Ruby flapped over and hit me in the face by accident.

"Whoa!"

She jumped back and laughed. Yanking off her headphones, she said, "Ready to go to the pier?"

As she raced around the messy room looking for her shoes, I glanced around and noticed she didn't have any stuffed animals. On top of the dresser she had a row of creepy dolls that I think her mom got for her. I carefully touched them and read their little tags. A porcelain one was named Queue San Baby, and a chinky-faced cloth doll had a label that said it was made by Ada Lum, whoever that was. The dolls looked dead and gave me the creeps so I found an *Aladdin Sane* T-shirt on the floor and put it over their heads.

"What are you doing?" Ruby asked.

"Nothing," I said, darting into the hall. We headed down a set of stairs. Just like in my apartment, at Ruby's there were two ways to exit—a stairwell that led to the storefront down below, and a separate set of stairs that led out to the street. We took the one that led directly to the sidewalk outside because we didn't want to go past her mom. As cool as Cissy was, we didn't need her asking us where we were going.

Out on the sidewalk, Ruby immediately began to sluttify her uniform by rolling down the waistband of her skirt, and hiking it up to shorten it. She then proceeded to undo the top buttons of her blouse.

"That's really hussy of you," I said.

"So what?"

I started to adjust my uniform, too, but she shot me an annoyed look. "Don't copy me," she said.

Some pervert passing by slowed down to check us out. "You two look like twins," he said. While Ruby shot back, "Fuck off," I was secretly pleased to be considered on her level.

We walked down toward the Maritime Museum, and eventually Ruby said, "Maybe you'll have nice ones someday."

"What?"

"Tits. I really like my tits." Ruby leaned forward a little, reached into her blouse, and rearranged hers.

As she walked a little bit ahead of me, I stewed over this comment. Was it my imagination, or did Ruby say stuff to deliberately make me feel like shit? Even though Ruby was my friend, I knew she kept me down. Maybe life was governed by the same laws as television, where there was always a good-looking person, and then a not-as-pretty sidekick. For every Lucy Ricardo was there an Ethel Mertz? Would Mr. Roarke be so powerful on *Fantasy Island* without Tattoo to kick around? Well, if I had to admit it, I was definitely the not-so-good-looking sidekick, much to my distress. But it was the truth. I ran a little to catch up with Ruby, and cast a sidelong glance at her breasts with their always-pointy nipples that reminded me of those small snail shells I sometimes found at Aquatic Park.

I knew that the plain-Jane sidekick on TV never got the dates, and unfortunately, this was also my reality. If life were *The Facts of Life*, I definitely wouldn't have been Blair, or even Jo, the tough girl. I wouldn't have been Tootie since I wasn't black, and there wasn't even one Chinese girl in the background of that whole sitcom, even though it was a girls' school with hundreds of kids. Chinese girls didn't go to boarding school, I supposed. We toiled away in obscurity at Chinese restaurants and maybe got to deliver take-out to Natalie, the fat, Jewish girl who stayed home baking cookies with Mrs. Garrett while Blair was off screwing boys from Bates, the boys' school next door. On one episode, Blair even got busy with a gorgeous guy who turned out to be mentally retarded. There was no doubt in my mind that Fat Natalie and I would both take a hunky retard over Mrs. Garrett any day, but such was the fate of porky Jewish girls and Chinese sidekicks of beautiful sluts.

Slut? Yeah. Ruby's sluttification of her uniform wasn't just for show. As of late she'd been much more a Playboy Playmate than a *Say, Say, Oh Playmate*, unlike me who was stuck in my middle-school groove. This jaunt to Pier 39 was probably going to result in Ruby ditching me for some guy. How did I know? Because she'd been doing it since the beginning of the school year.

Ruby kept saying she wanted to hang out with me, but invariably she ended up going off with some guy while I walked or took the bus home alone. I knew today would be no different. I was a stooge to keep falling for it, but I still did. I kept hoping that one of these times Ruby really might mean it when she said she wanted to hang out, even though I'd figured that she probably just didn't like to take the bus by herself.

"Hey," Ruby said, interrupting my thoughts. "Don't you think I have perfect-sized ones? They're not too big, and not too small." Looking straight ahead, she smiled to herself, seeming satisfied. Even though I made no comment, she added, "I just like them; that's all."

She had a way of always bringing the conversation around to herself, and I obliged. "Yeah," I said, "Remember when you had that disgusting wart on your finger? It was bigger than a pencil eraser and had a long hair coming out of it like a tail. Every time I happened to look at it I almost barfed. But nobody at school cared. They just stared at your tits because that was back when you didn't even wear a bra."

"Nobody stared," Ruby countered, but looked secretly pleased.

"Yeah, they did. And remember when you were picking at the wart and accidentally ripped it off, spurting blood all over the floor during 'The Life of Jesus'? The nuns didn't even make you clean it up. They made the janitor clean it instead. See, even the nuns think you're pretty. Sister Mary said you're 'an angelic child, like Bernadette of Lourdes.' Barf. Bernadette probably had perfect tits, too. The Virgin Mary probably only appears to you if your boobs are perfect. See, I'm screwed. Mary's never going to appear to me because my boobs already feel saggy."

Ruby laughed. "Why don't you diet? Just because we *are* fourteen doesn't mean you have to be a *size* fourteen. Between basketball practice and walking back and forth on Polk Street, you could lose weight if you stopped eating all those sesame balls and pot stickers from the to-go tray."

As I walked by her side, I simmered. I knew I wasn't actually all that much bigger than Ruby. However, I'd been a fat little kid, and couldn't shake the fatso mentality. I once read somewhere that amputees continued to experience the nerve sensations of their long-ago, sawed-off limbs, and in that same way, although I had lost major poundage since fifth grade, the memory of my poochy butt and sausage fingers lingered on, and I was self-conscious. You might say I *acted* fat, and hence, was.

Fat, that is.

Believe it or not, though, Ruby and I could actually fit the same clothes sometimes. But whenever I asked to swap outfits, she hardly ever agreed. First off, all of her non-uniform clothes were so much cooler than mine. Ruby shopped at Macy's with her dad's credit card, and had stuff like leather miniskirts, ruffled socks, and fingerless gloves. I bought basic stuff on sale at Piccadilly, the discount store, or at Clothestime. But I pined for Ruby's clothes and when I asked to borrow anything, she always said no. The fact that she said no just made me want them even more, but I told myself it would be too disgusting to wear her clothes anyway because her pants that she wore without underwear probably had dried pee crust on them and the mere thought of that gave me the heebie-jeebies.

On the rare occasion that I actually scored something cool like purple jeans, a KUSF T-shirt, or a silver-studded belt, Ruby not only helped herself to my things, but kept them forever. "That looks dumb on you," she'd say to me, or "that belt emphasizes your widest part." She'd gnaw at me until I was ready to throw the thing away, then she'd take it and keep it so long that she'd "forget" it wasn't always hers in the first place.

These inequalities had been built into our relationship for a long time. When we were little, she always talked me out of my best Barbies, too, latching onto my Superstar, and only letting me play with the shitty Midge whose legs didn't bend and were discolored brown with age while Superstar's flesh was new and piggy-pink. Years ago she'd glommed onto my Snoopy doll and all his outfits, including his doctor and Elton John costumes. I doubted she even remembered they were mine to begin with, but her taking the best of my stuff and me letting her, at this point, were a fixed part of life.

Ruby's prettiness and my fatness were a foregone conclusion as well. Ever since we were little, she was the pretty and dumb one, and I was her fat-but-smart sidekick. It's hard to say whether we came up with these definitions or if other people did. The descriptions just sort of descended upon us, but they stuck. At school, my good grades and her bad grades were accepted as the norm, and she was obviously attractive with her creamy skin, long hair, and perfect bod. I, of course, was not so perfect. Nor could I ever even think of myself that way. I was already ashamed of the little stretch marks around my waist and hips.

Truth be told, though, Ruby wasn't all *that* gorgeous with her crooked teeth and bitten-down nails, and I was only a *few* pounds overweight. Somehow though, our roles as The Pretty One and The Fat One just became the Truth, and somewhere along the line we silently had reached an understanding that these were the roles we would always play. If we were going to be Best Friends Forever, I assumed I had to be The Fat One forever if I was going to keep the Best Friend part, too.

But maybe it was just me thinking about these things. By all appearances, Ruby did as she pleased and didn't seem to ruminate endlessly on why life was so sucky. I figured her life was great so she didn't have to think about stupid shit like I did. Yet another way she was superior.

We kept walking and passed the Hibernia Bank on the corner of Vallejo Street. We went by the window and I could see Mrs. Martin, the teller, inside. As treasurer of my class, I visited this branch regularly with a passbook, and I occasionally borrowed from the class savings account if I was cash poor and there was a new cassette or album I wanted to buy. I was always careful to replace the money before anyone noticed. Of course, no one ever did because I was the only one with a passbook, and besides, good Chinese girls did not embezzle money. Secretly, I liked to do bad things, but maybe they weren't bad at all if no one found out.

Hopping on to the 19 Polk, Ruby and I headed to Pier 39. The bus ride was long but we shared an RC Cola that Ruby swiped from Quilici's Market.

"What are you doing this weekend?" I asked.

She took a gulp of soda and said, "I was supposed to go to my dad's, but thank God I don't have to."

Now here's a weird thing I didn't mention: Ruby's parents were divorced, and her dad, Mr. Ping, was the man who owned Eggroll Wonderland, where my family worked. He and Cissy weren't on friendly terms, but in their divorce settlement, she got the building where she lived and had her shop. For as long as Ruby and I had been friends, though, I never visited her when she was at her dad's, only at her mom's. Every few weeks Ruby would disappear to go stay with Mr. Ping awhile, somewhere in some unknown Richie Rich part of town. She always said she hated it there, and I wondered what it was like. It cast an extra aura of glamour to her, that she had some secret castle where she went off to. Shit, that was probably where all my good stuff ended up, come to think of it, because I never saw any of my former belongings at Cissy's place. And another thing, as much as Cissy was like a friend, Mr. Ping was

like a stranger, even though I'd known him all my life. To me
he was just the man who owned the restaurant and took care
of the plumbing occasionally. For all I knew, he didn't even
know that Ruby and I were friends.

"Have you been to the nightclub lately?" I asked. In addition to Eggroll Wonderland, Mr. Ping owned a bunch of busi-
nesses in San Jose. Ruby used to brag constantly about getting
to sit at her dad's bar drinking real, non-virgin daquiris, but it
suddenly occurred to me she hadn't mentioned it recently.

Ruby threw the empty cola can out the bus window. "No,"
she said. "I've been banned."

Now that sounded juicy. "Really? Why?"

She looked away, daydreaming out the bus window. She
had a look on her face that I'd been noticing more and more
lately. It was a hard expression, or rather, it seemed hard and
cold to me because it was a face that never looked my way. It
kept me out, like she was pondering some other world, one
that definitely didn't include me for some reason.

"You wouldn't get it," she whispered, staring out the glass.

A few seconds later, she turned to face me. "I hate going to
my dad's cuz he's such a Jesus freak, you know? And I can't
play any good music because he's always blasting freaky Chinese opera. And my grandma, jeez."

I nodded sympathetically, even though I'd never met her
grandmother. I wanted to talk more about the nightclub and
why she didn't get to go there anymore, but Ruby stood up
and pulled the cord.

Right at Fisherman's Wharf, we got off the bus and walked
the short distance to Pier 39. Years ago it had been nothing
special, but the area was recently refurbished as a tourist at-
traction with arcades, a carousel, T-shirt shops, and the usual
tacky stuff like saltwater taffy parlors and shit like that. We

sauntered past the colorful flags snapping in the wind, and headed into the darkness of the arcade where Ms. Pac-Man and the Bionic Woman pinball machine awaited us.

We immediately went for Galaga, but Ruby stopped in her tracks. She made a snotty face and said, "Those pimply W.P.O.D.s have staked their scuzzy claim on my favorite machine."

Ever since that Tubes song "White Punks on Dope" came out, Ruby called any guy she didn't like a W.P.O.D. We went over to Ms. Pac-Man, but it was also occupied, so we settled for Space Invaders.

"Got any quarters?" she asked, and I dropped two into the machine. Playing a few games against each other, Ruby whipped me by a mile because she was, like, the ninth best player and even had her initials listed on the scoreboard. The screen eventually flashed "game over" for me, but Ruby kept playing on her own. I watched for a while, but got bored of seeing the little plankton-spaceships dropping their bombs. I decided to go outside to get away from the popcorn-and-sneaker smell.

Pier 39 was mime ground zero. They were stationed every thirty feet or so along the rotting planks of the pier and all down the area where the ferries took off to go to Angel Island and Alcatraz. Groups of tourists were milling around everywhere, wearing shorty-shorts and poofy sweatshirts. They looked like marshmallows with toothpick legs as they chomped on churros and cotton candy.

I watched a clown in red polka-dotted pants as he attempted to make a balloon light-saber. He blew into the skinny piece of rubber and tied off the top, then tried to twist it to look like a sword. The balloon bent to the left and resembled an over-sized, red penis, not that I'd ever seen a real one. I continued to watch as he mangled it into a lumpy sausage, and the kid who was waiting started to cry. The clown said, "Jedi Knights don't cry," but the boy just started blubbering more.

When I returned to the arcade to look for Ruby, she was no longer playing Space Invaders. I wandered all over, until I noticed her uniform skirt and gangly legs poking out from the photo booth. The orange curtain was pulled shut, but I could see that she was sitting on some guy's lap. Through the part in the fabric, I could see that they were making out.

Gross. He was one of the pimply W.P.O.D.s.

I wondered if Ruby had just met him today, or knew him previously and had planned to meet him here all along. There was no point in barging in on them since I could already hear her instructions in my head, "Don't bug me. Just go home and I'll call you later." I was used to her ditching me for random guys, but it still stung every time. She was a dick magnet, and I was not, and that was the sad truth. Every time she went off with some guy, even if he was nasty, I felt a twinge of envy. I knew it was pathetic. As pathetic as spending my weekends frying eggrolls. As pathetic as kissing my pillow at night and pretending it was Adam Ant. As pathetic as grinding Jemima Puddleduck into my crotch.

Sneaking a last peek at the guy's hand on Ruby's thigh, I took off. I decided to walk to the grocery store up the street to buy some Pop Rocks, my favorite candy. I needed to stuff my face after being ditched. After buying a couple of packets, I ripped open the foil and poured a little into my mouth on the way to the bus stop. The crackles and sizzles on my tongue felt weird in a good way, and it was especially satisfying when a carbonated speck exploded between my cheek wall and one of my molars. I found a bench to sit on and spent the next twenty minutes watching shitty mimes and eating the two packets, dipping my wet finger into the foil when the dregs at the bottom became hard to retrieve.

The bus took a long time. I waited and boarded through the back door because the bus was really crowded and I knew I'd never get on in front. Swaying in the back with the high school kids from Galileo High School, I spaced out for a while. Between two big backpacks, and past an old lady's whipped-up hairdo, it took me a few minutes to realize that Ruby was on the same bus, up in front, sitting on the W.P.O.D.'s lap. In the time I'd gone to the Chinese market and sat on the bench stuffing my face, they must have gotten on at the bus stop before. They were making out, and Ruby's face was partially covered, but I could tell it was her.

Where were they going? In an instant I made up my mind that I was going to follow them. I didn't think Ruby would try to sneak him past her mom, so maybe they were going to his place, or somewhere to eat. The possibilities were endlessly fascinating to me. I'd never been on a date myself. Save for my midnight imaginings of Adam Ant, I had no idea what guys and girls really did together, and I wanted to find out.

It was warm inside the bus. I squeezed into a seat, and sitting at the edge, I kept my eyes focused, gazing at Ruby and the pimply guy. There was no way they could get off without me seeing them.

We rode for a long time. But then, on Market Street, suddenly I saw the two scramble off the bus, so I jumped off, too. Ruby and her W.P.O.D. climbed onto the 6 Parnassus that had just pulled to the curb, and I had to think fast in order to keep up. I ran and darted through the back door as a Mexican kid in black Ben Davis pants hopped off.

I wondered if they were going to Haight Street or Golden Gate Park, but they didn't get off near either place. I sat in the rear of the bus and slouched down behind a bunch of Cholos to avoid being seen.

The bus climbed up over the hills. Ruby and her pal were sitting near the front, in the seats reserved for handicapped people. He had his arm around her, and to the dismay of some old ladies, he periodically leaned in to suck on her tongue. Everyone on the bus couldn't stop watching them. They seemed to know they were being watched, too, and enjoyed the attention. The whole scenario made me wish I had more Pop Rocks.

Detaching his face from Ruby's, the W.P.O.D. wiped spit from his mouth, reached up, and yanked on the cord. They got off near the hospital on the hill, by the building that looked like a big waffle iron. I hesitated for a moment, not wanting them to spot me on the sidewalk. Then I jumped off the bus and hid behind a car. Ducking into some bushes, I then hopped behind a telephone pole before following them as they made their way up a few blocks. When they veered off the main street onto a service road that led into a forest of eucalyptus trees, I was pleased that the foliage made it easy for me to hide.

They hiked up the dirt path like they knew where they were going. Ruby stumbled and the guy laughed, stopping to cop a feel of her sweet ass. I followed, gazing up at the tree boughs in the wind. The leaves made a dry, swishing noise, like how I imagined taffeta prom dresses might sound brushing across a dance floor.

I followed them farther into the forest, through piles of fallen leaves, thickets of tangled branches, and lush swaths of dark green ivy. I scurried and dipped down through ditches to keep up until I heard the guy say, "There's the cave."

I hid behind a blackberry bush. Standing in a damp pile of

decaying bark, I arranged my feet carefully. Once I was fairly confident that I'd successfully hidden myself, I peeked through the tangle of branches to see what they were up to.

I watched as he climbed up and retrieved a rope from an upper branch of a eucalyptus tree. I stifled a laugh. *Hang myself when I get enough rope! White Punks on dope!*

Ruby kicked off her shoes and stepped onto the seat of the swing, pulling herself up. He slapped her butt cheeks, simultaneously giving her a shove into the air. Pushing her higher and higher, he palmed her butt every time. They looked like they were having fun.

Overhead, blades of sunlight split through the forest canopy. I hardly felt like I was in the city, and took a seat on a nearby, fallen log. It was a little wet from the rain earlier that day, but I sat and listened to the sounds of Ruby's laughter while I zoned in on an enormous banana slug feeling its way around the mossy tree trunk.

Watching the slimy creature, I listened to the sparrows, finches, and bluejays flitting around up in the high branches. They sang and tweeted, and pretty soon I no longer heard any noise coming from the rope swing on the other side of the blackberry bush. I turned around to take a look.

Ruby and the W.P.O.D. were making out, his hands kneading her tits, first outside her shirt, and then inside. He pulled up her skirt, and stuck his hand inside her underwear that, I noticed, were actually the bottoms to that striped bikini she bought last summer at Piccadilly. Figured. Ruby never had clean laundry.

He pulled the bikini bottoms down around her thighs, dropped to his knees, and in a quick maneuver, lunged his face right into her you-know-what. Holding her hips, he pushed his face between her legs, and I, watching, felt like a fat jerk. I heard my own shallow breathing, and imagined I was Ruby, feeling his mouth. Transfixed, I suddenly felt something gush in my underwear, even though I was fairly certain it wasn't time for my period.

He stopped to take off his jacket, and threw it down atop a pile of leaves. "Get down," he said, and Ruby did as she was told.

Still on his knees, he wasted no time in yanking off Ruby's bikini bottoms and tossing them. They flew up and landed about two feet from me, and I was watching so attentively I didn't care that my clothes were getting all dirty and my leg was starting to cramp. He undid his pants and I saw his one-eyed rat flop out.

"Spread your legs," he said, and Ruby lifted up her knees. I could see her face, but couldn't quite make out her expression. She just looked up at the pimply guy, and seemed neither happy nor sad, just plain, like she was wondering if it was going to rain. I watched his big hands clamp around her puny thighs as he pushed against her. Ruby turned her head to the side and made a sudden, distorted face like the time she took a swig of the distilled vinegar right from the bottle because I had dared her to.

The forest was quiet, and I didn't hear the birds anymore as I watched them Do It. I could hear the guy grunting as he pushed against her, but Ruby didn't make a peep. His butt looked flabby, and there was a dimple that puckered each time he thrust forward.

I climbed down and skidded across a narrow incline. Following the path back the way I came, soon enough, I was back down on Parnassus Street. Stopping on the sidewalk for a moment, I watched people walking by, going to work or to doctor's appointments. They didn't seem to care that I had just watched two people Doing It. Everyone looked lost in their own thoughts, and I turned and headed to the corner to catch the bus back to Eggroll Wonderland.

Candy-O, I Need You

The 19 Polk was crowded, but I crammed on, squishing past some old Chinese ladies and ending up somewhere in the middle, nowhere near a pole or seat edge to hold on to. The bus lurched into traffic, and I swayed with the crowd and couldn't help mushing my boobs against the stinky, drunk guy next to me. As all of us passengers stumbled against each other, I tried to steady myself, and the souse turned around and said to me, "Hey, Baby," his alcohol breath making me want to barf. I couldn't take it, so I hopped off near Broadway.

I wasn't too far from Eggroll Wonderland. Having walked this stretch of Polk Street so many times, I knew every storefront. After passing a realtor's office and a dentist, I slowed as I approached the copy place where I knew the Martin Fry guy worked. I saw him through the glass and spontaneously decided to go in.

The place smelled like ink and Windex. As I stood in the doorway, I realized I should have had a plan before coming in here. I tried to think of something I might've needed Xeroxed, but had no idea what. If I'd had a page of David Bowie lyrics, maybe that'd be cool, but it wasn't like I carried around record sleeves. Uh-oh. Mr. Fry was behind the counter, staring at me.

"What's your name?" he said.

"Candace Ong."

I blurted out my answer immediately, like I'd been called on by a teacher. Not cool at all.

"Really," he said. "Candy O."

Could he somehow tell that that was my favorite album of all time?

"You work at that Chinese restaurant. Come over here."

I walked toward him, and he watched me very carefully. His eyes followed me slowly, like the perverted guys on the bus. But there was also something about the way he was staring at me that I kind of liked.

"Nice uniform."

I could feel him staring at my legs. It was embarrassing, especially when my thighs started to feel hot. But it was a new feeling, tinged with something . . . good.

I couldn't think of anything to say, but then I didn't have to. He grabbed a blank card from the countertop, wrote something down, and handed it to me.

I took the card from his hand and saw that it was a phone number. And his name. His name wasn't Martin Fry. It was Andrew Fink.

"Call me," he said.

I looked at the card, then up at him. No guy had ever given me his number before. But he didn't know that. I didn't say anything, but turned slowly, knowing he was still staring at my skirt and legs as I walked away.

"See ya later, eggroll girl."

As I walked the rest of the way home, I felt kind of happy. I hummed "Don't Stand So Close to Me" by the Police since it had been on the radio a lot, and it had been stuck in my head all day. There was one line, "that book by Nabokov," that I had only figured out last week. I had called up the KRQR deejay and asked him about it. He'd said, "You don't know Nabokov's book, *Lolita*? How old are you, anyway?"

I didn't know any book by that name, and the deejay had seemed kind of pervy, so I hung up and went to the library to look it up.

Lo. Lee. Ta.

I saw the name written like that on one of the pages, and couldn't help but think the syllables sounded Chinese. At least the *Lo* and the *Lee* part, but I wasn't certain about the *Ta*. But two-thirds sounded Chinese enough, and I wondered if Lolita, the girl who was the fire of some old fart's loins, could have been Chinese like me. Not that I wanted skeevy old guys all over me. I didn't. I just wanted someone, maybe anyone, to feel something. About me, that is.

It was funny how music led me to things. As I proceeded down Polk Street, I thought of a couple of other lines from songs on the radio that had recently piqued my interest:

"Good heavens, Miss Sakamoto! You're beautiful!"

"I like Chihuahuas, and Chinese noodles."

"I think I'm turning Japanese, I really think so."

I was glad Thomas Dolby could love Miss Sakamoto because a Japanese girlfriend was at least one step closer to a Chinese one. And as far as the B52s were concerned, maybe someone who didn't have to cook Chinese noodles all day could like them, but not me. And as for the Vapors *turning* Japanese, well, I figured you either were Japanese or you weren't. Just like I was Chinese. Chances were I wasn't gonna turn into anything else, even if I wanted to.

As I kept walking, I nervously touched the jade pendant around my neck and thought of Auntie Melaura. I knew that my mom still kept some of her clothes in the closet, but mostly my parents threw all her shit away. I used to go to Golden Gate Park with Auntie Melaura and I'd once seen a Bowie cassette tape in her purse, even before I knew who David Bowie was. Actually, that was the whole reason I bought *Ziggy Stardust*, come to think of it. Lately I'd been listening to the tape more and more, hoping the lyrics would tell me something about life, or about her. I knew it was kind of lame to think I could get to know her better by memorizing that album. But shit, she was dead, and song lyrics were all I had.

Finally, I arrived back at Eggroll Wonderland. As I walked through the restaurant door, my mom screamed at me, "Why you stay out so late? You know you get rape?"

My mom was constantly extolling the virtues of perfectly fried eggrolls and an intact hymen.

"I haven't been raped," I said calmly. "I'm fine." I grabbed some tongs and flipped over some dried-out looking pot stickers in the to-go tray.

"You think you know it all," my mom said, turning over the *chow mein* with a giant spatula. "But you don't know. How can you know anything?"

I moved away, not wanting to hear the same old, tuneless Chinese music again. Walk where people can see you. Don't go out at night. Don't wear makeup. Only go out in groups, even though you're too young to go out. Don't wear jewelry. A man can grab you by the necklace, drag you behind dumpster. Rape you.

I reached up to my collar absentmindedly and touched the jade pendant again. My mom followed me into the kitchen and said to me, "Start to rain outside. You know what that mean."

I did. Rain meant that all the white people ordered *wonton* soup. The Chinese people, too, asked for *wor wonton, wonton mein*, sometimes with duck or *cha siu*. I actually liked it when it rained because I didn't have to fry as many eggrolls. I preferred folding *wontons* for soup instead of frying them because, when the oil was popping, I always imagined the grease clogging my pores and giving me blackheads.

Gathering all the ingredients I needed, pretty soon I was stationed at one of the back tables, folding *wontons* a mile a minute.

It was easy, really. The noodle skins came in a package, dusted with flour in between so they didn't stick together. My dad brought me a heaping bowl of meat that looked like raw hamburger, but it was really a mixture of pork, shrimp, water chestnuts, and some chopped chives. I put a dollop of meat into the *pei*, then dabbed water onto the corners so when I pressed the edges together, they stuck. I made row after row, and placed them on a cookie sheet. When my mom saw that I'd almost filled a pan, she came and took it away and brought me another tray to fill.

As I continued to make row after row of *wontons*, I looked back into the kitchen and saw my dad talking to Mr. Ping, Ruby's dad who owned the place. Every week he came by to collect money out of the back room, from the safe behind the oil painting of the Golden Gate Bridge. I listened as Mr. Ping and my dad walked from the kitchen to the front of the place. They were talking about remodeling the restaurant.

My mom barked out an order for eggrolls, so I stopped folding *wontons* and headed to my skillet station. Standing there waiting for the oil to bubble, I wondered why people were always ordering eggrolls in the first place. They weren't *that* good, for chrissakes. Like Chinese noodles, maybe they were tasty if you weren't the person cooking them. White people seemed to like them. Black people ordered them a lot, too. Hardly any Asian people ever ordered them.

I dropped six eggrolls into the bubbling oil, a double order. As I waited for them to be ready, I wondered how I could be more like Ruby, and less like my dork-ass self. Most likely, Ric Ocasek from the Cars was never going to come into Eggroll Wonderland and save my sorry ass. But then I smiled to myself, remembering an Adam and the Ants song where the lyrics were, "*Blackfoot, Pawnee, Cheyenne,*" but I swear to God, for months I was convinced he was saying, "Lunch with Bonnie Chiang." If Adam Ant could have lunch with some girl named Bonnie Chiang, maybe he would have lunch with me and then we'd run away together. Of course, that was just more of my lame-o wishful thinking.

After cooking the eggrolls and handing them to my mom who was going up front anyway, I stood in the open door-way that led to the back courtyard. The white clouds moved in slow-motion, out to sea, I imagined. The sun had come out and down here, in the concrete yard, the trees with gold light on their leaves hid several nests of birds. I listened to the chirping sparrows and wondered if they were like me, wait-ing for the rain to come back. It had been raining a lot lately. I watched the water ripple in the empty flowerpots where a couple of drowned cigarettes floated, evidence of my dad's habit of smoking when the restaurant was slow.

I hated the spare look of the yard. Back here behind the restaurant, there was no secret garden, just garbage cans, and I longed for heirloom roses and English countryside—all that make-believe, romantic stuff I'd read about in books. At that point, I would even have preferred the barnyard setting of *Charlotte's Web* to Chinese restaurant life. Not only was there no *Are You There God, It's Me, Mei-Ling?* but never in all my trips to the library since I was a little kid did I ever see one fairytale or nursery rhyme with Chinese people in them. Chinese girls were never the princesses and never got rescued. Was it too much to ask for one freaking story where a Chinese girl escaped chop suey drudgery?

I sighed as I scrutinized the terra cotta containers left out by Mrs. Lum, the upstairs neighbor. She was trying to grow some jade plants, but seemed to have forgotten about them. They were just gnarled little fists in dirty pots. I felt like a gnarled root that wanted to grow, too, but nobody was coming to water me, either.

Before the Pitbulls Chased After Me

It hadn't rained all night, and the next morning I was standing in the sunny schoolyard of St. Abigail's, waiting for the May Procession to begin. May was the month of Mary and we were all supposed to bring in flowers from our gardens to decorate a shrine for the Mother of Jesus. For my floral contribution I had taken some plastic carnations out of the bud vases on the restaurant tables. We were lined up, creating the semblance of a human rosary as the altar boys carried around the statue decorated with roses, lilacs, daisies, and my dusty sprigs of plastic crap. The whole eighth grade, followed by the seventh, sixth, and other classes, trudged slowly around the perimeter of the schoolyard, alternating songs about Mary with prayers. As the sun shined down on us, I was just glad to be outside. We recited the rosary until it was time to file into the church and sing hymns.

Lined up against the wall next to the church, I watched two girls in the seventh grade quietly playing a version of *Say, Say Oh Playmate*. They sang,

Say, Say, oh playmate/ I cannot play with you/
My dollies have the flu/ Boohoo, boohoo hoo
  hoo/
Ain't got no rainbow/ Ain't got no cellar door/
But we'll be faithful friends/ Forever more!

I wanted to find Ruby, but she was way at the front of the line, flirting with Chris, a cute boy in our class. Our procession had stopped as we waited to file into the church, and from a distance I admired the crystal rosary beads of Sandy, Christy, and Tina, who were girls on my basketball team. My rosary beads were plastic, just like the carnations I'd brought.

The line started to move, and I sang along with everybody else,

"Sing of Mary/ Pure and Lowly/ Virgin Mother
  Undefiled . . ."

We eventually went into the church and filed into our pews according to grade. We sat through mass, repeating the priest's words when we were supposed to, occasionally bleating back lines like "Lord, hear our prayer." At the end, all the Catholics lined up to take the Eucharist, but I sat in the pew while the holier kids stepped past me. I didn't think of the wafer as the Body of Christ, but more like a snack that I didn't get to have.

Later, back in our homeroom, as if it hadn't been enough that we'd just spent the last two hours in church and the whole hour before that saying the rosary in the yard, it was time for Religion class.

Sister Mary, a shriveled nun who looked like Mr. Toad from *Wind in the Willows*, was our teacher. Every day before Religion, she made a big show of taking the Bible off the shelf and kissing it. Her façade of holiness was such a joke. When she wasn't making out with the Bible, she was usually slapping one of us. A week ago she'd smacked me against the head for not being able to pinpoint Cork, Ireland, on the map. And a couple of days ago, when Gwen with the Greasy Bangs missed a math question, she had to walk around all day with the imprint of her own protractor on the side of her face.

"Boys and girls," Sister Mary said, "It's time to take out your 'Me' books. You have forty minutes to fill out the next section, and what you don't finish will be part of your homework. And I want quiet," she said. "This is personal time between you and Jesus."

A collective sigh rose from all of us. We took out our workbooks and started scrawling.

The book was called *Jesus and Me*. It was supposed to be about growing in our love for Jesus who understood that being a kid was hard. At least that's what it said on the cover. It was supposed to be like a journal but, of course, no one could write what they really wanted because Sister Mary read it even though she said she didn't. She claimed she just "checked" to make sure we filled it out. She said it was completely private, between us and the Lord, but we all knew that was a crock of shit.

Every eighth-grader received a blank *Jesus and Me* workbook at the beginning of the year. Like everyone else, I was supposed to write my memories from when I was little, and also jot down my current feelings. I wrote things like, "Wherever I go, I know Jesus is with me," and "Because Jesus is my friend, I know it's okay even if we lose the CYO basketball championship."

I looked around at the kids at the surrounding desks. They

were whipping through the pages in an attempt not to have any more homework than necessary, but I wasn't in the mood to write much and just doodled the words ROCK'N'ROLL SUICIDE over and over in the margins to pass the time. I had listened to that Bowie song the night before, and it had been stuck in my head all morning. But I didn't want to have to finish all ten pages for homework either, so eventually I did look at the first question:

What do you want to be when you grow up?

In my boredom, I almost scribbled ROCK'N'ROLL SUICIDE under the question, but when I saw Sister Mary's fat-bat silhouette out of the corner of my eye, I wrote ROCK STAR.

She peered over my shoulder and looked at what I'd written. She clucked her bloated tongue and stood there waiting for me to do something. I crossed out my answer, and out of nervousness, wrote,

NOTHING.

Sister Mary said, "Young lady, if flunking out is what you have in mind, I can send you right down to Sister Eugenia's office."

I crossed out NOTHING and hesitated for a moment, not knowing what to write. Sister Mary was still waiting. She opined, "You could be the owner of a restaurant. Or work in a laundry. That's very respectable work for an Oriental."

Did anyone know how much I wanted to bludgeon her to death with my *Jesus and Me* book? Just to get rid of her, I wrote,

SECRETARY.

She nodded and moved on as I slumped down in my seat. On to the next question:

Who is your best friend, and why?

I automatically wrote Ruby's name, but hesitated at the explanation. I left it blank, but wanted to write,

> *Because Ruby is pretty and screws boys in the forest and I want to be her. Plus, as you know, she has perfect tits and you think so, too, because you stare at her all the time, you fucking lesbian!!*

I was laughing to myself when the bell rang. The classroom erupted with the noise of slamming books and the opening and closing of desks. We all rose for the afternoon prayer, mumbled it in a rote singsong, and then gathered up our backpacks.

Outside, I caught up with Ruby.

"Hey," I said, "I have a student council meeting, but after, do you want to go to Pier 39?"

Chris came over and slapped Ruby on the butt.

She giggled and snuggled under his arm. "Well, Chris and I are already going. See ya."

They walked off, and I didn't know if "see ya" meant for me to join them later, or to get lost.

"HEY!" I yelled after them, but neither turned around.

I headed upstairs to the student council meeting room. Under a banner that read, "Leaders of Tomorrow," I sat at a table with my fellow class representatives around a box of donut holes from Winchell's. Gwen with the Greasy Bangs read the minutes from the last meeting and Christy, the Commissioner General, discussed the school's plan for Dress Up as Your Favorite Saint Day. Tina, the Commissioner of Safety, discussed too-fast traffic on Broadway and reckless cars making right turns with complete disregard for pedestrians. As the Commissioner of Finance, I reported the hefty sum of $392 in the eighth-grade coffer. The meeting adjourned at 3:35 p.m.

Out on the sidewalk in front of the school, I looked around but didn't see Ruby or Chris. A group of seventh-grade girls wearing leg warmers were sitting on a bench braiding skinny ribbons into their barrettes. "Have you seen Ruby Ping?" I asked, but they all shook their feathered heads.

I started walking and went by Ruby's house, but Cissy said she hadn't seen them. I decided to take the bus to Pier 39 to see if I could find them. Getting on the 19 Polk, I sat down in front, right behind the driver. After a few blocks, I was staring at the Maritime Museum up ahead, and heard laughing from somewhere behind me, but didn't look back because the bus was fairly packed, and kids were always sneaking on through the back door.

When I got off at Beach Street, I headed toward the entrance of Pier 39 where a troupe of clowns had a balloon stand. Some mimes in pastel unitards were doing a rodeo routine, and I watched for a little while before heading down to the stage farther down the midway where the high-divers performed.

I stood in the crowd and stared at a hairy guy with a medium-sized bulge as he jack-knifed into the see-through, Plexiglass pool of water. Right then, just behind a fat-kid tourist, I spotted Ruby's pretty hair behind a pretzel kiosk. Trying to make my way through the crowd toward her, I could also see cute Chris pawing at her titties, not doing a very good job of pretending he wasn't. When I finally managed to get closer, I heard squeals as Ruby and Chris ran away, zigzagging behind a cotton candy vendor to elude me.

I circled the immediate area, but didn't find them. Wandering back up toward the entrance to the pier, the only person I recognized was a curly haired juggler on a unicycle, who was a guy named Pete who came into Eggroll Wonderland every once in a while and used to ask me if I wanted to go bowling. It was very random to see him dressed like a clown, and I didn't want him to see me so I went into the arcade. I wandered over to Galaga and then Space Invaders, the same machines Ruby and I played all the time. When I didn't see her or Chris, I slowly faced up to the fact that they'd ditched me. I didn't want it to be true, so I decided to browse around in some of the shitty shops, hoping maybe I'd catch up with them somehow.

In the poster store on the upper level, I was minding my own business looking for pictures of Adam Ant when a huge Samoan girl bumped into me. The Samoan had two friends with her, one who was black and another who looked Mexican, and they came over and started shoving me for no goddamn reason at all.

The lady behind the counter, a middle-aged, Goth chipmunk on cocaine saw us and said, "Take that rough-housing outside."

I was scared, but didn't say anything because I didn't want to sound like a crybaby, which would have made the whole situation worse. The fat chicks shoved me out the door, and I glanced back at the coked-out rodent-lady pleadingly, but she just seemed to think we were all friends.

Outside, I walked along the wood railing that overlooked

the bay. The big girls kept trying to shove me as I tried to move away from them.

The black girl said, "What skoo you at, Chink?" and "What dat uniform?"

The three of them were dressed in a uniform I didn't recognize, and the plaid skirts and blue sweaters looked kind of funny on them because they were all so gigantic. As one of them kicked out the back of my knee, I stumbled, wondering simultaneously if they had to special-order their sizes at the uniform shop.

I ducked into a T-shirt store and the girls followed me. I was standing in front of a sweatshirt with a Jazzercising B. Kliban cat when the shopkeeper said, "Not you all again," perhaps assuming I was one of them, maybe because my plaid skirt wasn't completely unlike theirs, even though mine didn't have the green squares. People never noticed details, and I took a moment to disdain this fact rather than confront the reality that I was probably about to get my ass kicked.

Back outside against the wood siding that overlooked the water, pretty soon I was in an isolated spot with the three huge girls who looked like overstuffed armchairs in tartan upholstery. I knew it was stupid of me to have come this way, and I should have stayed around crowds, but there I was. They started shoving me between them, pulling at my clothes, and the Samoan yanked on my hair really hard, snapping my head back.

"Get away from me, you fat dog," I said, my voice wavering.

This statement, of course, infuriated the three snarling pit-bulls.

"Whad'joo say? Whad'joo say, you little chink?" said the Mexican girl.

I had heard of gang girls hiding razor blades in their fanned-out bangs, and I was scared.

"I gonna bust yo' chink fucking face," she said, lunging at me.

I was against the wooden fence that overlooked the water, so I couldn't turn around and run. The girl's fist looked like a hunk of roast beef as she raised it in the air. However, like a giant from a cartoon, her lumbering gorilla maneuvers were easy to anticipate. As she threw her substantial weight forward, I pivoted on one leg and spun away, just like I'd done a thousand times in basketball practice. The girl's prodigious rump bounced off the railing like a bumper car, but just as I was getting my momentum to run away, the Samoan girl grabbed at my shoulder and ripped off my backpack. I turned around, but before I knew it, the gorilla had thrown my bookbag over the ledge and we all watched it splash into the water. Quicker than one might expect, it sank without a noise.

"Moded!" one of them yelled.

While my attackers whooped and laughed, I figured there was nothing I could do now to retrieve my textbooks, note-pads, or any of my other stuff, so I turned and ran away as fast as I could before the pitbulls got a chance to chase after me.

My Velcro wallet had gone into the water with my back-pack, so I didn't even have bus fare or my transfer. As I started my long trudge back to Eggroll Wonderland, it started to rain but I was so numb I hardly minded the cold. One good thing about the rain was that the droplets disguised the fact that my eyes were leaking tears.

It felt weird to be walking without my backpack or any-thing to hold. After a half hour or so, I finally made it back to Polk Street and was soaking wet, the rain having pelted me the whole way. Almost home, I was near Carlene's of Maui when an old guy started following me.

He was dressed like a 1970s hustler with a brown leather jacket, a wide belt with a big buckle, and tan boots. He looked familiar. He looked exactly like the pimp in *Dawn, Portrait of a Teenaged Runaway,* the Afterschool Special where the actress who played Jan Brady was a teenage hooker.

"Hey, little sister, where you going?"

I ignored him, but he persisted.

"How old are you?" he said, walking right next to me. "Where you going so fast?"

Matching my stride, he tried to put his arm around me, but I moved away. I was frightened, but didn't want to be.

"Schoolgirl, huh? Mmm . . . ain't that nice?"

Jan's pimp rubbed his chin with his hand. "Where you going, again?"

In my head, over and over I told myself, "DON'T YOU DARE CRY."

I tried to walk fast, but he walked fast, too. When I picked up my pace, he kept up with me. Passing the Royal Theater, I wanted someone to notice that this guy was following me, but no one was looking my way. I thought about turning off Polk Street but remembered the thousand times my mom said to stay around other people or else I'd "get rape."

"Don't be that way," he said, still walking alongside me. "What's your name?"

I made it to Eggroll Wonderland, and ran inside. Jan's pimp didn't follow me. When I passed the glassed-in to-go counter, my mom saw me and shouted, "Crab Rangoon, table three!"

But I kept running to the back of the restaurant, my eyes welling up with tears. Up the back stairs to the apartment, I went to my room and pulled off all my clothes and got into my nightie, then into bed. I kicked all the animals off to the side, except for my gigantic beanbag frog, Big Mama, whom I placed over my face like an icepack.

The toy's weight was comforting, especially the sensation created by the beans inside sifting down from the frog body, filling up the frog legs that rested on either side of my head. Flipping over, I shoved Big Mama under my neck. Putting my arms around my pillow, I squeezed my eyes shut tight and told myself I wasn't crying.

Poor Little Greenie

I only felt free in the nighttime. I would listen for noises in the apartment and when I was fairly certain everyone was asleep, I'd put on a record and listen with anticipation as the crackles and pops of my warped records gave way to the comforting sounds I'd memorized—the first chords of a favorite song from *Changes One,* or the Burundi drumbeat from one of Adam Ant's albums. Tonight I leaned back on my radio and listened to "The Jean Genie."

I lay there wondering if Ruby and I were growing apart. I thought about her face as she was staring out the bus window, and I wanted to know what was in her head. She had asked me the other day if I was still writing MORRISON in syrup on my Eggo waffles, and I couldn't believe she didn't even know that my Jim Morrison phase had ended months ago and I was back to Bowie. If she was my best friend, how could she not have noticed that memorizing David's lyrics was my new life's work? Maybe because I didn't tell her. But that's because she didn't ask.

As a matter of fact, Ruby and I didn't even talk much anymore. She mostly just ignored me. Who *was* speaking to me? Only the disembodied voice of Mr. Ziggy Stardust, the Thin White Duke himself, Mr. Aladdin Sane floating through my crappy speakers.

I must have fallen asleep because when I woke up, light was coming through the window. I knew it was Saturday because I could hear my little brother, Kenny, watching *Superfriends* out in the living room. I figured I'd leave the house before the restaurant opened so I wouldn't get roped into working. Throwing on my clothes, I split.

I walked all the way down Polk Street toward Market, but then decided to head up to the Haight-Ashbury area. By now it was around ten in the morning, but the neighborhood was still pretty sleepy. Across the street I saw a neon sign advertising palm reading and psychic services, and I wondered if those kind of people could tell me anything about Auntie Melaura. Frankly, though, I'd been in Catholic school for nine years and I had a major fear of Satan. I thought maybe psychics and palm readers were, you know, into the devil, so I kept walking.

I wondered if maybe Auntie Melaura was a ghost and was following me right now. I wasn't scared of spirits the way I was freaked out about Satan. My parents had a little shrine in the house with pictures of all four of my dead grandparents and I always thought of them as friendly spirits looking down on me from heaven. Maybe I'd seen *Star Wars* too many times, but I imagined that Auntie Melaura would be like the Princess Leia hologram projected from R2-D2. Yeah, I could handle that. As I made my way down the sidewalk, I wished Auntie Melaura was walking next to me in a white robe. I could ask her questions and she'd be just like she was in real life, only see-through, and not nuts. I wanted to ask her if she'd ever had sex and if love was something real and not just something made up to make good songs. While I was at it, maybe I'd ask her if my parents were in love because they never even touched, except when they bumped into each other in the restaurant kitchen.

As I stopped in front of the donut shop, contemplating a glazed cinnamon twist, my eyes wandered to the next storefront. The door was shrouded by a thick, black curtain, and a sign above read, Holos Gallery.

Parting the curtain, I stepped into the dim, eerie space. Was this weird or what? It was a small room with pictures on the dark walls, all framed *holograms*.

I was convinced that Auntie Melaura was trying to tell me something. Maybe if I looked at the pictures long enough, my aunt might conjure herself like how the magic mirror in Snow White could talk to the Wicked Queen. As I stared into the 3-D images—one of a bowl of fruit, another of Janis Joplin—I waited for a sign from the beyond, but none came.

I gazed into a holographic image of Jim Morrison. It wasn't bloated, *L.A. Woman* Jim, but his skinnier self from the first album. However, the eyes were kind of off, which made him look a little retarded. During my Morrison phase, I had waited for him to appear to me, too, and he never did either. Losing patience, I finally slipped back outside and headed toward Golden Gate Park.

It was a short distance to the Children's Playground. I was surprised to see there weren't any kids around, but I figured it was maybe because of the rain. The sand was wet and pockmarked from raindrops. The swings and rocking elephants were wet and empty and I could smell the sweet tree blossoms from above.

I walked toward the streaked glass panes of the old merry-

go-round. Inside I could see a gryphon, dragon, and sea creatures. Making my way around the carousel building, I spotted
my favorite, the unicorn. It had silver scales, like medieval ar-
mor I once saw in a painting of a Chinese king.

"Wanna ride for free?" The operator was a young Asian guy
whom I'd seen before.

"Okay," I said.

"Since no one's here, I'll let it go around a few times," he
said, tossing his textbook onto the podium. He stepped onto
the carousel platform and went into the center area where the
gears were. After he disappeared behind a mirrored panel, I
heard the bell and the ride began to move. I gripped the unicorn's blue and silver neck, and soon I heard the hurdy-gurdy
jangle of the calliope music, no doubt the official soundtrack
for insane asylums everywhere.

The room spun around and around. At periodic intervals I
checked if I really was the only person riding. I couldn't see
the ride operator anywhere, and after a few minutes, things
started seeming pretty freaky. I told myself the guy was just
behind a partition reading his book or something, but the carousel creatures and pipe organ music and lonely feeling started
tripping me out.

Around and around I went, faster and faster it seemed. I pictured Auntie Melaura during the times she'd brought me here.
She had once jumped off the mythical bird she'd been riding,
and spun herself in circles between the creatures, laughing. I
imagined her smiling at me now the way she did then, pink popcorn in hand. I wished I could have asked her about sex stuff.
If she were alive, maybe I'd even tell her about seeing Ruby
humping the W.P.O.D. Unlike my mom, I think she would've
refrained from slapping me just for asking about nasty stuff.

As I sat there, the music suddenly struck me as way too loud. I shivered, shaking the image of Auntie Melaura from my brain. In my heart of hearts I knew no amount of wishing or looking at holograms was going to conjure my dead aunt in the Children's Playground. As I spun around, catching a glimpse of the sandbox area each time it whizzed by, I wanted to feel the feeling of being a little kid again. I wanted to jump on that metal squirrel seat on the curlicue spring out there and rock back and forth, but I remembered the last time I did, some lady with her kid told me I was too old for it.

At least ten minutes had passed, and the merry-go-round was still going. I wondered if the guy had forgotten about me, and the crazy music was really starting to get to me. I couldn't take one second more of the Ray Manzarek spacey carnival music so I slid off the unicorn and jumped off the carousel platform. From the ride's momentum to the cement floor I came to an abrupt stop and almost fell flat on my ass. Luckily, no one was there to see me almost wipe out.

I went outside and looked up to the billowy, cloudy sky with a jewel spot of blue in the distance. As I walked home, I thought about all the adults I knew: my parents, Mr. Ping, Cissy, Sister Mary, and the other nuns and teachers. No one was suitable to ask the stuff I really wanted to know. Was true love real? Why did people have sex with skanks? What was the point of being friends with someone when all friends did was steal your purple jeans and wear them with dirty, inside-out bikini bottoms?

I trekked back to Polk Street and wondered if anyone was wondering where I was. I doubted anyone cared where I went, what I did, or whom I hung out with. The pathetic thing, though, was that I didn't do anything, didn't go anywhere, and didn't hang out with anyone. I wanted all that to change. I didn't want to start high school in the fall as a total dork-ass, and since it was pretty obvious to me that I was dork-ass personified, I figured I'd better do something quick to interrupt my trajectory toward goody-two-shoes fat chick oblivion.

Deviled Ham on a Cupcake

I was supposed to be writing a short essay for Social Studies describing what happened at a potlatch, but instead, I took out the card with Andrew's phone number. I wanted to do the things Ruby did, and I wondered how old Andrew was, and if I could make him my boyfriend.

I decided to call him.

"Hello," he answered after only one ring, his voice sounding like he just woke up, even though it was four in the afternoon.

"Hi, is this, uh, Andrew? This is Candace."

I heard the sound of rustling sheets, and after about fifteen seconds he said, "Oh. The eggroll girl."

I still didn't like him calling me that, but he sounded pleased, so I took it as a good sign that he didn't think I was a total numbskull.

He said, "I didn't think you'd ever call."

I thought of a Bowie line and said, "I had to phone someone so I picked on you."

Nervously, I waited through the silence. I heard a yawn, and then, to my surprise, he said, "Hey, eggroll girl, let's meet somewhere."

Forty minutes later I was walking to the corner of Polk and Clay near Double Rainbow because I didn't want to be too close to the restaurant where anyone might see me. I was wearing a black-and-white striped shirt and a ruffled miniskirt, and as I went past Swan's Oyster Depot I saw him in the distance leaning against the wall at Paperback Traffic, waiting for me.

"You look good," he said.

My version of acting cool was to attempt to appear slightly bored, as if I met strange guys on the corner all the time. He was wearing black pants and a greenish jacket that struck me as very Ultravoxy. He didn't look too old, but older than high school, definitely. He was looking at me with the same half-amused, half-scornful look as the other day, and I wondered if he practiced this look in the mirror.

"You look . . . okay." I said, and he scoffed.

We walked to the bus stop and took the bus into North Beach. As I sat on the maroon seat, I snuck glances at him. His two-tone jacket was so cool, if a little threadbare. He wore an old watch with a brown leather band, like something from a grandfather or a pawn shop. Scuffs on his black shoes, as dumb as this sounds, were glamorous to me because they meant he probably didn't live with a mom or dad who yelled at him about keeping a tidy appearance.

Getting off the bus, we walked a short way to Café Puccini.

"Espresso," he said to the barista. "What do you want?" he asked me.

I had never drunken coffee before. "Bubble Up?"

"They don't have that."

"Orange Fanta?"

He smirked and said, "She'll have an Orangina."

I had never been to this kind of café, where people just hung around, not eating anything. People were reading or just sitting there, seemingly waiting for something to happen. I decided instantly that I liked the place, since I, too, was waiting for something to happen to me, although I wasn't sure what.

We had absolutely nothing to talk about. We drank our drinks and both stared out the window. But just when things seemed to officially be going terribly, he said, "Ever been to the Filbert Street steps?"

"Yeah," I lied.

"We could get a bottle of wine and drink it there together."

I liked the word "together."

"Yeah, wine's good," I said, sounding like an idiot. I'd never sipped coffee, let alone wine, but my brazen stupidity knew no boundaries.

We got up and walked down Columbus to a liquor store.

"Money," he said, and held out his hand.

I didn't know how much wine cost, so I gave him a five-dollar bill.

While I stood outside and waited, I considered that maybe he liked me a little bit. I wondered if he'd put the moves on me at some point, which, frankly, I wouldn't have minded because Heathcliff the raccoon, my nighttime lover in all his Dacron polyester-fill glory, was getting a little old.

A few minutes later, Andrew swaggered out with a bottle in a sack and two plastic tumblers. It was about six'o clock, and getting a little chilly, but I didn't have a jacket. When we got to the steps, my miniskirt was so short that when I sat down I was just sitting on my underwear, which was kind of uncomfortable, but I acted like I was too sophisticated to be bothered.

I didn't like the taste of the wine but drank it anyway. After a while I didn't feel drunk, just somewhat sick. It was pretty cold but I didn't complain.

"Are you chilly?" he said, maybe noticing me shivering. "C'mon, let's go to my place."

We ended up going to his apartment, which was on Pine Street between Larkin and Polk. On the outside it looked like a regular San Francisco flat, but upstairs it was kind of scummy with a hallway and lots of doors, which I realized were people's rooms. At the end of the hall was the bathroom. I never knew people lived in apartments without their own bathrooms.

Andrew's place was the first one that faced the street. We went inside and I smelled dirty laundry, which reminded me of Ruby's house. I saw bottles of hair dye and Tenax styling gel by the only sink, which doubled as the kitchen with a hot-plate and cans of deviled ham. The only place to sit was on the queen-sized bed, which took up the whole room. Sitting on a corner of the red bedspread I got kind of a bordello-flophouse feeling. Not in a fashion magazine kind of way, but in an actual poverty kind of way.

The first thing Andrew did was pick up the telephone to call one of his friends. He talked about meeting for band practice that night, and then quickly hung up and excused himself to go take a bath, which seemed like a really weird thing to do. He gathered up a towel, a bathrobe, and a toothbrush, then walked down the hall, leaving me in his room with the dirty laundry smell.

I just sat there and didn't really know what to do. Imagining that the restaurant was probably really busy at that very moment, I wondered if maybe my parents were worried about where I was.

Probably not. I did have the good sense to lie, and had told them I had a kickball game. They were too busy cooking, cleaning, and managing to-go orders to notice that it wasn't even kickball season, for chrissakes. I liked to tell lies that were easy to catch, to test them, but they failed all the time, never noticing my fibs no matter how obvious. Their lack of attention used to bother me more, but now I had to admit, it was convenient. I wasn't supposed to be out past dark, but in the afternoons like today I mostly came and went without too much hassle. But once in a while I wished they'd at least ask how my day went, and shit like that. They didn't even know that my basketball team had won consecutive CYO championships in the last two years and that we were on our way to our third. But who cared, really? I was in a guy's apartment.

I tried to open a window to let out the sock smell. City traffic was zooming by outside and I wondered if anybody driving by was somebody I might know, like Cissy or Mr. Ping. As I stared out the window for a while, Andrew eventually came back, and he was wearing only his white bathrobe. He came over and sidled next to me on the bed. *Sits like a man but he smiles like a reptile.*

I wasn't sure how it happened but all of a sudden he kissed me really hard, pushing his tongue into my mouth. I always imagined the tongue part would come after just putting the lips together, but he skipped that step. Whatever was happening, I liked it.

As we made out, my tongue seemed small in his mouth compared to how big his teeth and tongue were. He was kind of slobbering all over me, and I liked how into me he was, moaning and sucking on my tongue and licking my gums. It was kinda gross, but funny, too, like watching someone devour a banana split, except it wasn't ice cream, but my face. I started to giggle, and when I did, he pulled his mouth off me and asked, "Do you like that?"

And that's when I saw it. His robe fell open and I saw his Thing.

With its head poking out from behind the terry cloth, the Thing reminded me of the hairless, newborn hamsters at the pet store that blindly rooted around for a mother to suckle. The Thing was really pink, maybe because he had just gotten out of the bath. I couldn't help but think of the parts my dad pulled out of raw chickens to give to our neighbor, Mrs. Lum, to feed her cats.

"Down, boy," Andrew said, then folded his robe over the creature, but it sprang out again. He noticed me staring at it, and smiled.

"Eat me," he said.

"Fuck you, Asshole."

When the words came out of me, I tried to sound tough, but the truth was I was really just chickenshit. For all my curiosity, when it really came down to it, I didn't want to touch his freaky rat, and I certainly didn't want it anywhere near my mouth. What did he mean by "eat me," anyway? The only time I'd seen or heard those two words together was in a children's book, written in icing on a cupcake.

Sitting there with his legs spread and his overgrown pinky rat exposed, he said, "That's okay." He reached under my blouse and pawed at my bra, putting his hand inside and squeezing really hard. Reaching over, he pulled me against him. I had never seen a naked man, let alone rolled around in bed with one. While we made out some more, I remained fully clothed, which was fine with me. The small, stuffy room was steamy with the smell of Old Spice, soap, and deviled ham. When we stopped kissing, he said, "I'm going to touch it and you can stay and watch if you want. You don't have to do anything."

Sitting back against the wall, I considered my situation.

"Okay," I said.

What followed was somewhere between thrilling, revolting, and boring. First he licked his hand and then stroked the rodent with his spitty palm. He moved his hand along the length of the Thing, alternating the motion with grabbing the top part. I was fascinated at first, watching as he squeezed the hairless animal and moved the skin back and forth. But then my mind started to wander and I thought of the time the drawstring of my hooded sweatshirt got stuck and I had to squish the cord through the hem until I could yank the tip through the grommet. Sitting there for what seemed like a long time, I started to worry about getting home and considered whether I should take the Jackson Street bus or the 47 Van Ness.

"Do you want to touch it?" Andrew asked, his breathing heavy. "Do you want to cup my balls?"

"Uh . . ." I tried to think of something that might encapsulate all my feelings—squeamishness, excitement, total nausea. I settled on being as polite as possible.

"No thank you," I said, having read somewhere that good manners were never inappropriate.

"Yeah, that's awright," he said. "But don't leave," he added, still stroking. "Stay till the end."

The end of what? I didn't want to be rude, and felt obligated to wait. One leg crossed over the other, sitting on the edge of the bed, I rested my chin in my hand and continued to watch. The novelty had worn off, and I looked at the clock.

Like a Muni bus, he took forever to come. Spacing out, I turned my head when I heard a groan, and saw whitish stuff spurting from the hairless rodent's feeble mouth. Andrew took a deep breath, then calmly reached down to the floor, picked up a sock, and wiped himself off with it.

He said he had to get to band practice so I got up to go, and he didn't react at all to my leaving. With nothing else to do, I straightened my clothes, and walked out the door.

About five minutes later I was trudging up Pine Street by myself, back to Eggroll Wonderland. I could still feel my face burning a little because his scratchy beard had chafed my cheeks. I liked the way it felt, and wondered if this meant he was my boyfriend.

Back inside the restaurant, my mom was ringing up a bunch of to-go orders and barking into the microphone. When she saw me she didn't even ask if my team won our kickball game, and it bummed me out, as much as it would have had I actually played and not lied to go out with some guy who ended up choking his chihuahua in front of me. *I like Chihuahuas, and Chinese noodles.* I trudged into the back, put on my apron, and fired up some crab Rangoon.

We Are the Champions, My Friend

I told Ruby all about Andrew and the stuff we did.

"I can't believe you had the chance to do it, and you didn't do it," Ruby said. After another second, she asked, "Was it big?"

"Yeah," I said. "Kinda gross."

She smirked like I was just a baby. "You should've done it," she said.

Standing outside the gym, we were in our basketball uniforms. Our team was one game away from being the league champions for the third year in a row, and today was the final game against St. Michael.

"Pop Rocks?" Sandy offered. Ruby and I held out our hands as she shook tiny amounts of granulated candy into our palms. We collectively enjoyed the crackling sensation in our mouths as we waited for our rides.

The carpool moms drove us to an area of town where all the streets were named for cities like Paris and Lisbon. When we arrived at St. Michael's and went inside the gym, the place was packed to the gills and the stomping cheers for St. Michael's made my stomach feel simultaneously hollow and filled with lead. All the kids on the other team and all the families in the bleachers were black, but none of us mentioned this obvious fact.

Ruby, my teammates, and I all wore our prim school blouses under our nylon basketball jerseys, but our opponents wore nothing under their tank tops, letting their armpits show. Plus, they were all at least six inches taller than we were, looking like full-fledged teenagers, adults even, with hairy pits and sweaty smells. In comparison, we looked as threatening as declawed, yappy dogs, except for Ruby who somehow managed to look chic in our maroon and gold uniform.

We watched in awe as the St. Michael's girls practiced doing layups, making each shot, one after another. Scanning the crowd, I saw black moms dressed in heels and fur coats standing under the scoreboard setting up a huge sheet cake. It was so big I could read the frosting from where I was standing. It said, "Congratulations, St. Michael's 1983 Champions!" as if they'd already won. In the visitor section, only three moms from our team were there to cheer for us—Mrs. Rinaldi, Mrs. Rossi, and Mrs. Balestreri. They were clapping politely, but even though they tried to look chipper, it was obvious that they were pretty freaked out. They knew we were doomed.

Amidst chants and clapping, Sandy lost the first tip. A tall black girl grabbed the ball and bombed it downcourt with a powerful pass. Before anyone on our team even knew what was going on, St. Michael's had made a quick two points. Noise ricocheted off the four walls of the gym as roars erupted, our opponents and their fans fairly assured that the game would end in a quick and painless victory.

Ruby, though, was actually a pretty good basketball player, and this kind of competition was her strong suit. Her natural meanness was an asset on the court. After Sandy bounced the ball to her, Ruby dribbled fast across the court and passed the ball to Christy who was no slouch either. A girl twice her size tried to psyche her out by raising up her fist and pretending to sock her in the face, breezing an inch from her head. But Christy didn't cower. Her dad was, seriously, a major gangster, and she grew up in his South of Market bar and had learned how to handle herself. She dribbled the ball straight toward the girl and got called for charging. Cheers rose up from the spectators, and they began to stomp their feet as St. Michael's took possession of the ball.

In our little white collars, we were just getting warmed up. Our team had played together for four years straight and we knew how to capitalize on each other's strengths. Plus, we had a secret weapon in the form of our coach, Mr. Torino, the biggest dork who ever graduated from Catholic school, and incidentally, a master planner when it came to our team.

Mr. Torino had no girlfriends and no life outside his job at the Marina Safeway, and as a result, he lived and breathed eighth-grade girls' basketball. When he wasn't working, he spent all his time driving around the parochial schools to watch other teams play against each other. He scribbled detailed notes about the girls we'd be up against in the upcoming weeks, devised elaborate strategies to foil them, and brought diagrams outlined on Safeway paper bags to our practices.

We had the master nerd on our side, all right. Of course, now that I think about it, on some level he was probably getting some pervy jollies watching us girls get all sweaty. But his coaching strategies always worked. Our team hadn't been champs all these years for nothing. All his repressed sexual feelings got channeled into his coaching, and his meticulously drawn diagrams resulted in victories for us.

"Don't be scared of them," he said. "They tire easily and leave the baselines wide open." Good Catholic that he was, Mr. Torino also advised, "They fight dirty, but God won't approve if you don't fight fair. Remember, be like Jesus and turn the other cheek." As he swiveled his head back and forth with dramatic flair, I recalled that Mr. Torino had always wanted to be the dance teacher, but the nuns thought that that was deviant so they gave him coaching duty instead.

Anyway, back to the game. Tina took an elbow to the gut, but kept on going. The St. Michael's referee conveniently looked away and didn't call a foul, but Tina drove up the center and made a basket anyway. On the other side of the court, when a St. Michael's player shot and missed, Ruby and I went in for the rebound. Girls from the other team scratched our arms so hard that red welts formed immediately.

"This is bullshit," Ruby said to me, looking from her scraped arm to the referees who acted oblivious.

For the next two quarters, our team endured hair yanks, more scratching, and shoulders thrown against our comparatively puny bodies. At one point, the center for St. Michael's actually took her chewing gum out of her mouth and stuck it onto Sandy's head, smearing it into her hair. The crowd cheered wildly although they were only leading by six points.

At six foot, five inches tall, Mr. Torino was freaky-looking with his handlebar mustache and floppy, white-man Afro combed over and clipped with a bobby pin. Suddenly, he jumped up on a metal chair, and whirled his pointed index finger over his head like he was drawing a huge circle in the air. "Sneak attack!" he yelled, his Coke-bottle glasses bouncing off his head. This outlandish signal told us that we were to switch to "man-on-man" defense, and we instantly moved into our new formation.

The St. Michael's team was temporarily confounded, either by this sudden switch in our strategy, or by the gigantic, skinny-ass white man whose spontaneous disco maneuver suggested he'd lost his mind. The girl who was dribbling the ball stopped to stare at Mr. Torino, at which point Ruby stole the ball and tore up the right side of the court.

I was the only one left down on our side of the court because I had stopped to tie my shoe. I watched Ruby dribbling in a dead sprint toward me, the thunder of many feet behind her. As the stampede of thoroughbred girls threatened to knock her to the floor any second, she shot the ball to me in a move we had practiced a million times both at school and in the cement courtyard behind Eggroll Wonderland. I caught the ball and eyed the basket.

In addition to free throws, the baseline shot was the one basket I could consistently make. I often missed easy shots right off the backboard from two feet, but this one, from way outside and on the right, was always my baby. As the girls charged toward me, I pinpointed my target, bent my knees, and threw the ball high and straight. It arced like a rainbow over the heads of five girls, and dropped precisely through the hoop, the net hardly moving as it swished through.

But there was no time for congratulations. Ruby slapped my arm affectionately as we ran back down court. Looking quickly at several of my teammates, they struck me as nervous and exuberant gazelles barely outrunning a pack of lionesses set on tearing us apart. We couldn't slow down now.

Luckily, having played basketball together for so many years, we had memorized each other's maneuvers. It was automatic knowledge, stuff like who was the fastest, and who had the best hook shot. Ruby knew that I could make that basket from the baseline and I didn't need to tell her how to throw it to me—slightly forward and with a particular flick of the wrist so it would spin into my grip. As we ran back down the court, we shot each other lightning-quick glances across the key. We knew we could win this game.

The St. Michael's girls seemed sluggish and tired. They were a lot slower than they were in the first quarter, and now their coach was yelling, "Run them white asses down!" He added, "Don't be playing like stupid bitches!" For a tired team who up till now had relied on their height advantage to score, these words didn't appear to inspire them.

In contrast, Mr. Torino wasn't getting hotheaded, just revved up. From his perch on the side of the basketball court, he called forth from his vast repertoire of semaphore, and signaled to us the various plays he'd choreographed to defeat this team of titans. As I looked in his direction, he was employing Fosse-esque "jazz hands" to tell us to return to normal defense.

But then the referee got into the act. Every time someone on our team so much as stood next to a St. Michael's girl, he called a foul. By the second half of the fourth period, three from my team had fouled out, and I was one infraction away from being benched myself. The score was thirty-one to thirty, in favor of the home team.

But then, with five seconds left in the game, something happened to me. I was standing in the key, anticipating catching the ball as Ruby fired it at me from half-court, when a sharp jab to my head knocked me to the floor. I wasn't sure what had happened, but I heard the whistle, and as I sat on the floor holding the side of my melon, I saw the referee running over.

Turned out, even he couldn't pretend some Amazonian girl didn't just knock me the fuck down on purpose.

Ruby smoothed her hair down behind her ear and gave me a sly smile. I had once made twenty free throws in a row during practice for which I won a bag of Corn Nuts. I knew that she knew that this shot would be easy for me. But that was at our home gym and this was, well, totally different.

Scrambling to my feet, I felt a little wobbly, and tried to take a deep breath, but the air in the gym was stiflingly hot. Many feet in the stands began to stomp until the noise was so deafening I could't even hear Coach Torino's shouts from the sidelines. But I didn't need to hear him because I could see him strutting around like a gigantic goonie-bird, his arms outstretched and his limp hands twittering at the wrists. I knew he was shouting, "PSW!" which stood for Polk Street Wrist. It was his way of telling me to toss the ball gently with the flick of the wrists like I was a gay dude saying hello to his boyfriend. Seriously.

Ruby was standing at the front of the key, and gave me a wink. Although I had doubted my free throw ability a second ago, Ruby's confidence bolstered me back up. I heard the whistle and quickly tossed the ball toward the basket without thinking too hard. It hit the back rim and fell through the net. While my teammates cheered, one of the St. Michael's girls yelled, "Aw, fuckin' pussy!"

Someone tossed the ball back to me, and I made sure not to look at anyone. I didn't want to see my teammates' eyes that said the game was tied and I had to make it. Nor did I want to see the face of anyone who was going to call me a fuckin' pussy in hopes I'd miss. I didn't even want to look at Ruby. Without glancing down at my hands, I tightened my grip on the ball with the tips of my fingers, and rotated it a couple of times, telling myself it was just like in practice, and after I made it, I could go home and watch *Edge of Night*, a soap opera that I particularly liked. I told myself if I made it, I didn't have to fry any eggrolls that night.

I tossed the ball with the best PSW I could muster, and it was all over before I could die of anticipation. I knew I'd made it when I heard a St. Michael's girl say, "Motherfuckin' pussy!" The words, "motherfuckin' pussy," meant we had won the game.

"Yeaaaahh!" I heard my teammates screaming, and over in the bleachers, Mrs. Balestreri was jumping up and down and her gigantic bosom in the lavender sweater set was all over the place. Hands were grabbing me and hugging me and slapping me on the back. I really wished at least one of my parents was there.

The mothers of the home team discreetly blew out the sparklers on the gigantic victory cake. People filed out of the exit doors as we lined up to shake our opponents' hands. The St. Michael's girls dug their nails into our palms, except for one girl, who had slathered her own hand with Vaseline and smeared it onto our fingers.

Outside in the parking lot, Mr. Torino handed all of us Cokes. Sandy, Tina, and some other girls were excitedly talking about the game, and I looked for Ruby, but didn't see her. As I scanned the yard, I eventually spotted her smoking behind a dumpster, and ran over to her.

To my disappointment, the closeness I felt to her just a while ago on the basketball court had evaporated. I wanted to talk about the game, tell her she played great, and hug her like our teammates were doing over by the cars, but the way she was standing, so cool and detached-looking, made me feel like a retard for wanting to give her a high-five.

"Good going, Fatty," she said.

I didn't understand how I could be pumped up and struck down by the same person all in the time frame of fifteen minutes. I just nodded, trying to take in the compliment while ignoring being called fat.

"Wanna hang out at my house?" I asked.

Ruby pointed with her chin toward Mrs. Rossi's car. "Nah," she said, stomping out her cigarette. "I'm going with Sandy and Christy to Round Table."

She grabbed her duffel bag and walked away from me. I headed back to Mrs. B.'s station wagon and got in.

The game was all over, and it was time to go home. While the other girls crammed into Mr. Torino's and Mrs. Rossi's cars and headed to Round Table Pizza in the Marina to celebrate, I told Mrs. B. to drop me off at Eggroll Wonderland. I knew I had told myself that if I made the free throws I wouldn't have to fry any eggrolls, but that was just talking, and no one else heard me anyway. Like every night, I knew my parents were expecting me to work, and besides, I wasn't in the habit of making promises to myself and keeping them.

Reaching Up, My Loneliness Evolves

When I was little, I used to have a pet duck named *Op*, which meant duck in Chinese. I used to feed it bologna sandwiches and Whoppers. Then I came home from school one day and asked my mom what was for dinner.

"*Op*," my mother said.

I should've suspected back then that things and people I loved would end up dying, being taken away, or in this case, getting served with *hoisin* sauce. When I was little I had really trusted my mom, but after The Op Incident of 1979 I don't think things were ever really the same between us. "Why you so secret?" she'd once asked me when she found me hiding a swallowtail butterfly that I'd caught in the concrete yard. I wanted to say, "I don't want it to end up as a garnish next to the *Ma Po* Tofu!" But instead, I just opened my cupped hands and let it fly away. It hurt me that my mom was always so practical, thinking of Op only as a potential dinner, and not as my friend. Didn't she notice me rushing home from school every day and running to the yard to hug my pet, whispering my secrets into its snowy white head? It was obvious to me that my mom was only able to see *me* in a practical Chinese way, too. I was her only daughter so she was obligated to love me. I figured she wanted me to be safe and have enough to eat, but it wasn't as if she liked anything specific about me.

But then again, maybe my mom did realize I was wrecked about her cooking Op, because they did eventually get me a new pet, a hamster I named Twinkiechubs.

Lying on my bed now, I watched the hamster in her penthouse Habitrail. In the rodent condominium with its interlocking yellow tubing, my pet crawled through a passageway to a separate plastic cubicle. I watched her scurrying around, looking for an escape route, but there was none. She climbed up a skybridge, and then hung from the airholes of the metal grate, trying to gnaw herself to freedom.

My parents never said they loved me, but they did buy a lot of Habitrail parts to add to Twinkiechubs's estate. For Christmas I'd get extra plastic tubing, or for birthdays I'd receive snap-on room attachments. Most recently, they shelled out for the rodent penthouse. Half of my room was taken up by the hamster's plastic village. Although I wasn't into hamsters as much as I used to be, I knew my parents were trying to show me they cared. They even bought Twinkiechubs that roaming ball that let her meander through the apartment while encased inside a hollow plastic chamber, just like *The Boy in the Plastic Bubble*.

Frankly, though, the whole pet thing was becoming tiresome, and a little stinky. I was fairly certain that the girl on the cover of *Candy-O* didn't have a roomful of hamster stuff.

I watched as Twinkiechubs scrambled up the three-by-five inch penthouse where she seemed to feel safest. Most days she sat atop the mast of her Habitrail ship, propped all day and night in the crow's nest. I called it the poopdeck because that's all she ever did up there. She pooped and the resulting turds resembled black grains of rice. Too fat and lazy to bother retrieving food pellets from the main cage, she periodically reached down under her mattress of shredded Kleenex to gnaw on a little turd, the perfect handheld meal.

Actually, there had been two Twinkiechubses before this one. The first hamster they'd bought me after The Op Incident of 1979 had died suddenly. I'd come home one day and stared at the stiff little body nestled in the tangle of Kleenex. Checking for any subtle shift in the rodent's sleeping position since the morning, I noted that all food pellets and turds were in the exact same piles as the day before. The next day the hamster's fur looked a little mangy and an overall boniness appeared around her back thighs, which up till then had always looked relatively plump.

My parents had whispered in the kitchen to each other as I vocalized lengthy monologues to my "hibernating" pet. Deep down inside, I knew it was "living impaired," and although I'd only had the thing for a week and hadn't cared much for it, now that it had died I somehow convinced myself that I loved it. I told the little corpse that it was my best friend, and I berated myself and felt guilty for not having given it the best time on earth ever.

By the next morning my parents had disposed of the hamster and replaced it with a new one. Arriving home from school, I was greeted excitedly by my parents.

"Look! It wake up!" my mom said.

My dad added, "Boy, must be tired!"

They ushered me to the Habitrail and carefully watched my reaction. Twinkiechubs Two was a totally different variety than the original Twinkiechubs. Nonetheless, I was impressed that my parents went to all the trouble. I knew they probably borrowed a car, drove all the way to Sears on Masonic Avenue, and spent at least $2.99, because Twinkiechubs Two was a long-haired teddy, and not the short-haired, regular kind like the first hamster. When that one also died unexpectedly, about six months later, they reenacted the same scenario and I, once again, pretended not to notice that the new rodent, my current Twinkiechubs Three, was a totally different color.

Now that I thought about it, I had to admit that the demise of Twinkiechubs One and Two, and their subsequent, Lazarus-like resurrections were fairly decent proof that my parents cared about me, at least a little. But I never forgot that first betrayal, the cooking of my pal, Op. Maybe to spite my parents I never did love any of my hamsters the way I let in that duck, but then again, maybe I was just cheating myself out of twitchy hamster nuzzles. Either way, I was bummed out that my parents could only see me in the role of a hamster-caretaking child. I had had enough of cute and fuzzy. I wanted to rock and roll, dammit.

Bored with Twinkiechubs Three's antics, I looked at the clock and saw that it was eleven. Since my parents were still downstairs cleaning up, I figured it was the perfect time to sneak out into the living room to watch television. I tiptoed out into the dark, and managed not to knock over any of my little brother's toys. As I stepped around his stuff, I wondered if Kenny was already in bed, or running around with his group of preteen gang kids in Chinatown.

Making my way toward the television, I stepped on a metal car with my foot and slipped on some long plastic strips that were part of a Hot Wheels racetrack. I wondered if my parents knew or cared that Kenny was already a measly pawn for the Wah Ching gang, selling firecrackers on the street. Not that I cared what he did with his time, as long as he stayed out of my way. I was mostly unconcerned with his Chinese boy world, but I did think my parents should've kept better track of him. They never told him what to do, or when to be home. Apparently, hoodlum Chinatown boys weren't in danger of "getting rape."

But no matter. It was time for television. I was pretty happy because about a year ago, a mini miracle had occurred. Somewhere a mistake was made, and my family now got cable for free. One day, it was just there, beaming up all those channels beyond Channel 12, giving me access to a steady stream of late-night movies. Tonight, however, I had my heart set on watching music videos.

"She Blinded Me with Science" came on, and I waited patiently for my favorite part. Thomas Dolby said, "Good heavens Miss Sakamoto, you're beautiful!" The woman in the video danced with her long, black hair swaying over the small of her back painted in black ink, and he played her like a cello.

A few minutes later, "China Girl" came on and I lay on the floor and listened as David Bowie sang, "I'll give you television, I'll give you eyes of blue." A homely Chinese girl was dressed in an ornate wedding headdress like the one in Cissy's antique store. Bowie watched her sleep and she sat up and screamed. I waited for some kind of profound meaning to dawn on me, but it didn't.

Several songs later, I watched the video for "I Want Candy." I was scrutinizing Annabella Lwin's dark complexion and flat nose, when I heard my mom and dad coming up the stairs.

I turned off the TV and raced back to my room. I didn't want them to see me in the living room because then I'd have to talk to them. Hopefully, they would both just go to bed.

Crouching in the dark, I listened to Twinkiechubs trying to gnaw the lid off the Habitrail. I waited for bathroom and teeth-brushing sounds. No one came in to check on me, and after a while I heard sink noises and toilet flushings, and then only quiet. I hesitated a few more minutes before attempting to go back out and watch more videos.

But only my mom had gone to sleep. My dad was in the kitchen. He went to the cupboard and took out the tall Aquaman glass I got free with a hamburger at Burger King. He filled it two-thirds full with the whiskey he kept in the cabinet along with the soy sauce. I was disappointed when I saw him park himself in front of the television. He could be there for hours, which meant that my night was screwed.

Crawling into the hallway on my belly, I snuck in for a closer look. After a couple of war movies flashed by, my dad stopped flipping channels and I saw neon lettering move across the TV screen. I thought of the opening line of David Bowie's "Sound and Vision," where he said that blue, blue, electric blue was the color of his room. I thought of that because the words on the screen were *Electric Blue*, but it wasn't a Bowie video as I'd hoped, but rather, the name of a porno show on the Playboy Channel. I watched my dad staring transfixed by the sight of two naked girls feeling up each other. He was sipping from my Aquaman glass, and for some reason it really bothered me that he was using my special cup while watching smut.

A few minutes went by as I watched the slippery, tan bodies of the blond porno ladies, and my old Chinese dad sipping whiskey. I was only about ten feet away from him, but the angle was such that he couldn't see me behind him.

A brunette started spraying her crotch with a shower nozzle. I started to crawl away to head back into my room, but before

I shut my door I snuck a final peek at my dad watching the girl soap up her ass with a pink frothy sponge. He had downed his liquor within two minutes and now my empty Aquaman glass was sitting on the end table.

The idea of my dad getting off while watching those skanks made me want to barf. Did dads even get boners? Gross! I thought it was disgusting because he was so old. I even thought it was nasty to see old people on *Falcon Crest* and *Dynasty* making out. If movies could be rated R so I couldn't see them, why weren't there laws about old people seeing sex stuff, too?

Totally revolted, I went into the bathroom to take a bath. I locked the door and ran the water, not taking off my clothes until the tub was half-filled. After undressing, I stepped into the water and shut the sliding door immediately.

I lay in the water, my feet feeling prickly from the heat. Sliding down to wet my hair, I thought about Ruby and how she told me she looked at herself naked all the time and even walked around in her room without clothes on. I figured, yeah, if she had any *clean* clothes maybe she could wear them. I didn't know what to make of her liking herself and her body so much.

As I lay soaking, I thought about how Auntie Melaura had once told me that what was inside was what counted most. She said we weren't our bodies, and that inside I was a diamond. I was a precious, flawless diamond, she said. She said I was the only one who could know the inside of myself.

As for Ruby, she wasn't a diamond on the inside, but a ruby. And not on the inside, but on the outside, all the time. A red siren, cherry on top, stop sign, candy apple babe for everyone to see, and everbody, it seemed, wanted a piece of her action.

In rock songs, too, a ruby was always the gem of choice:

"Ruby, Ruby, when will you be mine?"
"Goodbye, Ruby Tuesday."
"Sunday dress, ruby ring."

As I toweled myself off and got into my Holly Hobbie nightgown, I thought about how people liked to touch sparkly things, and it seemed everyone wanted to touch Ruby. If I really was a diamond on the inside like Auntie Melaura had said, I would have willingly ripped off my own flesh to have gotten half the action Ruby got.

That Waxy Lipstick Smell

"I still can't believe you didn't fuck that guy."

Ruby and I were standing in front of the copy place, staring through the plate glass window at Andrew Fink.

"Let's go inside and say hi," I said, seeing him look up from the counter. He smiled at us, and I wanted to feel the sensation of his tongue poking in my mouth again.

"I'm not in the mood," Ruby said, not taking her eyes off him. "Let's just go to Swensen's, then watch TV."

I shrugged in agreement, relenting as usual. I was always a little afraid Ruby would stop being my friend if I said I wanted to do something other than what she wanted. After all, I figured Ruby could be friends with anyone. Even Sandy and that clique would have welcomed her.

We walked up the hill to Swensen's, and saw that inside, Dean, the Saint Ignatius boy, was working today.

"Well, look who's here," he said.

Ruby pulled up her blouse and flashed him her bra. He probably sprang a boner right there, but played it cool. He said, "Mr. Swensen doesn't hire girls because he says they're not strong enough to scoop ice cream."

Ruby loved a challenge. She ran behind the counter and grabbed the scoop, which forced Dean to wrestle with her a little bit. I saw him press against her, and they laughed together as I stood there feeling like a troll.

After a second, Ruby sauntered out from behind the counter triumphantly. Dean scooped our cones, and gave them to us for free.

Licking our ice cream, we left the place and Ruby said, "He's just a W.P.O.D."

Trudging back down the hill, I felt a little jealous. "Hey, maybe there's an Afterschool Special on," I suggested, trying to get the image of Dean bumping up against Ruby out of my mind. While I walked, I thought about calling Andrew once I got home.

We reached Empress Wu's Antiques, and bypassed Cissy by going up the other set of stairs. Up in Ruby's room, I tripped over a white wicker daybed and tumbled into a pile of her dirty clothes, landing on the telephone.

"Hey, let's make our crank calls," she said, looking over to her alarm clock to see what time it was.

Peter B. Higgins, the afternoon deejay on KRQR came on at five. In addition to occasionally asking him to decipher song lyrics, we called him every few days or so, pretending to be different girls requesting tunes. We took turns dialing, and it was my turn today.

I dialed the number and he answered, "KRQR."

I tried to think of what to say, but mostly something that would impress Ruby.

"I really like my tits," I said, then hung up fast.

Ruby rolled her eyes and said, "You're so stupid."

She got up and went to her dresser. Looking in the mirror, she started to put on some makeup.

"New lipstick? Can I try it?" I asked.

"NO!" Ruby practically shouted. I didn't know why she was so upset.

"Look," Ruby said, turning around and planting her hands on her hips. "I want you to stop following me, trying to act like me, and trying to copy me all the time. OKAY?"

"Shit, I just wanted to try your lipstick."

"Aarrgh!" She replaced the cap and threw the tube at me.

"Hey!"

Ruby looked across the room at me, mad at first, but then her face softened into a calm little smile. Where a second ago she'd been pissed, now she wasn't. She said nicely, "Hey, why don't I give you a makeover?"

"Um, okay," I said, just glad she seemed to get over her tantrum.

"Here, sit here," she said, dragging over a chair. "Lean back. It'll be like in a salon. You close your eyes and I'll be the attendant working on you."

I sat down and put my head back on a towel that Ruby rolled up like a cushion.

"Just relax," she said. "I'll start with a concealer to hide this puffiness here."

I felt the soft pressure of a makeup brush and a sponge wisping across my face.

"Wow, this looks really good," she said.

"I want to see," I said, pushing myself up a little.

"NO!" she yelled, and then lowered her voice. "I mean, not yet. Wait till I'm done."

She brushed her hand across my face like she was smoothing on some powder. After a moment, she said, "Hmmm."

"What?"

"Nothing. Well, actually, I don't know."

"What?" I said again, my eyes still shut.

"Well, it's just that my mom has this really expensive hair stuff. You just rub it on and it makes your hair amazing. But I'd have to sneak into my mom's room to get it. Do you want me to?"

"Let me look at the makeup first."

"No!" Then more calmly, she said, "I mean, you don't want to ruin the overall effect, do you?"

"I guess not."

"Good."

Ruby ran off. I sat there with my eyes closed and even though I wanted to look, I stayed still. After a few minutes, her thumping feet came back. Even though my eyes were still closed, I could smell the familiar corn chip smell of her socks.

"Found it," she said. "This is really expensive stuff. My mom'd kill me if she knew we were using it."

I could feel her fingers rubbing something smooth into my hair. But after about thirty seconds, she started laughing, just a little at first, but then her giggles turned to squeals.

I opened my eyes and jumped up from the chair. I looked in the mirror and saw blue eyeshadow circling my eyes, raccoon-style. Bright rouge on my cheeks and pink lipstick smeared beyond my lip line made me look like a clown with a third-degree sunburn. My hair was slicked with mayonnaise.

Ruby stopped laughing. "There!" she screamed. "Buy your own fucking lipstick and stop copying me!"

I ran out the door. Not stopping to put on my shoes, I flew down the hall, under the curtain, and past Cissy, whose back was turned. I ran on to the sidewalk in my socks, on to Polk Street. I didn't care who saw me.

I wasn't going to cry. Not until I got back home, anyway. I ran for a block, feeling my jade pendant on its gold chain inside my blouse, bobbing as I dodged pedestrians. Eventually, I had to wait at the stoplight because traffic was whizzing by. As I stood there, I tried to wipe off my face with my hands and sleeves as best as I could, but I was just in my short-sleeved uniform blouse, so it was hard. In my stocking feet, I could feel pebbles from the blacktop as I crossed the street. When I reached the Chelsea Square mini-mall, I ran into the bathroom.

It was quiet in the ladies room as I cleaned off my face with a rough paper towel and powdered soap. Looking in the mirror at the blue eyeshadow, I felt like a hooker in a shitty movie. As I washed my hair in the unfamiliar sink, I turned my head so that the water dripped down my forehead, and from there I could see my socks, dirty and wet from running down the street.

Flipping my head back over, I cranked the handle of the towel dispenser, and squeezed the water from my hair. I repeated this process several times until my hair was as dry as it was going to get. There was no hand dryer, so I combed my fingers through the tangled mess and stared back at myself. Looking sallow under the fluorescent lighting, I really wished I knew what was so wrong with me that made Ruby hate me.

I left the restroom imagining no one could see me. Still in my socks, I walked up a little ramp and onto the sidewalk. No one could see me, I told myself again. Heading home, I no longer ran, just walked at a regular pace. I was invisible. No one could see me, and even if they could, I just didn't care anymore.

Wandering back to Eggroll Wonderland, I was aware that not one person on the street made eye contact with me. Gay hustlers were emerging from the residence hotels and taking up their stations on the various corners of Polk Street. People getting off the 19 bus looked distracted, dying to get home and eat their leftover Salisbury steaks, or whatever white people ate.

No one could see me, I told myself again as I approached Eggroll Wonderland. I almost missed the restaurant because workmen were setting up scaffolding in front of the window. As I walked through the door I stopped for a moment and saw a sign in my dad's handwriting saying the restaurant would be closed in a few days for remodeling.

It was a strange moment in time. As I stood in the doorway, I didn't see anyone in the restaurant. No one was watching the place. My mother was not standing behind the steaming to-go trays like she usually was, and there were no people eating.

What luck. With my invisible powers I'd made everyone disappear. Or maybe it just happened to be slow that night, just before the dinner rush, and maybe my mom just ducked away to go the toilet. I walked past the cash register calm but fast, not wanting to be around should my mom pop out of the bathroom at any second.

I quickened my step, taking the stairs two at a time, lunging, at last, into the safety of our apartment. Once I was inside my room, I rubbed my face with a clean T-shirt and squeezed the excess water out of my hair. Pulling off my socks, I went right to *Where the Wild Things Are,* which is where I kept the card with Andrew's number. I dialed him, but there was no answer, so I flipped the card over and called him at the copy place.

"Xerox," he said.

"Andrew?"

"Yeah."

"It's me, Candace."

There was a long pause, like he had no fucking idea who I was. My stupid fucking feelings were beginning to crumble when he said, "Oh. What's up?"

"I was wondering what you were doing."

I heard muffled noise, like he'd put his hand over the receiver for a second. I thought I heard laughing. He said, "I'm at work."

After more muffled laughter, he came back on and added, "Hey, my band is playing tonight at the On Broadway. Do you want to come? Starts at eleven."

"Okay," I said, excited. He hung up without saying goodbye, but I felt better already.

My Back Molars

I was unenthusiastic about facing the deep fryer, so I decided to go to the Main Library, which was just a few blocks away on Larkin Street. There, I could watch movies for free on the fifth floor, stuff I might not necessarily get to see, even on cable. Nobody checked if films were R rated; I could just grab one and pop it into one of the Betamax or VHS machines they had in one of the viewing rooms. In the past few weeks I had watched *Cat People* and *Liquid Sky,* and also *Breakfast at Tiffany's, Pretty Baby,* and *The Rocky Horror Picture Show.*

As I walked to the library, in my head I was screaming, I DO NOT WANT TO WORK IN A CHINESE RESTAURANT ALL MY LIFE. Through the heavy door, I walked up the grand staircase, past the bums sleeping on the sides. I looked overhead to the arched limestone ceiling, and saw pigeons fluttering above, but I kept going, finally reaching the top of the steps from which I could see the giant card catalog.

"Oh, hi," said Trudy Lum, the lady who worked at the information desk. Incidentally, Trudy was also the niece of Mrs.

Lum, our upstairs neighbor who was the recipient of the restaurant's chicken innards she fed to her cats.

"Hi," I said, glad for this little exchange. I knew Trudy would no doubt tell Mrs. Lum that she saw me, who would then turn around and report to my dad that her niece saw me at the library. This corroboration of witnesses helped reinforce the image of me as Homework Girl, the best thing a Chinese girl my age could be. But I wasn't there to do homework. I crossed the library floor and went up the steps that led to the open stacks.

The floors were made of frosted glass panels. Although the building was old, this one part seemed modern with steel beams holding up the icy-looking floor. The bookshelves were high; so when I was standing in an aisle, I could easily hide.

Not feeling much in the mood for a movie anymore, I browsed the stacks for an hour, glancing at the spines on the shelves. Really, I just wanted to kill time before going to the club to see Andrew and his band. I could tell it was getting dark outside by the diminishing light from a side window.

Turned out, I wasn't the only one who liked to hide in the stacks. In the next row, something weird was happening. A guy was doing something to another guy because I heard a lot of moaning and slurping noises. I didn't want them to see me so I looked around for something to read while I waited for them to leave. Trapped in the anthropology section, I picked up a book about Ishi, a Yahi Indian captured in the California foothills.

I tried to ignore the groans and gasps as I read, my brain alternately absorbing the textbook's dry information and the wet utterings from the next aisle over. I read that Ishi was studied by a man named Alfred Kroeber, up on the hill near UCSF. Ishi lived in the forest up there, and had a cave where he sometimes hid out. "*Yeah, you like it like that?*" The captive Indian accepted that people liked to gawk at him and performed for their entertainment. His only request of his friend, Kroeber, was that when he died he wanted his body buried whole and intact according to his religion. "*Oh, yeah, suck it.*" He was a living exhibit, but never revealed his true name to his captors. "*Harder, Motherfucker.*" The Last Stone Age Indian of North America died of tuberculosis in 1916. Alfred Kroeber allowed the Smithsonian to remove Ishi's brain before they cremated him. "*Swallow that cock!*"

After the commotion in the next aisle died down, I placed the Ishi book where I found it, and left. Seeing no one as I ducked down the stairs, I headed back to the main floor, and finally outdoors.

It was still too early to go to see Andrew's band, so I decided to head back home. No sooner had I walked through Eggroll Wonderland did my mom bark an appetizer order at me. I raced to the back, threw down my stuff and found myself, once again, standing over the wok waiting for the bubbles to rise in the oil. I had a triple order of crab Rangoon to fry.

Cranking up the heat, I craned my head and looked up through the doorway and saw Mr. Ping scrutinizing some paint samples while holding them up to the greasy wall.

I finished frying. After dumping the three crab Rangoon orders on separate plates, I arranged the ramekins of sauce. My dad happened to be walking by with a tray of chow fun, and offered to take the appetizers to the tables, which was fine with me. My mom yelled over the microphone, "Three order, eggroll!" and as I was cooking those, my mom yelled for two more. When I was finished, I peeled an entire bag of onions, then washed a stack of dishes, including some big pans, which

I especially hated. Before I knew it I had been standing there for hours. It had been a really busy night, and looking at the clock, I suddenly saw that it was ten-thirty.

I knew my parents took about an hour to close up so I either had to sneak out while they were still sweeping and doing dishes, or I had to wait until after eleven forty-five, which was the approximate time they went to sleep, unless, of course, my dad was up watching the naked channel. If they checked up on me, they'd notice I was gone. But I figured it might be worse if, once they got upstairs, they watched television and then I wouldn't be able to sneak out at all.

I decided it would be best to go upstairs, change my clothes, and sneak out while my parents were still closing up the restaurant. I jogged upstairs and pulled on jeans and my fuzzy, green sweater that always reminded me of Oscar the Grouch.

I tiptoed down the stairs that bypassed the restaurant and led directly to the sidewalk. Out on the street were a mishmash of people. None of the shoppers who were around in the daytime were out, and working folks had already gone inside their apartments. After walking to Union Street, I caught a bus that took me over the hill and within walking distance of the On Broadway.

In North Beach I walked past bars and nudie places. No one noticed me walking around, maybe because my clothes were dark or they just didn't care. I passed beneath flashing bulbs and neon lights illuminating the silhouette of a nude girl on the Garden of Eden sign. Across the street, Carol Doda's boobies blinked on and off, but the left boob was burned out.

Finally, near the Mabuhay Gardens, I saw Andrew standing out front, right next door to the On Broadway.

"I was wondering if you'd show," he said.

"I'm here, aren't I?"

Smiling, he led me up to the ticket booth and told the person behind the glass, "Give her the double x's."

Andrew slid some money over while the guy took a permanent marker and drew an "x" on the back of my left hand and then did the same to my right. We went up the stairs.

Tragic Mulatto was already playing, but there was hardly anyone there. We took seats in the middle of the cavernous place, which was like a movie theater with the band up higher on a stage. Behind them was a screen playing some kind of film, but I didn't pay too much attention as Andrew immediately attached his mouth to mine and reached his hand inside my sweater. I liked the sensation of his tongue slithering inside my mouth with a kind of urgency, like we were in love, and I wondered if I was.

I passively sat there and let Andrew feel me up until, after a while, he abruptly stopped kissing me and then sat there like we hadn't been making out just a second ago. In a way, I was glad he had stopped groping me because I had my period and had a thick maxipad between my legs. Just when I was thinking this, I felt a big blob of blood ooze out and I prayed it all got sopped up by the pad and didn't soak through my pant leg.

Looking over, I saw that Andrew was watching the band. Sitting up, I stared up at the stage, too, like I was interested. I wondered if I should reach over to him and hold his hand, and as I was thinking about it, my eyes focused on the imagery on the screen behind Tragic Mulatto. At first I thought it looked abstract—the pink, red, and black colors. Then the picture resembled body parts, a heart pumping maybe, or something hairy. Eventually I realized that it was a close-up of two people Doing It. The movie didn't show any other parts of the people, but I was fairly sure that that's what it was. I could't see the top part of the man—just his Thing that looked like a tube as it went in and out really fast.

We didn't make out again before his band went onstage. During the intermission, he and his friends set up their drum kit and other instruments. I sat alone in the dark theater with only a couple of other people I didn't know in the back. I really wished Andrew would come back because he hadn't even said one word to me since we'd come inside. I sat for about a half an hour longer and wondered if my parents at home had opened the door to my room and found the pile of stuffed animals I'd left buried under the blankets to resemble my flabass body.

Finally, Andrew and his band started to play. I recognized the drummer and the bass player from the copy place, but I hadn't seen the guitarist before. Andrew was at the microphone, kind of sing-talk-wailing, and looked kind of sinister up there under the blue light. Also, he looked old. I wondered if the person I'd been making out with could really be that old guy up there who wasn't a very good singer. He no longer looked much like Martin Fry from ABC to me, but maybe because I always imagined Martin Fry would at least be, well, nice.

They played about a dozen songs, each of which, I had to admit, was terrible. There were no catchy beats or even intelligible lyrics, just clangy chords that made the silver fillings in my teeth hurt. I heard him sing something about "autocracy" and I wasn't sure what that was, but it sounded boring.

After their set was done, the show was over. I was the only one sitting there now watching as they dragged their instruments offstage. I got up from my seat and walked over to Andrew who was by the side door talking to the guitar player

I didn't know. He didn't introduce me, which I found kind of rude.

"What are you going to do now?" I asked.

"Go home," he said. I wasn't sure if he was saying that he was going to go home or if he was telling me I should go home. Either way, he didn't invite me to hang out with him. He picked up some of the sound equipment and joined his friends loading their van parked out by the side door.

Standing there, I felt stupid and didn't want to feel like a hanger-on so I turned and headed up the ramp and then down the stairs, out the way I came in, except now I was by myself.

Back out on the street, it was late but I didn't know what time exactly. I didn't see any buses coming so I started to walk and ended up cutting through Chinatown. I passed dumpsters and lots of *bok choy* and cabbage strewn about the sidewalk. Grant Avenue was narrow and quiet, and in the living quarters above the storefronts I saw old Chinese people sitting in their underclothes watching television. In one window of a brick building I saw a little girl staring down at me. She lifted up her chubby hand and waved at me with curiosity. I gazed back at her, too, but just for a second. I looked away, embarrassed.

Heading up Sacramento Street, I expected the 1 California bus to come, but it never did. I ended up walking all the way past the fancy Nob Hill places until I reached Polk Street, the whole time scanning the doorways for anyone who might mug me. Approaching Eggroll Wonderland I saw all the lights were out in the restaurant as well as in our apartment above.

I went in and tiptoed up the stairs. Everything was quiet, and I sensed that my parents were asleep. But I was wrong. Making my way to my room, I saw someone shuffling around in the dark so I quickly ducked into the bathroom and shut the door slightly.

"Who is it?" my mom said gruffly in Chinese.

"Only me," I answered in the dark. "Just going *chee-saw*."

The light flicked on. My mom, squinting, looked at my clothes and in a split second figured out that I hadn't been sleeping all this time, but had been out.

"Where you go?" my mom screamed. "How many time I have to tell you? You go out and get rape!"

In her ratty nightgown with the worn-out areas around the armpits, my mom grabbed me and started shaking me.

"Let go of me, you crazy bitch," I yelled back.

"What you call me?" My mom yanked me over to the small bathroom sink and started to wash my mouth out with Irish Spring. Although I was actually bigger and stronger than her, I didn't fight back. I let my mom wash out the inside of my cheeks and alongside my gums and teeth. The soap tasted a lot worse than I expected, burning my tongue as I tried not to swallow. I could feel it leaking down my throat, making me want to gag, but as a point of pride, I choked it back.

"I teach you to shallup you mouse!" my mom said, which was her version of saying, "Shut up your mouth." Her agile fingers scrubbed my mouth like a cup. She made sure to get into the corners behind my back molars, and even under my tongue. My eyes were watering by now and I was about to throw up.

I hated her. I couldn't believe that for nine months she'd carried me in her womb like Mary did Jesus. He was the fruit of her womb, but I felt like a different species than my mother. As she jabbed her hand inside my mouth, I pictured my infant-self tearing my way out of my mom's flesh like that thing in *Alien*.

I heard my dad, sleepy-eyed in the hallway. "What going on?" he said.

As my mom turned, I took the opportunity to wrench myself away and escape to my bedroom. From behind the door I could hear my mom yelling in Chinese.

Spitting and coughing into a balled-up T-shirt, I tried to get all the soap out of my mouth. Through my tears I saw two beady, shiny eyes staring at me from behind yellow plastic. It was Twinkiechubs, wide awake and seeming to wonder what was wrong. "Can I help?" the little eyes seemed to ask.

I removed the lid to the Habitrail, and reached inside to grab the hamster's water bottle. Twinkiechubs managed to somehow hook herself onto the nozzle and hitched a ride as I lifted out the plastic tube. With a flick of the wrist, I flung her off and she landed somewhere in the corner with a boneless thud. As I unscrewed the cap and rinsed out my mouth, she ran under my dresser and hid. I didn't bother to chase after her as I gargled the water and spit it out into the T-shirt. I cried very softly against the door and waited until I heard my parents go back to their room.

When my eyes adjusted to the darkness, I saw that everything was how I'd left it. All the stuffed animals were in the exact same position, so I was pretty sure that my parents never came in and checked on me. I pulled off my clothes and got into my nightgown, then into bed, kicking all the animals off to the side, except for my gigantic beanbag frog, Big Mama, whom I placed over my face, once again, like an ice pack. As I lay there, I really wanted to get up and brush my teeth and wash my face but I didn't dare.

Removing the frog from my face, I put my arms around my pillow. I pretended I was hugging Adam Ant and asked him, "What am I going to do?"

I rolled over and reached for Mr. Toucan. I wanted to stuff

him into my underwear and mash his soft beak between my legs, but I remembered I had my period. I checked to make sure my maxipad wasn't soaked through, then flopped back onto my bed. Staring out into black space, I listened to my own shallow breathing, too scared to reach over and put on a tape.

Pliant, Little-Nobody Body

Standing in the schoolyard the following Monday, I looked up to the windows of the adjacent apartment buildings. I wondered what the people who lived there thought as they looked down on us schoolkids all day, every day. Once I saw an old man in his underwear eating a piece of toast. Another time, a teacher-looking lady was putting on underarm deodorant.

Speaking of which, I had been needing deodorant myself lately. My armpits at the St. Michael's game had been totally sweaty and a little stinky. Stinkier than usual. School-wise, I figured I stank more than Tina with the Perfect Perm, but less than Gwen with the Greasy Bangs. I needed deodorant but didn't want to dip into my Barbie Corvette savings just for that. But then again, I couldn't bring myself to ask my parents for money because they'd ask me what for, and then they'd tell me that Chinese people didn't need deodorant; only white, black, and Mexican people did. Come to think of it, I needed razors to shave my legs, and also Ten-O-Six astringent, and Love's Baby Soft perfume, which was what I would need to smell like if I ever really did meet Ric Ocasek or Adam Ant.

At lunchtime, I was sitting on a bench, carefully touching part of my ear that still hurt from my mom's smackdown the night before. Ruby was absent, and I thought about her and the shitty thing she'd done to me as I listened to a couple of sixth-grade girls by the hopscotch singing,

> Say say oh enemy/ Come out and war with me
> And bring your pistols three/ I hope you skin your
>   knee
> Slide down my warpath/ Into my dungeon door
> And we'll be hateful friends/ Forever more,
>   more . . .
> Kick you out the back door!

Chewing a nail, I heard someone yelling over to me.

"Hey Candace, play tag with us," called Christy.

Even though we were on student council and the basketball team together, Christy and I never socialized on the regular schoolyard. Our fiefdoms were separate, and an offer to play tag with her clique was akin to being asked to tea at Bucking-ham Fucking Palace. Never once since the third grade had she ever asked me to play, so I figured, hey, why not?

"Okay," I said, and stood up to join my classmates.

The game was the usual exercise in pain and humiliation. Any teacher walking by would be unaware of any hostile shenani-gans, but the aim of the schoolyard chase was to either pull up the skirts of the girls, or knee the boys in the crotch. My class had been playing this kind of "tag" for two years now, since sixth grade, but the game's specifics had been inherited from many an eighth-grade class before ours. Guys got their nuts kicked by anyone and everyone, and girls' underpants were exposed to the delight of all. Catching the person was only part of the fun. The true pleasure, all chasers would agree, came only if and when the victim started to cry. No one ever objected to the cruelty of the game. It's just the way it was.

I became "it" after one boy grabbed me and snapped my bra. I held down my uniform skirt before he could pull it up, so luckily, no one saw my Wonder Woman Underoos. But it bothered me to have been caught so fast, and I could still feel my sore ear, seeming to throb worse now that I'd been running around. The kids were all moving fast, eluding me with fake-out dashes one way, followed by sprints in the opposite direction. Everyone seemed impossible to catch, and I wished I hadn't agreed to play.

I wanted the bell to ring or for someone else to be "it." I'd gotten tired and Percy Menky was taunting me with his albino monkey face. His sharp, pointy, canine teeth jutted out like stalactites from his red, candy-rotted gums.

I decided to go after someone small, slow, and harmless. I spotted Ella Ng in the distance and took off running in her direction. Suddenly, I was a torpedo launched from a submarine, headed dead straight toward the pathetic little dinghy that was sixty-two pound Ella Ng, bobbing in the outer area by the four-square court.

I imagined that Ella was a target painted yellow, just like the limp, lace-covered dress that hung off her skinny frame on picture day. Ella was oblivious to the fact that I was headed right toward her. When she finally did realize that I was aiming for her, she just stood there and screamed without running until I knocked her over and she went flying like a bowling pin.

When I pulled up her skirt, I felt her pliant, little-nobody body go slack. She didn't fight back or try to get away, and her passivity, for some reason, infuriated me. I pulled down her underpants as well, and her knees got quickly tangled up in the yellow panties with pink flowers, and she fell to the asphalt.

As the other eighth-graders circled around Ella and laughed, I calmly walked back into the school building, up the stairs, and into our classroom. I sat at my desk for the remainder of lunch, and when the bell rang, my classmates came back in, refreshed and ready for Religion.

Life Is a Pop of a Cherry

*L*ater that afternoon, I was standing in the back of the restaurant washing a thousand dishes. Because of all the steam and hot water, I was sweating. As I stared at a teetering stack of platters with food still stuck on them, I hated how dirty and sticky I felt. I could tell I smelled like fish sauce.

Ripping off the rubber gloves, I decided to walk to Record Factory to visit my friend, Albert. I was glad that Ruby had been absent from school that day, and I figured I needed to start cultivating other friendships since things were obviously getting totally fucked up between her and me.

Albert Carrasco was cute, Mexican, and gay. When I first started visiting him at the record store, those were the only things I knew about him. But by now I'd known him at least a year, and had learned that he was eighteen, and the grandson of the former vice president of Mexico. He was the bastard son that his dad had had with a soap opera star. His dad used to feel generous and sympathetic toward his existence, but recently sent him a letter saying he wanted nothing to do with

him. Albert was determined, though, that one way or another
he was going to be wealthy someday and pursue his dream of
being a world-famous mime, like Robert Shields, only Mexican. But for now he was just a clerk at a not-so-good record
store.

"Hey," I said, perusing the 45s.

"Hey. I get off in five minutes. Wanna hang out?"

"Okay," I said.

As I waited and browsed, I snuck peeks at Albert. He was
wearing his favorite outfit—a tight, red T-shirt, and black peg-
leg jeans. He had a shaggy haircut and looked like a pretty
Mexican girl, except with a huge bulge in his pants, Ziggy
Stardust-style.

"Be right back," he said, striding toward the back room,
presumably to get his stuff.

A minute later he returned with his leather jacket and sunglasses on.

"Ready, Angel?" Out on the street, I liked the feeling of
walking and being free from Eggroll Wonderland. We walked
farther and farther, down Polk Street and then up and over
Russian Hill until we were in North Beach.

Albert lived in an alley called Varennes, off Union Street. Up
some rickety steps, there was a warren of tiny apartments in a
really old wooden building. The place looked like it could fall
down any moment, and I took note of the peeling paint, transom windows with big cracks, and old hexagonal tiles that used
to be turquoise, but now were so worn away that they were
white and smooth with only faint green-blue corners in hard-
to-see places like right up against the wall behind the radiator.

Inside Albert's apartment it smelled like clove cigarettes. As
he straightened up the place, I looked around.

First off, Barbie dolls were everywhere. They were arranged

around the room with all the current accessories that I had seen advertised on television. Malibu Barbie was in the elevator of the three-story townhouse, bubble-haired Midge was having her hair done in the beauty parlor, and Superstar and Skipper were frolicking in the day spa and gazebo, respectively. In a plastic camper, with the little gold crown fused to her blond bun-head, Ballerina Barbie was naked and spread-eagle with Sweet Sixteen's face mashed between her legs. The white, satin tutu was artfully ripped, resting on the hood of a pink dune buggy.

"They drove to the beach, and lust overcame them," Albert said, noticing me admiring his diorama. "Look, I've even added pubes." He carefully separated the dolls and showed how he'd glued tiny, nylon hairs between their legs.

"Check it out," he said, "I trimmed her bangs to give her some fringe down there."

I smiled, thinking he was a freak. Stepping away, I left him to rearrange the scenario while I checked out the rest of his small apartment.

"Don't you have a refrigerator?" I asked, standing in a corner that was supposed to pass as a kitchen.

"No," Albert said, coming over and adjusting an overturned milk crate. "But food can last unrefrigerated longer than you might think. Eggs, about a week. Milk, three days. Want a bowl of Lucky Charms?"

"No, I'm not hungry," I said. I actually wouldn't have minded eating something, but it seemed weird to drink milk that hadn't been in the fridge. Albert shrugged, shook out some cereal into a bowl, poured milk over it, and started to eat.

"Go ahead and look through my tapes," he said, noticing me eyeing a stack of cassettes visible in his closet behind a partition.

"Okay," I said. I stepped over a bare-breasted Francie doll on all fours getting humped by a Magic Sideburns Ken.

Picking through the plastic cases, I stopped to admire Split Enz and the Kinks. Albert had pasted pictures from magazines over a lot of the cases, some with movie stars, and others with just weird images. One had no words on it, but was decorated with a picture of this huge, fat lady, like three-hundred pounds, and she had her fat-lady dress hitched up to her waist, and her big legs were spread and there was a cord, like one from a hairdryer, going from a wall socket to the inside of her, between her legs. It was all hairy down there and I looked closer at the picture and could see dark purplish folds of skin, and could see there was something inside the fat lady. She was holding her hand down there and making a weird face that freaked me out. After five seconds, I couldn't decide what to think, so I just put the tape down.

"Anything in there you want to borrow?" Albert said, his mouth full of cereal.

"No, thanks," I said, but for some reason I pocketed Adam and the Ants' *Dirk Wears White Sox.* Even though Albert would have just lent it to me, it just sort of felt good to take something.

Emerging from behind the partition, I saw some Polaroid pictures on a wall and stepped closer to study them. Albert wandered over.

"There's me and Billy Flash at the Castro Street Fair . . . Steaven and Armando at the Patio . . ." As he narrated, he pointed to his friends, all tan and gorgeous.

"Who's this?" I asked, staring in awe at a photo of a thin blonde with chiseled features. "He looks exactly like David Bowie."

"Doesn't he?"

"How do you know him?"

"Fred? He's . . . the man who fell to earth."

I wanted to know more, and gave Albert a look.

"Fred has the unique talent of telling people exactly what they want to hear. And he's gorgeous, of course. Has the best clothes. Oh, and he lives in an amazing castle over on the other side of town."

"A *castle*?"

"Yeah, right here in San Francisco. Can you believe it? It's out in India Basin, and it used to have a windmill in the back. All the chicken coops and stuff are gone, but beneath the main house is a cave and an underwater spring."

"Take me there sometime?" I asked.

"Well . . . maybe. I'm not sure you could handle it."

I hated when Albert tried to pull his mysterious, older and wiser shit on me. Puh-lease. After all, he was the one with all the Barbies. And besides, he was only four years older than me. Sulking, I sat down on the floor next to a stack of records and flipped through them.

I hung out a little while longer, and right before I was about to leave, I noticed out the window that it had started raining.

"Fucking weather," Albert said. "I don't have an umbrella, but do you want to borrow a jacket?"

"Nah, it's okay."

I took the 41 Union bus over the hill, but when I got to Polk Street, the 19 was nowhere in sight. I walked the rest of the way, periodically turning around in hopes that the bus was on its way, but it wasn't. By the residence hotels, I passed doorways with boy hustlers hunched in the rain, but they didn't bother me.

It was getting dark out. The rain had been light at first, but was now steady. I was getting drenched and really wished I had an umbrella. Cold air penetrated my clothes and seeped right through to my skin. Lost in thought, when I walked by the Leland Hotel, I didn't realize that someone was trying to get my attention.

"Hey," he said, grabbing my wet arm. "You're soaked, come inside."

I stepped under the awning and looked at who was talking to me. He looked vaguely familiar, but I couldn't place him.

"It's me," he said. "Pete."

"Oh," I said. He was the juggler from Pier 39. I didn't recognize him without his juggling pins, unicycle, or an offer to go bowling.

"Let's get you inside and dry. You're drenched, Babe."

I was only a couple of blocks from the restaurant, but I was freezing so I ducked into the lobby with him. I was glad to be out of the rain, even for a moment. I wasn't planning on staying, but he beckoned me to follow him, and I did, walking up some stairs with crappy carpeting that smelled like dogfood.

"You live here?" I asked.

"Yeah, I pay weekly. It's pretty cheap," he said.

We got to a brown door with a brass number on it, and we went inside.

"I have some towels," he said. "Do you want something to eat?"

Looking around the place, I wasn't sure why I'd agreed to come up to this depresso lair. Just like Andrew's apartment, it was all just one big room with a sink in the corner, no bathroom. There was a tiny cube of a fridge, and Pete started pulling stuff out, making something. As I rubbed my face on a not-too-clean-smelling towel, he talked over his shoulder at me.

"Yeah, I thought it might rain today, and I was right. So I

knocked off early. But this is much more fun, wouldn't ya say? Don't you think you should get out of those wet clothes?"

There was a warped, full-length mirror leaning up against the window and in the reflection I could see that I was soaked to the skin, and through my wet uniform blouse I saw that anyone could see the outline of my chest fairly well. Pete looked over at me with a goofy expression, and as he stirred chili that he was heating up on a hot plate, I knew I didn't want to be there.

Unable to think of any polite way to excuse myself, I watched for when Pete looked away, and when he did, I walked fast over to the door, turned the knob, and walked out. I heard him yell, "Hey, wait a minute!" as I started to run down the hall.

Right before I got to the stairs, I nearly collided with a guy in a Roxy Music T-shirt.

"Hey, aren't you Andrew's friend?" he said.

Standing there, I said, "Who are you?"

"David. I play guitar. Didn't you come to our show at the On Broadway?"

Just then, Pete came walking fast down the hall. "Hey!" he called down toward us.

The guitar player touched my arm and said, "You know *the juggler*? That guy is a total molester!"

Watching the gangly limbed, floppy-haired juggler pick up speed and come running toward us, I yelled, "The juggler is after me!"

David shuffled me quickly around the corner and into his own room down the hall. Slamming the door behind us, I felt exhilarated, like I'd just escaped from a villain in a movie.

David popped open a root beer and gave it to me, and for a

while we just looked out his window and watched the rain. It was really pouring now. As a curtain he had a Greek flag, and he pulled it aside so we had a better view.

He said, "At first I wasn't sure if you were the girl who came to the club, or that other Chinese girl that Andrew hangs out with. You know, the pretty one. I mean, sorry. Um, not that you're not pretty, too."

"Who?"

He chewed a nail and thought a minute. "She wears the same uniform as you so I figured you must be friends. What's her name . . . uh, is it . . . Ruby?"

I stared at him, dumbfounded for a second. Since when had *Ruby and Andrew* been hanging out?

Then all of a sudden, David leaned over and kissed me. I was so agitated to have inadvertently found out that Ruby was trying to hijack my boyfriend that I stuck my tongue in David's mouth and we started to make out. I put my arms around him and he started mashing against me. It felt good to have someone being nice to me for a change. I wasn't sure why I didn't think he was a sleaze, but I just didn't. He called me "sweetie" and didn't try to take off my clothes or anything. We just kissed and rolled around and it felt good.

After a while, David turned on the TV and we watched the *Flintstones*. We laughed and agreed that the Great Gazoo was totally gay.

"What is it now, Dum-dum?" David said, imitating the green Martian. We laughed and kissed some more.

From his clock I could see that it was getting late, so when there was a break in the rain, I told him I had to go. I still couldn't believe what he'd said about Andrew and Ruby hanging around together. He kissed me goodbye and said,

"See you around." He didn't walk me down to the lobby, but that was okay.

Darting out onto the sidewalk, I arrived quickly at Eggroll Wonderland. I put on my apron right away and started to help my mom. I dished up a large portion of Mongolian beef and also an order of *gah-lee guey*, and packed a medium steamed rice into a paper carton as my mom rang it all up for a bald guy.

It was a typical night in my life. When the dinner rush died down, my dad browned five pounds of ground pork in a huge wok, and shook the meat into a huge Tupperware container. He also shredded huge mounds of cabbage and about twenty carrots, placing it all in a storage tray. These ingredients, sprinkled with a majorly unhealthy dose of monosodium glutamate, went inside the eggrolls.

I dolloped the ingredients inside the wrappers made of thin wheat dough, and pinched them shut just-so. I would undoubtedly be the one frying them, so if I didn't assemble them right, I'd be the one who was going to suffer. It sucked when the eggrolls unraveled and spewed bits of stuff into the clean, bubbling hot oil, and I hated fishing out the flotsam and jetsam with the slotted spoon. I made sure to roll them right so I didn't have to deal with that headache later.

Tonight, as usual, I set up a station at one of the restaurant's back tables. Just like with wontons, I could assemble eggrolls without looking, making row after row on a cookie sheet that I'd later cover with foil and slide onto a lower shelf in the refrigerator.

As I worked, I watched the people in the restaurant. There was a group of people at the big table—a Chinese man with his white wife or girlfriend, and it looked like their families were meeting for the first time. The white people used chopsticks, and I guessed that they were wanting to show the Chinese people that they could. The Chinese people ate with forks, maybe figuring they didn't need to prove they could work chopsticks. I smiled to myself, watching the white people trying to act nonchalant, like they ate slices of beef tongue and jellyfish all the time. But I could tell they were freaked out by the way they pursed their skinny lips around the meat and tried not to gag.

Over at another table, I saw someone I knew. It was a nine-year-old girl who always looked kind of skanky, that is, if someone who was nine could even be called skanky. But yeah, she was. I often saw her wandering around Polk Street. Her mom was a road dog who looked like a homeless Grace Slick, and the kid cruised around all day, her mom kind of using the shopkeepers as a babysitting collective.

I didn't know her name, but the girl was pale and skinny. Tonight she was wearing a denim jacket, a really short miniskirt, and lipstick. Her hair was all fucked up, like she couldn't see the back well enough to comb it. She was sitting with her hands folded, and although I couldn't completely hear what she was saying, I could tell she was trying to be polite and chirpy.

She wasn't with her mom, but with a fat, old guy at table three. He was really hairy and nasty-looking, and I could tell he wasn't her dad or even remotely related to her, just by the pervy way he was eyeballing her. Periodically his eyes darted around the room to see if anybody was looking at them.

The guy didn't seem to see me because I was in the corner. Or maybe he figured that since I worked there, I didn't count as a real person. Or maybe Chinese people were invisible. Anyway, the girl looked like she was wanting food because her eyes kept wandering over to the nearby to-go counter where the pot stickers were sitting in a chafing dish. I imagined she was wondering if it might have been easier just to swipe a couple of dumplings when no one was looking rather than sit there with that gross, old guy, waiting for him to give her his leftovers. As for the guy, he was starting to look sweaty, like he was pondering what he could get from the girl without going to jail.

I thought of *Lolita* and felt bad for the girl because her mom just dumped her off on the street and wouldn't come back for hours. Who knew where the hell they lived? I empathized with her because the Polk Street Humbert Humberts followed me, too. But at least I could hide in the restaurant and had somewhat normal parents and food.

I felt sorry for her. A little girl shouldn't be so skanky. She was a poor little greenie, just like me, and it made me sad that no one was looking out for her. As I watched her fidgeting, it was like watching a nine-year-old me. There was something behind her wanting-to-please eyes that I recognized in myself. She was working the twinkly eyed angel angle. She smiled to maximize the cuteness of her dimples. I knew her tricks so well because mine were exactly the opposite. As I studied her, I noted that she giggled where I would have looked down and away. When she batted her eyelashes and winked, it was where I would have scoffed. I thought she was playing it all wrong. But then again, maybe she was just too fucking hungry to play it cool.

Feeling like I had to do something, I got up from my chair and abruptly walked over to their table. The lipstick-wearing nine-year-old didn't even see me. She was too busy trying to charm her meal ticket. Unexpectedly, even to myself, I grabbed the girl's hand and yanked her to her feet, dragging her out the front door.

"Hey!" the guy yelled, but I kept going, the girl in tow.

Outside, a few storefronts down from the restaurant, I said, "Do you know that guy?"

The girl shrugged, then scanned the street, maybe looking for her mom. After a second, she said, "Do you know those little fruit pies? Will you get me one at the liquor store? Cherry, okay?"

We walked down to the corner of Bush Street and went inside Sukkers Liquors. It smelled like rat poison, cigarettes, and air freshener. The girl wanted a cherry-flavored pie, the kind with Twinkie the Kid on the package holding a lasso. I bought it for her, and outside the liquor store she ripped open the wax paper and scarfed down the pie messily, the red jelly-filling smearing together with her pink lipstick.

When I returned to Eggroll Wonderland, the fat guy was gone. The big group had left, too, and there was nothing left to do but resume assembling eggrolls. I sat down and rolled together about thirty more, and then a family came in and ordered some, so I jumped up to fry a plateful, but not from the new ones on the cookie sheet, but from yesterday's stack in the fridge that I knew to use up first.

I worked until ten o'clock, side by side with my mother. It actually turned out to be a really busy night for the restaurant, and as my dad cooked the orders in the back, my mom and I had a good rhythm going. We switched off, taking turns dishing food into containers, working the cash register, and calling through the microphone to my dad, telling him which things we needed more of up front.

At the end of the night my mom asked me if I had any homework to finish, and I lied and said I didn't. The truth was, I'd actually skipped doing homework for a whole week, something I'd never done before, even when I had the chicken pox in fourth grade. I was in total denial that my books and backpack were gone, tossed into the bay by the girls who threatened to break my chink fuckin' face. I wanted to tell my mom what happened at Pier 39, but didn't want her to blame me for wasting my time, or tell me it was my own fault, or say I was lucky I hadn't been raped.

I said, "Yeah, all my homework is finished."

"Good girl," she said, and we both pretended she hadn't screamed at me or washed my mouth out with soap a few nights ago.

Whipped Me Across the Face
with the Hot Wheels Track

I was alone in my stuffy bedroom. Big Mama, my beanbag bullfrog, had sprung a leak, and I was trying to glue shut the tiny hole that had begun to fray along one of her legs. As I squeezed a dot of glue onto the fabric leg, I tried to hold the edges of the hole shut, but the cotton just absorbed the white goo and nothing would stick.

Thinking of Auntie Melaura, I reached up and absentmindedly touched the jade pendant she'd given me. Deciding that the hole in Big Mama's leg was too big for glue, I figured I needed to find a needle and thread.

I headed down the hall. My parents were downstairs in the restaurant, but I knew that my mom kept the sewing stuff in their bedroom. I went there and found the travel sewing kit in a drawer, but then figured I might as well snoop around to see if I could find any photos of Auntie Melaura. I rummaged around in the dresser drawers, but there was nothing but so-worn-out-they-were-see-through undershirts and my mom's stretched-out, high-waisted, granny underpants.

Opening the closet door, I pushed my mom's old jackets to the side and spotted the black garment bag I knew she kept there. Inside were some of Auntie Melaura's dresses. I'd seen my mom looking at them once when she didn't know I was watching. I reached into the back of the closet and lifted out the bag. It was long and heavy, and I had to hoist it up so it wouldn't drag on the floor.

Gently, I laid the garment bag on the bed and unzipped it slowly, as if Melaura herself were lying inside it. Cocooned in plastic, the red brocade cheongsam was immediately recognizable. As I parted the plastic, I was certain it must have been the dress she'd worn at the Miss Chinatown pageant. I lifted the dress out by its hanger and held the silk to my face, feeling its softness. I caught a whiff of Auntie Melaura's old perfume, still embedded in the fabric after all these years. As I inhaled, the immediacy of her death flooded my senses. Death smelled like Rive Gauche and talcum powder.

I arranged the dress back onto the hanger, zipped up the garment bag, and crammed it back into my mother's closet. Straightening the bedspread, I accidentally kicked something under the bedframe. I reached below the frame to see what it was, and pulled out a Playboy magazine. Feeling around, I found a whole bunch more.

Careful not to crease them, I silently turned the glossy pages. I was disgusted that my dad could look at these magazines, but I was simultaneously fascinated by them. There were cartoons of girls with boobs that looked like rockets, and real pictures of naked girls with white tan lines from bikinis. There was one spread with cheerleaders in various states of undress, some wearing silver cowboy boots, and nothing much else. Scrutinizing a rosy-cheeked butt, I detected a sudden drop in the room's atmosphere, and suddenly the air felt different.

It was my mom. "*Ai-ya*! What you looking at? *Hom sup nueyr*!" Translating in my head, I thought my mom just called me a perverted girl, but just then I noticed something in my mom's hand. She started belting me with orange strips of Hot Wheels racetrack, and I felt them whip across my legs and wrap around my thighs with each blow.

"Get off me!" I yelled at my mom.

"Why you act so craze?" she hollered back.

I tried to cover my legs as my mom beat me like a disobedient dog. I wanted so bad to hit her back, but instead I screamed, "Crazy like Auntie Melaura?"

As an unspoken rule, when my mom hit me, she never aimed for my head or face. However, at the mention of Auntie Melaura's name, my mom got an insane look in her eyes. She raised up her arm, and smacked me across the face with the Hotwheels track.

Holding my cheek and lip, I saw my mom's cold, hard stare and grim mouth. I wanted to hurt her like she was hurting me, but instead of balling up my fist and punching her, I screamed, "I think you secretly want me to get raped! Yeah, I want to be raped, and get it over with, so maybe then you'll just shut up."

I wasn't really sure why I said this, but when I saw my mom looking confused and worried, I liked it. I suddenly felt powerful. I took my words a step further, and said, "Yeah, I'll get raped like Auntie Melaura, then I'll jump off the bridge and kill myself!"

It was the most evil thing that came to mind. I added, "I'm going to kill myself like Auntie Melaura and then you'll finally be happy."

Seeing the rage in my mother's eyes made me feel stronger than I had ever felt before. Victorious, I breathed the air from the room, imagining inhaling every last molecule of oxygen as my mother suffocated in the silence.

My mom, looking deflated, dropped her arms to her sides. The Hot Wheels tracks fell to the floor like giant strips of orange licorice. She began to walk away, but then turned around and said to me, "You are very bad girl."

Standing there in a heap of wrinkled and ripped nudie magazines, I kicked them under the bed without folding or stacking them. When did I become a very bad girl? I used to be my mom's plum blossom. That's what she used to call me when I was small. I guess I wasn't a plum blossom anymore. Auntie Melaura used to be a plum blossom, too.

Drifting into My Solitude,
Over My Head

I had to get out of the apartment. I ran down the stairs and out onto Polk Street, standing stupidly in the middle of the sidewalk for a minute. On the one hand, I really wanted to find out if Ruby and Andrew were hanging out together, but I hadn't seen her since the "makeover" incident, and I wasn't looking forward to going back to her place. If she and Andrew had been hanging out, that meant that Ruby had gone into the Xerox store behind my back and started shaking her tits in his face, which was totally something she would have done.

I headed toward Andrew's. I still held onto the improbable notion that David, the guitar player, was wrong about my Best Friend Forever and my would-be boyfriend. The cliché of it all was just so retarded. If David *was* wrong, then maybe Andrew and I would even make out again and I might see his Thing once more. As I turned left on Pine Street and made my way toward his place, I considered that maybe I'd touch it this time if he asked me to.

When I got there, a delivery person was just leaving and held the door open for me. I walked quietly up the stairs, but when I got to the top, I saw that the door to Andrew's room was ajar. Maybe he was talking on the phone to his bandmates or had just taken another bath, in which case he'd be coming down the hall in his bathrobe any minute. I got excited thinking about his Old-Spice-and-Tenax smell, and suddenly wished I had put on makeup or something before having come over here. I took slow steps toward his door edging myself along the banister so he couldn't see me. As I approached, I heard voices.

"I love eating cheap Chinese," I heard him say, followed by the sound of giggles. Girl giggles. Unmistakable Ruby Ping giggles.

I could see her on his bed, half-covered by a blanket. He was scooting up closer to the pillows, emerging from the tent created by her legs and the sheet. He rolled over on his back and I got a good look at him.

Seeing Andrew instantly brought back the sensation of his mouth on me. I leaned up against the wall, remembering the way he shoved his hips into mine when we had made out. Pressing my thighs together, I didn't want to remember that feeling or acknowledge the fact that right now I felt a certain wetness between my legs. I stayed still against the wall and listened.

"Whatever happened to your little friend?" I heard him say.

"Who? Oh, her. We're not really friends anymore."

I almost died when I heard Ruby say this. Like the moron I was, for a second I believed she couldn't possibly have been talking about me.

"Oh, well," Andrew said. "She came to one of our gigs once."

He tossed off this comment nonchalantly, like he barely knew me. Was that all? Didn't he even remember making out with me, or rubbing his hands all over my tits, or sticking his tongue in my mouth and asking me to eat his fucking, disgusting pinky rat?

And then I heard him say, "Yeah, she did kind of smell like Chinese food," and then they both burst out laughing.

I peered inside and saw Ruby's smug little face plastered on her tiny pinhead. She was laughing so hard with her head thrown back, I could see the silver fillings in her teeth. They started kissing, and when she wrapped her arms around his back, I focused on her bitten-down fingernails and the spot on her ring finger where the ugly wart used to be.

On the floor I could see her inside-out dirty underwear. Suddenly I hated her guts and conjured all the disgusting things about her that I'd always overlooked, like her gross habit of wiping her ass from back to front. We'd gone to the bathroom together once and I'd seen her do it. First, it was revolting that she even took a crap in front of me when I thought we were both just going to pee, but when she wiped the wrong way, that was the most unsanitary thing I'd ever seen. I wondered if Ruby ever got shit in her pee-hole.

Standing there a few feet from them but out of their line of sight, part of me still pathetically hoped she and I were still friends. I wanted to ask her if he stuck his dick inside her and what it felt like. What did it feel like to hump a real person and not just a stuffed animal?

Motionless against the doorjamb, I could tell the room reeked of putrid mushrooms and corn chip socks. I flew down the stairs, and slammed the door behind me. Outside on the sidewalk, I took a deep breath and wiped my face on my sleeve.

So that's how it was going to be. Ruby and Andrew could both die miserable deaths. Their coffins would be lined with black satin sheets and smell like Fritos.

My mind was quick to conjure reasons why I was so much better than they were. I told myself I was going to be a rich and famous pop star. I was going to have a red Mustang convertible, one of the old ones. I'd drive out to the deserted highway somewhere and leave my old self in the middle of nowhere. I would somehow transform myself into the beautiful and confident Candy-O, a girl just like the one the Cars sing about on that album.

Candy-O was permanently seventeen, I imagined. Driving my red car, I'd leave Candace Ong by the side of the road. Unlike the fat dork in the school uniform, Candy-O would wear chic things like silk slips and stiletto heels with pointy toes. I would shop at Matinee, Old Vogue, and La Rosa, and own Art Deco things like jeweled pillboxes instead of piggy banks, ceramic flamingos, and plastic barrettes shoplifted from Pay'N'Save.

When, exactly, would this transformation take place? I didn't know, but I hoped soon.

The Jaundiced Glow
That Made Me Feel Safe

The only thing that was going to make me feel better was if I shoplifted something. I knew just the thing I needed, too. I absolutely had to have jelly shoes. They came in different colors of translucent, malleable plastic, and were all the rage that spring. If Candy-O were a real person, she would've definitely been wearing a pair already.

I was pissed at Ruby for swiping Andrew from me. Yeah, he was kind of a molester, but he was *my* molester, for chrissakes, and she had no right to screw my deal. As I turned back onto Polk Street I could smell the freshness of the coming summer mixed with the street: gasoline, a little trash, and water evaporating off the cement. Walking several more blocks up, I was determined to rip off something because I, after all, had just been totally ripped off by Ruby and her perfect fucking tits.

Sauntering into Red Peppers, I inhaled the happy smell of coffee and plastic. It was a novelty store that sold Gumby and Godzilla toys, Kit Kat clocks with moving eyeballs that tick-tocked back and forth, and an array of other fun stuff that nobody really needed. Except, of course, jelly shoes. I definitely needed them, all right, and I spotted them in the back of the store.

There were different styles and colors, and I tried them all on. Some looked like regular high-heeled shoes, only purple or yellow and made of a pliable petroleum product. Others were like fisherman-style sandals, but I was looking for the ones that looked like ballet flats. I desperately wanted to wear them with short, ruffled socks for that slutty-baby look. Or maybe I'd wear them with lacy stockings and fingerless gloves. This was, seriously, the latest style.

Standing in the aisle behind rows of shoeboxes, I snuck a peek at the tall, slender New Wave guy at the counter. Black shirt, piano-key necktie, and not paying attention. I took a bright oilcloth purse from a display, threw in the shoes I wanted, and breezed toward the door. Just as I was about to make it outside, I heard him behind me.

"Hey," he said.

I turned around and gave him my most innocent look.

"Seen you around here before," he said, smiling, not looking at the purse I just lifted, but rather, at my bod. I gazed past his head to where rows of porcelain Pierrot masks stared out blankly behind him, some with stars in their eyes, others with tears.

"Yeah," was all I said.

He winked at me. "Well, don't be a stranger."

He didn't stop me as I left the store, and as I walked out I felt the thrill of having turned someone on as well as having gotten something for nothing.

I rationalized that the New Wave guy either saw me and let me take the shoes and purse, or else he was too horny to notice my thievery so it served his pervert-ass right that I ripped him off. To my benefit, no one ever expected a Chinese girl to be a shoplifter.

Feeling better, I stopped by Record Factory to see Albert, my friend, whose dream it was to become the most famous Mexican mime.

"Sorry, you just missed him," said the guy at the register. "His last day was yesterday and he just came by to clean out his locker. But maybe you can catch him across the street."

"Okay, thanks," I said. Jaywalking toward Chelsea Square, I spotted Albert in front of the gelato place called *Perche No!*

But he wasn't dressed like his usual self. Gone were the skinny, black jeans and red T-shirt. He seemed to have undergone some kind of punk rock deprogramming. He was now wearing paisley-patterned pants, a turquoise Polo shirt, and a white cotton blazer.

Standing in the courtyard, I studied Albert's appearance. If I didn't know his face, I wouldn't have recognized him. Sipping an espresso from one of those tiny cups, he seemed so grown up. If I didn't know better, I would have thought he was rich, standing there looking so tan and confident.

"Hey," I said. "What's up?"

Albert smiled and said, "Money. My philandering dad had a heart attack while screwing some *puta* in a Mexico City whorehouse. Left me a *buttload* of *cashish*."

"Wow."

"Yeah, I've moved to a new loft, quit my job, and can be a mime now. What's up with you?"

I showed him my new plastic shoes and he insisted that I put them on right away. I sat down and switched out of my sneakers, and threw my old shoes into the bag I'd also stolen.

Then I proceeded to tell him that I'd just found my best friend in bed with my would-be, dreamboat statutory rapist.

"I don't know what to do," I said.

Albert didn't miss a beat. "There's nothing to do but hope he gives her herpes, chlamydia, gonorrhea, and genital warts. All of them. None of which are pretty. Trust me." He didn't seem to know how to further console me, so he said, "Come on. Let's go shopping."

We walked down Polk Street and went into a shop called H. Dumpty. It was a deluxe toy store that struck me as demented child molester ground zero. The walls were covered in oversized circus banners depicting old-fashioned clowns with ruffled collars, red wigs, and floppy ragdoll bodies. With the giant posters and freaky knickknacks, even though there were no other customers in the place, the store felt crowded. At every turn were menacing mannequins, one dressed like Scoopy the Clown, that scary white-faced mascot of ice cream cones. I shuddered and clutched Albert's arm tighter.

We browsed the aisles lined with wind-up rockets and metal robots. Life-sized, stuffed tigers and lions were displayed in elaborate cages painted silver and sprinkled with glitter. On the far wall were papier-mâché trophy heads of rhinos and gorillas. The overall effect was that of a terrifying childhood nightmare brought to life, as if the shopkeeper resurrected P.T. Barnum from the dead to be his interior decorator.

"Look!" Albert said. "Here's what I came to show you."

In the corner was a display of life-sized movie dummies from *The Wizard of Oz*. Dorothy, the scarecrow, and the tin man stood on a painted yellow-brick road, teetering mid-skip. They looked expensive, like real Hollywood promotional figures from the movie. But from the neck up, Dorothy was not

Judy Garland. Nor were the scarecrow or tin-man sporting human faces. Atop the shoulders of the mannequins were incredibly lifelike chimpanzee heads. The scarecrow and Dorothy had wigs, hers complete with braids and blue ribbons.

Albert waved his hand in front of my glazed eyes, and I snapped to attention.

"Sorry," I said, "I was spacing out on that fucked-up monkey."

"Do you need help?" a small man called out to us, rushing over with a feather duster.

"No, thanks."

The man smiled and said, "You want to be like Dorothy? Don't we all wish?" He reached beneath the monkey's gingham apron and squeezed her firm breasts. After a second he seemed to forget that Albert and I were even there. With the feather duster he began to tickle the monkey's face and started talking to it.

"Let's get the hell outta here," I whispered. As we tiptoed toward the door, we passed a glass case, inside which gleamed a pair of original *Wizard of Oz* ruby slippers. A spotlight from the ceiling shone down on the dainty heels that gleamed with jewels, and right then I wished I was wearing them instead of my comparatively shitty red jelly shoes.

Outside, Albert pointed to the sidewalk right by the exit, to something we hadn't noticed on our way in. A beam of pink light projected a holographic image of Glinda the Good Witch onto the pavement. *So hologramic, oh my TVC–15!*

I thought of Auntie Melaura and the day I went to Holos Gallery expecting a sign from her. As Albert bent down and waved his arm through the ghostly Glinda, I imagined Melaura, lit up there. I thought about my auntie and how she must have looked in her Miss Chinatown cheongsam with its red sequins and golden birds snaking down the side slit. I wondered if she wore a tiara like Glinda the Good Witch. I didn't picture her smiling, though. How many times had my mom pinched my face when I was little, telling me to smile more? Auntie Melaura never once told me I should smile more.

"That's the magic I want to create as a world-famous mime," Albert said wistfully.

Walking for a really long time, we crossed Market and headed down Ninth Street past the El Dorado Hotel. This part of town was all industrial spaces, warehouses, and just one sad-looking grocery. Its name was even sad, Asad Market. Finally, we reached a nondescript door and went in.

Up a steep flight of dark stairs, Albert's new loft was as large as two basketball courts. The walls and wood floors were painted white, and the high-ceilinged interior was bright with sunlight. The side that faced Ninth Street was an entire wall of glass panes, several of which opened out to let the air in. Through the transoms I could hear the steady hum of traffic and see the flickering Best Western sign lit up even in the daytime.

Albert stood there for a while, letting me get an eyeful of his new digs.

"So, what do you think?"

"Where's your Barbie stuff?"

Albert paused for a moment and replied, "Let's just say that that kids' stuff is no longer part of the vision."

"Yeah," I said. "I like it."

"Oh damn," he said, looking at a clock. "I'm late. I gotta go, but you can hang around as long as you want."

Albert took his pants off right in front of me and changed into a new outfit from a big pile of clean clothes on the floor in a corner. Apparently, a disorderly closet was still part of "the vision." In another minute he was racing down the stairs, and yelled, "Just close the door behind you when you leave!"

I could hear his footsteps clack-clunking away, and then it was quiet. I liked the sound of the place empty. By now it was late afternoon, and the space was oven-hot. The sunlight filtered through the glass panes, creating wobbly squares of light on the walls.

I decided to explore. There was a trapeze set up in the corner and a balcony overhead where I guessed a kitchenette and sleeping space might be. On one side of a thirty-foot wall was a swath of fabric like a colorful sail attached to a beam on the ceiling. It billowed and sighed with a shy silky sound, slapping the air with its saffron softness. It moved with fluid motion as the breeze blew through the loft, and I imagined the fabric was made of sewn-together moth wings.

Instead of leaving, I sat down on the floor. Five minutes turned into a half an hour, and then into an hour. I didn't want to go home.

Sitting and staring out the transom windows, I watched as the light of day changed to early evening. Having sunken below the horizon, the sun no longer cast wobbly colors against the wall. The heat swirled through the space like a spirit exploring the corners, getting snagged here and there—on the table, a stack of papers, and on a beat-up leather chair—until finally the whole cavernous loft seemed to bluster with a gentle, hot wind.

It was getting dark, and I noticed that on the floor, lined up against the windows, were row after row of red candles in glass holders, like the kind in Mexican restaurants. The sky was turning dark blue and I didn't see any lamps so I found some matches and lit all the candles. They flickered, making the room glow high above Ninth Street within the urban tangle of cars and freeways.

Sticking my neck out the window, I saw fog and storm clouds. Cold air now came through the open windows. I tried to close a couple of transoms, but they were stuck.

Over the course of the next hour, the loft's daytime warmth swiftly beat it out of there, dashing off from its day job to moonlight somewhere in the darkness of a sweaty Folsom Street nightclub. The heat was replaced by chilly air that seemed to know it had the night shift and was ready for work. Albert didn't come back, and I just sat there in the dark with the candles. I stayed on the floor and enjoyed the knowledge that my parents didn't know where I was.

Climbing up a tall flight of narrow stairs, I explored the bedroom, which was just an area separated by a curtain. There was a futon on the floor and an end table with New Age-y stuff on it, like a picture of a pyramid with a third eye and a statuette of a Hindu god with a lot of arms. I lay down on the bed for a moment and wondered if Ruby and Andrew were still at his place screwing.

From the bed, I could still see out the windows to the clouds blowing toward a bright moon. I recalled a scene at the end of *Peter Pan*, when Wendy's father dreamily looked out his bedroom window and saw the outline of a pirate ship floating in the sky. In the cartoon, he seemed to remember himself as a young boy, the point being that only people who believed could see magic things. I wanted to believe, too. But I didn't know what kind of magic was going to deliver me from my humdrum, *egg foo young* existence.

I fell asleep. Waking up around midnight, I didn't know where I was for a moment, then remembered. I got up and headed down the stairs. It was dark and quiet outside, but peaceful in an urban way that was comforting. Traffic coming off the nearby freeway ramp softly murmured, and as I crossed the street, the Best Western sign illuminated the sidewalk with a jaundiced glow.

The sight of weary motorists filling up their tanks and buying chips at the gas station made me feel safe. Walking up to Market Street, I caught the 19 Polk as it pulled to the curb, and as I got on, the driver said, "You lucked out. This is the last ride for the night."

Tits on a Ritz, Mmm . . . Good Cracker

I was squinting in the sunshine and taking in the familiar scent of the damp cement when I noticed some fifth-
graders across the schoolyard. They were playing *Oh, Mary
Mack* and I was pretending to be engrossed in their game as
I listened to Ruby and Christy telling each other dirty jokes.
Their voices floated in and out as I tried to eavesdrop on their
conversation:

"Then his dick got cut off and fell into a pickle barrel . . ."

"The old lady said, 'That's the most delicious cucumber
I've ever tasted!'"

" . . . Liquor in the front, poker in the rear!"

"Beauty is only skin deep, but ugly goes down to the
bone!"

"Mommy, Mommy, turn on your headlights. Daddy's snake
is going into your forest."

I rolled my eyes, having heard all those stupid jokes before.
But still, I felt left out. A minute later, I felt something hit
me on top of the head, and when I turned around, Ruby and

Christy were laughing. The bell suddenly rang, and as we all lined up, they pointed and snickered, laughing so hard that the P.E. lesbo nun had to shush them.

The line began to move. As we snaked past the water fountain, I felt a tap on my shoulder, and turned around to see Ella Ng looking at me consolingly.

"You have something in your hair," Ella said, and I reached back and touched something wet and gooey.

"Go down to the bathroom. No one will notice," Ella whispered. I didn't bother to say thanks, just detoured down the stairs. I'd assumed that Ruby or Christy had thrown something at me, but in the girls' bathroom I discovered that a pigeon had shit on my head.

It was white and sticky, with green and black stuff that had slimed down the side of my hair. I practically had to stick my whole head under the sink and claw at the caramel-like birdshit with a handful of pink soap to get it out. As I rinsed it clean with water, all I could think about was how I was the one who told Ruby she had gotten her period that day when she was wearing white pants while waiting in line to collect her Shamrock Shake, and I could've laughed and pointed like everybody else, but never would have because we were friends. Or used to be.

Luckily, I could dry my hair using the hand dryer. When I finished, I walked back to the classroom, and slid into my seat, late. But at least the birdshit was gone and my hair was clean and fairly dry. I thought I heard stifled giggles behind me, but didn't turn around.

I opened up my *Jesus and Me* book, and like everybody else, scribbled out a couple of bullshit paragraphs about loving my neighbor.

Two hours later at recess, I caught up with Ruby and Christy in the schoolyard.

"Thanks a lot," I said sarcastically.

"What? We weren't laughing," Christy said.

"It's not like we *made* that bird shit on you," said Ruby.

It occurred to me that Ruby didn't even know that I had seen her and Andrew together, and I wanted to call her a boy-friend-stealing ho-bag, but I was chickenshit. Instead of confronting her, I skulked away from everyone and headed toward the opposite side of the yard. I wiped off the damp bench with my sleeve before sitting down like a lump to consume my snack, which consisted of a couple of leftover green onion pancakes from the restaurant.

As I ate, I watched the kids across the yard. Ruby, Christy, Gwen with the Greasy Bangs, and some other girls were standing in a conspiracy circle by the garbage cans. They looked over at me, and after a brief huddle, Gwen waved to me, but I pretended not to see.

Pretty soon the whole bunch of girls sauntered over in a pack.

Christy said, "All the boys say you give good blow jobs. We all wanna see you give Bruce Fung a blow job."

The other girls stifled their laughs, except for Ruby, who just looked right through me. I knew I'd better say or do something quick because the wall of girls was closing in around me.

"Don't be stupid," I said. I couldn't for the life of me think of why Ruby hated me so much now. Not only was she letting this happen to me, but she seemed to be the one who had put the other girls up to teasing me.

"I'm not stupid, you are," said Gwen, her greasy bangs totally repulsing me as they drooped over her pimply forehead.

Even though she was on student council with me, I knew why Gwen was happy enough to go along with this bullying. On our last multiple-choice test in social studies, she had tried to cheat off me and I'd tricked her. I had circled the wrong answers on purpose and let her copy them, then I went back and erased the answers and circled the correct ones. She flunked and had been pissed at me ever since, but I figured it served her right for being a cheating dumbo who was too lazy to wash her nasty-ass coif with its dandruff morsels glued on with hairspray.

Greasy-headed numbskull shoved my shoulder. Then another hand came out of nowhere and hit me in the right boob. More hands came toward me in attempts to pinch me, but I evaded the mean fingers by turning away. I started to run, and the chase was on.

I could hear the frenzy in the pitch of the girls' voices as they ran after me, chanting, "Blow job! Blow job! Blow job!" It was a hyena howl, but like any repeated word or phrase, the syllables eventually ran together and became mere sounds. I hoped some nearby teacher might be able to distinguish the chant and put a stop to the hunt, but I knew there was a slim chance of that happening. As I fled, blowing past my ears were the usual schoolyard noises—squeals of delight and shouts of joy—and I doubted that any passing nun would bother to distinguish the difference between screams of delight over cupcakes or shrieks of delicious hope that I might fall flat on my face or, better yet, start to cry or pee my pants or something.

More girls, even some seventh-graders, joined the pursuit. As I ran, cutting through the air, I heard and felt the excitement in the girls' breath. The line chasing me grew longer and longer until it was so snakey and stretched-out that I almost collided with some of the kids at the end of the rabid conga line. Like the tail end of a roller coaster, those bringing up the rear seemed to move faster with tail-snapping speed, static electricity and menace bonding the line together as the kids flailed in a loop-de-loop across the schoolyard, running me down.

I ran toward Bruce Fung who was innocently sitting on a bench at the far end of the schoolyard. He was obliviously eating a red apple, biting around the fruit in a gnawed ring. The yellow flesh where he had bitten had turned brown, and strangely, I noticed this, and figured the apple wasn't very crunchy.

"Make her do it!" someone yelled.

The chant changed. Now they were all yelling in synchopated rhythm, "Do it! Do it! Do it!"

Rushing toward Bruce, I quickly reached him and grabbed the nylon hood of his jacket, yanking him to his feet. The apple went flying from his hand as, mid-gape, his mouth seemed to wonder where it went. As quickly as I'd pulled him up to a standing position, I now started to spin him through the air, his neck snapping back awkwardly. I noticed Bruce's small, old-man-style, buckled shoes barely touching the ground as I went for humiliation gold. Soon enough, both of his feet were skipping through the air, desperately searching for, but not finding the playground asphalt.

As I spun my victim, I heard the jeering encouragement of girls whose faces whizzed by in a blur. But in the rotating, still space of just me and Bruce, in the silence of our inner circle, I could see in slow-motion his dorky glasses, bright pink gums, and small front teeth, one with a tiny white spot on it. I could see his teeth so clearly because his lips were stretched back in sheer fright. I wondered if he was still wondering where his apple went.

I hated what I was doing to him, but didn't know how to

stop. We were spinning so fast now that I couldn't just let go. But that's what I did. I let go. Bruce flew through the air in a sideways somersault. His arms and legs out, he spun like a ninja star and crashed into the railing by the boys' bathroom. He hit the rail face-first and his bright pink gums spurted red. He wasn't spinning anymore, or even moving at all.

I made a run for it. Across the schoolyard, I didn't look back. The sun shone above as I pumped my arms and legs, trying to ignore the dizziness. I ran past the basketball court, hopscotch squares, and dodgeball circle. In my head was my own chant, "Poor Bruce, poor Bruce, poor Bruce."

I ran out the side gate, past the teacher parking lot, and was soon out on the sidewalk. As I ran toward home, it was thrilling to be running free when I was supposed to be in school. I ran as fast as I could until I started to feel winded, then slowed down and walked the rest of the way. As I passed the familiar shops, I wanted to stop time. I wanted Ruby and me to still be friends, and for her to stop preferring pimply dickheads over me.

I was still into my stuffed animals, so what?

Even though I wanted to know about sex, I wasn't ready to fuck every W.P.O.D. I saw. I didn't wear cool clothes, but how could I dress sharp when everything good I ever got Ruby tricked me into giving to her? I wanted to say all these things to her, but couldn't.

As I headed home, I detoured to avoid walking by the copy shop where Andrew worked, but I did stop in front of Ruby's house. Since it was Monday, though, Cissy's store, Empress Wu's Antiques, was closed. I stood in front of the window and gazed at the sparkling sequins of the opera costumes, and in an opposite display, I saw a statue of a Chinese goddess sitting inside the petals of a porcelain lotus blossom. A hundred arms encircled her head. Its ghostly white, fleshy appearance made me imagine that the statue came alive at night when no one was looking. And right here and now, the statue seemed to be taunting me. As I stared back at her, I felt that I could almost hear her whispering in my ear. I gazed deeper into the store's window, and saw jewelry illuminated in the case, and papier maché puppets on the floor, their silk bodies crumpled in a heap. They looked alive, too. As the morning breeze lapped under my skirt, I had an ugly feeling deep in my bones.

International House of Dead Girls

$\mathcal{B}$ack at Eggroll Wonderland, I stopped at the door and read the handwritten sign that said the restaurant would be closed the next two days for repainting. Inside, workmen had already set up dropcloths and had moved all the tables and chairs. I walked past them and up the stairs that led to our apartment.

My mom heard me and stopped me in the hall as I headed toward my room.

"Why you home? What you do wrong?" she asked. The way she immediately assumed I'd done something bad annoyed me.

"We had a half-day today," I said. "For teacher conferences."

My lie was a pretty good one, I thought, but she stood fuming, her hands on her hips and her nostrils flaring.

"Jesus," I said. "Take a chill pill."

My mom looked confused. She raised her voice, yelling, "What is pill of chill? You take drug?"

"NO!"

I didn't mean to shout, but I did.

My mom shouted back, "TV commercial say watch out for teenage smoke mari-jewanna. You smoke mari-jewanna? You know people who smoke get a dickhead?"

I laughed, covering my mouth with my hand. I figured my mom meant to say *get addicted*, but with her accent it sounded just like *get a dickhead*. Standing in the cramped hallway, we stared at each other.

A few seconds elapsed, then she seemed to conclude that we reached some kind of stalemate, but she had to have the last word. She said, "Restaurant close today for repainting."

"Yeah, I already know that," I said. I could already smell the strong paint fumes wafting up from downstairs. I wriggled past my mom and darted into the bathroom without saying anything. After peeing, I poked out my head to make sure she was gone, then went into my room and hid out. The paint fumes from downstairs were getting stronger, and I just wanted to get outside and breathe some fresh air, but I didn't want to see or talk to anyone.

I sat in my room for a couple of hours, doing nothing. Eventually my mom pushed open my door without knocking and said, "Since restaurant close today, and you here, we go see Auntie Melaura. We borrow car and go to cemetery. Your father say maybe you confuse about death. Maybe that why you act so craze."

Without waiting for me to agree or disagree, my mom walked away, leaving the door open. The paint fumes were overpowering and I really wanted to get out of there, but I didn't want to go to the cemetery. I figured I'd just split, so I got up and bolted out the door. I should have taken the stairwell that led straight to the street, but in my hurry I forgot and went down the stairs that went through the restaurant.

Stepping around tarps and ladders, I breathed through the collar of my shirt and almost passed out as I walked through the newly painted space. Once I got out the door, I paused on the sidewalk by a parking meter to catch my breath, my eyes stinging just from the five seconds of being exposed to the paint fumes.

My lungs felt tight as I stood there taking deep breaths. I watched the painters inside, rolling shiny white paint onto the walls, and I wondered how they could stand being in there. Even outside with the breeze blowing, I felt dizzy.

My parents and Kenny came downstairs, and when I saw my little brother, I couldn't recall the last time I'd seen him. Then I remembered. A few weeks ago I'd seen him digging up salamanders in the back courtyard. He was tying them to firecrackers and blowing them up, their body parts exploding and splattering against the back wall. Today he struck me as strangely docile and kid-like next to our parents. He looked sleepy and innocent, and not at all like the shitty little Wah Ching punk that he was.

"What are you doing out of school?" I asked, talking to him for the first time in a month. I realized my question might reveal my own lie about school being a half-day, but nobody seemed to catch it. Guess he was ditching, too. I didn't know if his lie conflicted with mine, but we just looked at each other and decided not to say any more. For a long time now, our only sibling bond was that we knew not to wreck one another's cover. Our common virtue was shutting the fuck up.

My parents weren't paying attention when Kenny gave me the finger. Then my dad said, "We go IHOP, and afterward go to doctor for Kenny booster shot. Then we go cemetery."

The International House of Pancakes was my dad's favorite

restaurant. He looked at me with a hopeful expression. "You coming?"

In my head, I weighed the pros and cons of chocolate chip waffles versus having to sit in a booth with my slap-happy mom, amphibian-killing brother, and porno dad.

"No," I said, "Go without me."

"We come back and pick you later to go cemetery," my dad said, obliviously omitting the word "up."

"You come cemetery with us," my mom reiterated, leaving out the words "to" and "the." Why couldn't my parents talk like normal people?

I stood and watched as my family piled into Mrs. Lum's car across the street. The crapmobile rattled to a start, and my dad maneuvered it out of the space. As I stared, I hated that my dad clutched the steering wheel like a nearsighted turtle, and Kenny was staring back at me through the glass, mouthing "Fuck you, fuck you, fuck you."

After they sputtered away, I turned my attention back to the painters. I had nothing to do and didn't feel like talking to anybody, so for a while I just sat on the hood of a parked car and stared out into space. I watched the clouds moving slowly overhead and wondered when the rain would start again.

Lightheaded and spacey, I didn't know how long I'd been sitting there when I noticed the painters cleaning up. I figured the fumes were finally getting to them, too, and they looked like they were knocking off for the day. As I watched them pack up and leave, I felt a smack on my shoulder.

"Hey."

It was Ruby.

I had nothing to say to her, but she just stood there and wouldn't leave. I pretended to stare intently across the street.

Meanwhile, she fumbled in her LeSportSac, and inside it I could see all sorts of crap like eyeliners, an eyelash curler, Wet'n'Wild lipsticks with their caps lost, and loose tampons. Eventually, she found what she was looking for, a cigarette.

"Got a light?"

"No."

"Figures. I should have known better than to ask you for anything, you fat, fucking fatty."

For a second, I considered hauling off and slugging her in the gut, but she looked away and when she turned back to me, tears were welling up in her eyes. I figured it was another one of her manipulations.

She was standing close and breathing on me. Her breath smelled like cherry Pop Rocks.

"Are your parents upstairs?"

I had no idea why she was trying to make stupid conversation.

"No. They went to IHOP."

Ruby leaned up against the parked car and started sniffling, wiping back more tears, which kind of freaked me out. Out of nervousness, I said, "My mom is really pissing me off."

"Really?" Ruby brightened, and looked at me expectantly like she wanted to hear more.

I added, "Yeah, she's always telling me not to get raped. But if I did, it'd be my fault."

"Have you ever been?"

"What?"

"Raped."

Ruby looked at me plainly, like she'd just asked a simple thing such as whether or not I shaved my legs. The weirdest part of her question was the way she asked it, like it was the most logical question, as if most fourteen-year-olds had not only Done It, but had been raped. Like, "Have you taken the P.S.A.T.?" Check. "Applied to high school?" Check. "Been raped?"

I wasn't really sure how to answer, and wondered if Ruby was just messing with me.

I blurted out, "I know about you and Andrew. Why are you such a slut?"

"What do you care? He's just another W.P.O.D."

Flipping her hair, she went on. "You know," she said, "You need to grow up about guys. Are you seriously still thinking that someday your prince will come?"

I felt defensive, and was fed up with people, especially her, making me feel stupid. I said, "I'm not a jaded slut like you. Don't you believe in anything? Someday maybe *my* prince will come."

"Yeah, sure! He'll come on your face!" She laughed and rolled her eyes. "That's all the fairy tale you're going to get, dumb-ass."

I didn't say anything. As I stood there leaning against a parking meter, I wondered how I ever could have thought she was my Best Friend Forever.

An awkward minute passed. Eventually, she asked me again, "Got a light?"

"I said I didn't."

And now she was mad again. "You don't know anything," she said, her voice tense. "You're just a fat, fucking waitress in a Chinese restaurant." She looked away, seeming totally disgusted with me.

More than anything, I wanted *not* to be stuck being a waitress in a Chinese restaurant my whole life, and Ruby knew that. As she flipped her hair nonchalantly, I felt my face flush hot as my voice rose.

"Why would I have any matches if I don't smoke?" I said, and then, louder, "If you're so desperate to die of lung cancer, just go inside the restaurant and light your fucking menthol with the flame on the stove . . ."

I yelled, "And rearrange your perfect tits in the bathroom mirror, you backstabbing ho-bag!"

I could hear the echo of my words in my head. Ruby stared at me in shock for a second, then shot me an evil look. She stormed inside Eggroll Wonderland, and I could see her wander into the kitchen, way into the back. She bent down and fumbled with the dials of the oven, and I figured she probably didn't even know how to light a pilot light. I turned my head away in disgust, figuring any minute now she was going to come back out and ask for my help.

I suddenly realized I hated the girl with the perfect tits and sweetheart ass who had just sashayed into Eggroll Wonderland like she owned the place, which, I supposed, she did since she was Mr. Ping's daughter. But it was *my* family that cooked all the food, waited all the tables, swept the floors, and washed all the dishes. And *I* was the one who almost singlehandedly fried every fucking eggroll. Ruby's dad just collected the money. I wished it were the other way around. I wished Ruby toiled at the hot, greasy, grimy fry station. I wished my dad collected the money and I was the one with the red miniskirts and cascading black hair like Miss Sakamoto in the Thomas Dolby video.

I wanted to yell, "Get the hell out of my restaurant!" but I just turned away and leaned up against the parked car. I wished I were eating waffles with Adam Ant or Ric Ocasek right now. I knew someday I was going to be punished for telling my mom I wished I was dead like Auntie Melaura, and I conjured the image of my aunt in a Miss Chinatown USA *cheongsam* with worms crawling out of her eye sockets. Maybe at the gravesite my aunt would reach out of the dirt like *Carrie*, and drag me down to hell with her. I remembered the nuns at school saying that if a person committed suicide, there was no way they could get into heaven.

The next moment, fast and sharp, I felt a searing pain against the back of my neck. A delayed millisecond later, a huge noise exploded around my head, followed by a muffling in my ears that spread like an inkspot, pierced periodically by crackling noises. The sound was that of breaking glass, and splinters like icicles were flying through the air. In the strange, slow-motion time, I saw a sliver of glass pierce my arm like a dart into the sponge of a dartboard, and I watched as a tiny dot of blood spread into a line.

My observation was interrupted as a second blast lifted my whole body and hurled me into the street. I was thrown to the ground so fast and hard that I was knocked out. When I regained consciousness, I had no idea why I was sitting on the asphalt. Propping myself up on my elbows, I noticed that Eggroll Wonderland was engulfed in fire. Black smoke was pouring out of the windows, and I saw the recently purchased, never-turned-on neon sign snap in two and melt into oblivion in a matter of seconds.

I crab-crawled as far from the fire as possible. My skin felt like it was peeling off, and I managed to get halfway up the alley across the street. Although my eyes felt like they were sizzling in oil, I spotted Mrs. Lum across the way, running out in orange slippers with curlers in her hair, holding four cats in her arms.

The street looked like it had barfed up a hundred people, everyone with open mouths like they were yelling and screaming, but I couldn't hear anything, as if I was underwater. I didn't know if I'd been lying there for two minutes or two hours. My eyes kept closing themselves, but an ember flicked onto my leg and I felt the precise pain burning through my skin until I brushed it off in a panic.

Looking up, I noticed three fire trucks blocking the street. I saw flames and blue-black smoke, cars, and people running. Eventually, I made out one figure across the street. It was my mother. Tiny and frantic, she was jumping up and down and pounding on the arm of a burly fireman who was shielding his body with both arms like he was being attacked by a silver-backed gorilla instead of a hundred-pound Chinese lady.

Despite the blasting heat, I imagined that I was a newly hatched penguin in the Antarctic. On a TV show I'd learned that baby penguins were highly attuned to their mother's call because they had to be able to locate each other on the ice in the middle of all those identical birds. I was thinking of this because through all the sounds and yelling, I could distinctly hear my mother's shrill voice shrieking, "*Bi Bi*! Where is *Bi Bi*?"

I thought my mom was looking for my little brother. In my delirium, I wondered if Kenny was okay. And then I heard the little hoodlum's voice. "Here she is, Mom!"

I was suddenly being hoisted to my feet by my dad and little brother. My mom, so seemingly devastated a moment ago, hustled over in her black pants, cheap sandals, and quilted jacket, and started slapping me all over, starting with my arms, and then on my back and shoulders.

"Stupid *Bi Bi*! Worry me sick!" She was laughing, hitting, and crying all at the same time. The hits just kept on coming, and I, fairly numb anyway, was too tired to fight back.

My dad held up his hand to shield me from my mother's blows.

"Is okay, is okay," he said, and the next thing I knew, my

mom was trying to hoist me onto her back, as if I were still a baby to be carried in a cloth sling. The attempt resulted in a clumsy maneuver, and I almost flopped to the ground just as two paramedics appeared, lifting me onto a stretcher. They slid me into an ambulance, and I could hear my mom yelling at them in Chinese.

Goodness, it felt nice to be lying down. After the doors slammed shut, I thought I'd just take a short nap. As I shut my eyes and tried to breathe into the thing on my face, I realized I should've just gone to IHOP.

Grabbing the Snoopy

The girl who really liked her tits was gone. The girl who liked her tits, had a heart-shaped butt, and played a mean game of Galaga, was blown to smithereens. They said it was the oil-based paint and the fumes in the confined space. They said something ignited the blast.

No one asked me anything. I was lying in the hospital bed, and no one asked why Ruby had been inside the restaurant or if I had snidely suggested that she light her cigarette on the gas burner to hasten her death by lung cancer. As for me, I had some scrapes on my head and a gash on my arm, but there was pretty much nothing wrong with me.

All I could think about was who was going to pay for my stay in the hospital. Maybe if I told everyone I was fine and just got up and left, my parents wouldn't be charged anything. Looking around the room, I saw my shredded clothes crumpled in a plastic sack next to the bed. I sat up and sipped from a cup of water just as my parents and Kenny came in.

Kenny had a mouthful of Marathon Bar and said, "One

time, in the Ping Yuen basement where they stored the fire-crackers, it all caught fire and it all went KA-BOOM to high heaven!"

"Don't talk no more," my dad said, thwacking him on the head with a knuckle. Turning to me, he said, "How you feel? If you feel okay, doctor say can go home."

Shooting a look at my mom, he continued, "Problem is, can't go to apartment yet. Damage pretty bad. Kenny go stay at friend house. I stay YMCA. Ma stay with Mrs. Lum at the niece place—you know, one who work at library? But still, not much room there."

"How bad is it?" I managed to croak.

"Apartment all smoke damage everything. Water damage, too. But some area worse than other. Our room not so bad, clothes and furniture still can save. But your room . . . not so good. Most all gone."

I needed more water, but the cup was empty. My throat felt scorched, but I managed to utter three syllables. "Twinkie . . . Chubs?"

My dad and mom exchanged worried looks, but Kenny piped up, "Roasty toasty, toasted hamster!"

"Shut up!" I wanted to yell, but my throat felt raw, like the worst sore throat I ever had.

My mom dragged Kenny out of the room by one ear, and my dad wrung his hands. His rough palms make a sandpaper sound as he rubbed them together.

"You know," he said slowly, "Ruby . . . Mr. Ping only daughter. Very sad, tragic accident. I arrange with Mr. Ping, that since nowhere for you to stay right now, well, he agree that you stay his house."

I had a thumping headache, but even still, I knew that this was a bizarre idea. "I'm going to stay *over there*? What *for*?"

My dad shook his head. "Don't ask so many question. Very generous offer, so just go there, and we figure out later."

I remembered that I didn't want my parents to have to pay for an overnight stay in the hospital, so I nodded. My dad patted my hand, and left the room.

A couple of hours later, I was discharged from the hospital. From the apartment, my parents managed to salvage a pair of my jeans and a sweatshirt, which reeked of smoke. The cheap, white tennis shoes that they bought for me from the Dollar store in Chinatown smelled like mothballs. Nonetheless, I had no choice but to wear the stupid ensemble with hospital socks.

Outside, my parents and brother headed off together in one direction, leaving me at the Geary Street bus stop. When the bus arrived, I climbed onto the 38 Express and rode off toward the fancy Seacliff neighborhood where Mr. Ping lived. My dad had given me a scrap of paper with the address on it, and as I stared at it all I could think about was how Ruby said she hated staying there, and that her dad was a religious freak. As the stores and houses on Geary Boulevard whizzed by, I wondered what it would be like there, and how long I'd have to stay.

First off, I could barely think about poor Twinkiechubs, cooked alive in her plastic poopdeck. And Big Mama, who, yeah, was only a beanbag frog, but was also my friend. All my records and tapes, too, and the yellow mass of plastic tubing that made up Twinkiechubs's Habitrail town were gone. Well, at least now I could say all my school textbooks burned in the fire so I didn't have to tell anyone about the pitbulls at Pier 39 who wanted to bust my chink fuckin' face.

My illicit lovers had burned, too. Mr. Ferretface, Jemima

Puddleduck, Señor Mouse, and Mr. Toucan with the convenient beak for late-night crotch massaging were all gone.

And Ruby was dead.

The bus was getting close to the ocean, so I knew my stop was coming up. I wondered what Mr. Ping's house—*Ruby's* house—would be like.

"Last stop, everybody off," the bus driver said.

I pulled myself up and almost fell flat on my face as I jumped to the curb.

"Easy there, China girl," the driver laughed. He pulled a lever to make his seat deflate, and the cushion made a farting noise.

I had to walk the rest of the way because the Pings lived in a fancy neighborhood where buses weren't allowed. I shuffled along the winding, perfectly landscaped yards and clean sidewalks. Squinting at the number on the piece of paper again, I headed toward a white mansion with immense pillars and marble fu dogs out front, like Tara from *Gone with the Wind*, but Chinese-style.

I rang the bell, but there was no answer. After ringing two more times, I checked the gold handle and the door was unlocked, just like doors in the movies always were. I went in.

I had never been to a rich Chinese person's house before, and once inside, I stood on a huge plush rug that looked like it cost more than a car. Looking up, I saw an enormous chandelier, glimmering down onto the marble floors, giving me the feeling that I was in the lobby of a bank.

Between two gigantic cloisonné vases that were taller than I was hung a freaky oil painting of a blond-haired, blue-eyed Jesus with sun rays blasting off his head. On the opposite wall was an equally enormous painting of an angel flying over clouds, clutching in his muscular, holy hand an American flag snapping mightily in the wind. Some weird Chinese Muzak was playing on invisible speakers, and I wondered if anyone was home.

"Hello?" I called. My eyes traveled up a staircase where I could see rows of doors along a balcony overlooking the foyer where I was standing.

"Hello?" I said again, and when there was still no reply, I decided to have a look around.

The house reminded me somewhat of the Cathay funeral parlor, but maybe I was just freaked out to be in a dead girl's home. I walked past a room with a pool table and a giant television, and in the corner was a popcorn machine on wheels, like the kind I'd seen at Pier 39. I walked from room to room, each one larger than my family's entire apartment, and I saw cabinets filled with dinnerware sets and fancy punchbowls that looked like no one ever used them. I could tell they were the expensive antique-y kind because they looked like stuff I'd seen in Cissy's store. The furniture was all oversized, upholstered in gold and white satin, and covered in thick plastic, reflecting the light from electric, candle-shaped sconces on the walls.

In the spacious, empty kitchen, I opened one of the stainless steel refrigerators and saw that there wasn't much food, just rows and rows of some kind of soda from Hong Kong. The cans had Chinese writing, but then in English, said "Energy Drink." On a lower shelf, I saw stacks of Chinese restaurant to-go containers. From Eggroll Wonderland, naturally.

Tracing my path back through the house, I decided to go upstairs to see if anyone was there. The plush, padded carpet was so soft and spongy I actually bent down to touch it. I'd never been any place as luxurious as this house, but instead of feeling welcome or lucky to have a place to stay, I felt like I'd stumbled into some kind of Hotel California scenario where I was going to find pink champagne on ice and would never find the portal back to the real world.

Slowly, I approached an open door. I heard nothing but could feel there was someone in the room. Standing in the doorway, I looked at the canopied, king-sized bed and saw an old Chinese woman propped up on satin, ruffled pillows. She was wearing an ornately embroidered silk robe covered in phoenixes and peonies. The woman, in fact, was draped so heavily in finery that she resembled a disembodied head floating against piles of fabric. Lower down, her bony fore-arms looked like petrified wood manacled with jade and pearl bracelets.

The woman's face was cartoonish with black eyeliner and too-bright lipstick. On her hands were rings with stones as large as marbles, or eyeballs. Upon seeing me, she attempted to smile, and bared her animal-like teeth. Overcoming my fright, I approached the edge of the mattress. "Hello," I said.

The woman said, "Ruby?"

"No, I'm Candace Ong." I wondered if the old woman was blind, but didn't think so. Maybe she was just drugged up.

"Ruby is my granddaughter," the woman said, still not looking at me.

"Glad to meet you, Mrs. Ping. Thank you for letting me stay in your house." I could make polite conversation when I wanted to, and whipping out some manners seemed like the right thing to do when hanging out in your dead ex-friend's house talking to her grandmother who looked seriously de-ranged.

Mrs. Ping stared expressionless at the far wall as I shifted my weight from foot to foot.

Half a minute passed before her head swiveled like a ventriloquist's dummy. "Listen," she said to me. "Be careful. There's a man who lives here." She looked around the room, then added, "He's a filthy ape!"

I nodded my head, figuring she must be referring to Mr. Ping, her son. As I turned to leave, she said, "Put your things in Ruby's room. You'll sleep in her bed."

I stood ever so still to hide the panic I felt. Why, when this house had so many rooms, did I have to sleep in Ruby's bed?

"All right," I said. "Thank you."

I backed out of the room and solemnly closed the door.

In the hallway, I turned the doorknob of the next room, and found the bathroom. Splashing some cold water on my face, I noticed the fixtures on the sink were 24-karat eagles' heads, and the spigot was a crystal rectangle carved to look like a waving American flag. After drying my face and hands on a plush, perfectly folded hand towel, I headed back out to the hallway to find Ruby's room.

It was the second door after the bathroom. Like in Mrs. Ping's room, there was a canopy bed, but this one was done all in white, with a ruffled bedskirt and frilly pillows. There was a big Snoopy doll on the bed, and as I stared at it, I realized it was mine. It was one of the things that, over the years, Ruby had conned me out of. I spotted a bureau loaded with My Little Pony and Strawberry Shortcake figurines, and it dawned on me that Ruby was more of a dork than I suspected. Because of the bitchy, slutty way she'd been acting lately, I'd forgotten that she was, like me, still part-kid, and seeing her stupid dolls reminded me that she wasn't so grown-up at all. Except, of course, she was dead. And I was here.

Throwing down what few things I had brought, I sat on the bed. Here I was. I was doomed to sleep in a dead girl's room, and the why and what for were a total skanky mystery.

But I was so tired. Exhausted, I didn't have the energy to soak in the complete freakiness of my situation. I lay down and rested my face against the pillow, grabbing the Snoopy around the neck to hug it.

I was extremely sleepy, but my mind was wide-awake. I wondered what Auntie Melaura was thinking as she fell through the air from the ledge of the Golden Gate Bridge. Did she close her eyes, or were they wide open all the way down? Did she gaze at the blue bay water as she sped toward it? I wondered what clothes she was wearing and if her shoes came off mid-air. As best as I could recall, she always wore heels, and those didn't stay on too tight.

From the moment Auntie Melaura jumped off the ledge, it must have taken several seconds before she hit the water. I wondered if she immediately wished she hadn't done it. Was she going so fast that she could feel her clothes flapping in the wind? When she smashed into the water, did she feel herself going down, or did it all end suddenly, her bones breaking on impact? Most likely it wasn't a gentle fade to black. Maybe a smack to black. Or maybe everything went white, like ice.

Then I thought about Ruby. What was her last thought as she lit her cigarette on the burner? Oh, yeah. Now I remembered. She had called me a fat, fucking waitress. How typical that her last act on earth would be to put me down. But then again, maybe she'd said that because I'd called her a slut. I guess it was my fault that she stormed away. I had been pretty certain, standing there in front of the restaurant, that she wouldn't have known how the pilot light worked. Maybe I had wanted her to have to ask me for help, or at least to know what a drag it was that I had to cook eggrolls all day while she screwed my boyfriend in her stinky socks.

I realized right then that I was definitely going to Hell.

It was my fault that Ruby was dead.

Not able to sleep, I listened for sounds in the house, but there weren't any, just the demented Chinese Muzak piping through the halls. Eventually my stomach started growling so I snuck out of Ruby's bedroom, through the hall, and down to the kitchen. I checked the fridge again, but wasn't in the mood for Chinese food or a Hong Kong energy drink. I checked the freezer and found several pints of ice cream, all different flavors. Picking a pint of Alice Marble Fudge from Swensen's, I snuck it back up to my room. In the cavernous kitchen I had looked everywhere but couldn't find a single spoon, so I ate the ice cream with a plastic, Great America keychain I found in Ruby's bureau drawer.

Quick Like a Bunny

I woke up the next morning and realized it was a school day. I hadn't talked to anybody since my chat with crazy Mrs. Ping the day before. My parents hadn't called, either. It didn't occur to me to *not* go to school, so I opened up Ruby's closet. There I discovered all the clothes Ruby had ever manipulated, cajoled, and shamed me into giving to her. They hung there waiting for me, as if a fairy godmother knew that all my stuff at home had burned and granted me a brand-new wardrobe. But they were all my own clothes, just stuff I never got to wear: my purple Très Jolie jeans, red miniskirt from Piccadilly, KUSF T-shirt, a men's tuxedo shirt from Matinée, and a pair of red jelly shoes that were the predecessors to the ones I'd most recently swiped from Red Peppers. It was great to discover all my old, cool clothes, and for a guilty split-second I was glad that Ruby was gone because that meant I could finally wear them.

But not today. Today I had to wear a school uniform, and I was relieved to find two white uniform blouses and two plaid skirts. I took down one of each, and found some socks and underwear in the dresser. I put on a pair of Ruby's shoes I found on the closet floor.

Dressed, I opened the bedroom door a crack. Mr. Ping must have come home in the middle of the night, because the Musak was off and the chandelier was unlit. There was only dim, gray light coming through a skylight overhead, and the sound of a lawnmower outside.

I had no backpack or anything, and just walked out the front door wearing Ruby's school sweater. It felt weird to be wearing someone else's clothes, even though they were the same blouse and skirt I had worn for years. Nonetheless, they didn't quite fit. I could tell that Ruby had sluttified every piece of the uniform because the top buttons were missing off the blouse, the sweater had been nipped in at the waist, and I could feel the hem of the skirt skimming the back of my upper thighs even though Ruby was a full two inches taller than me.

As I walked to the bus stop, I looked at the sky, the houses, and the sidewalk. I wasn't thinking much about anything— not about a funeral for Ruby, or how long I'd be staying at the Pings'. There was only a week of school left, but I wasn't even thinking about graduation. Nor had it occurred to me whether anyone at school even knew about Ruby being blown to pieces or Eggroll Wonderland burning down. For a second I thought of Twinkiechubs, but squelched the thought as I stepped onto the 38 Geary.

On the bus I played the same game in my head, the one where I pretended no one could see me. It pretty much worked, I was glad to find, except for some pervert who was staring at my thighs from across the aisle. I got up from my seat and walked to the back, wishing I had some McDonald's hash browns.

Poor Twinkiechubs, poor Ruby, and also, poor Op, my old pet duck. And poor Auntie Melaura. I reached up to my neck and felt the jade rabbit around my neck. It felt warm against my throat.

After hopping off the bus, I walked a little ways until I was outside the school building. I didn't have the nerve to face the kids in the schoolyard, so I ran inside and up a flight of stairs. I just wanted to go straight to the homeroom, and I bolted past the office and the teachers' lounge.

"Candace!"

I skidded to a stop, nearly hitting the wall. It was Mrs. Field, the fifth-grade teacher.

"Where are you going in such a hurry?" she asked.

I stood there speechless with my arms at my sides. Mrs. Field was the only nice teacher at the school. I had had her three years before, and I suddenly felt like telling her everything. Did she know that Ruby was dead? Should I tell her how I chased Ella Ng and pulled down her underpants? Should I tell her what I did to Bruce Fung, or how those girls at the pier wanted to bust my chink fucking face? I wanted to tell someone all these things. I wanted to tell someone about the Hot Wheels tracks, and about my mom hugging me and calling me *Bi Bi* while she hit me. I wanted to tell someone that Twinkiechubs and Big Mama burned up and so did Ruby, and I wanted to tell someone that none of it was my fault even though it was.

I almost started to cry, but then Mrs. Field said, "The teachers' lounge is out of coffee. The bell won't ring for another four or five minutes. Be a good girl and go across the street to Peter D's and get me a cup? Cream and sugar, please."

She held out a dollar, and I took it. As I turned to walk away, Mrs. Field said, "Run quick, now! Quick like a bunny!"

I took off running, this time across a different hall that led to a side exit. I ran outside and onto the sidewalk on Franklin Street, and noticed I had a green light to cross Broadway. Sprinting toward the green light, my eyes were fixed ahead at the wide, white-painted lines of the crosswalk. Jumping off the curb, I saw the white lines still, but then there was more white, shinier and glossy. I could tell it was glossy because it was now up against my body, and then my face. I was sliding across the hood of a white Cadillac, careening through herky-jerky space. I could suddenly see a glass windshield and the confused face of an old white man. White hair, whites of his eyes, and a crisp white shirt. His mouth made the shape of the letter "O."

I heard screeching brakes, and then I was on the ground. The street was, not surprisingly, extremely hard. Yet somehow, it did surprise me. The palms of my hands stung, and when I lifted them to my face, I saw there were bits of black embedded there, and bloody scrapes.

A chrome bumper gleamed as it slowly maneuvered around me. The shiny, white Cadillac accelerated, and soon I saw the back of it, the jewel red of the taillights. I was worried there might be a line at Peter D's, and tried to remember if Mrs. Field wanted cream and sugar, or just cream. Or maybe just sugar.

"I'd better get up," I told myself, but my legs didn't quite feel like working. I saw a shoe in the intersection and wondered whose it was, but then realized it was Ruby's. That confused me even more till it dawned on me that I was wearing her loafers, and so the shoe was actually mine. Still lying in the crosswalk, I watched the Cadillac move farther away.

"Heavenly Father, have mercy!" A trio of nuns lifted me off the asphalt. I was still worried about Mrs. Field's coffee, but forgot about it when I looked down and saw that my ankle looked all Elephant Man.

The nuns carried me to the nurse's office where, once in the fourth grade, I had barfed up a bologna sandwich in the sink. I lay on the spongy cot and listened as Alma the Admin Lady called the doctor.

After a minute, Alma hung up the phone, turned to me and said, "Dear, we have to call your parents."

"Our house burned down," I blurted, and simultaneously, the tears came.

"We know all about it," Alma said. I wondered if she meant that everyone at school knew Ruby was dead, or knew that I'd killed her.

Alma left the room. About an hour later, a doctor who looked like a human version of Fozzie Bear came in and checked out my ankle. He handed me two aspirin and watched me as I swallowed them with water. To no one in particular, he said, "Mmm-hm."

Sister Eugenia, the principal, came in. Somehow, she had Trudy Lum's phone number, and dialed it from the desk at the foot of the bed. I listened.

"Mrs. Ong, something has happened," said the nun into the phone receiver. "But there's naught to worry. Candace still has all her limbs."

Lying there, I secretly hoped my mom was worried sick. I wanted to overhear panic or hysterical crying echoing through the receiver, but I was too far away to hear anything.

"She has been bumped by a car. She has a few scrapes and a twisted ankle, and we think it best if you came to collect her." Sister Eugenia said "collect her" like I was a bunch of dismembered body parts in a box, like C3PO in *The Empire Strikes Back*.

"Oh, I see," she continued. "Not until later this afternoon? Well, we'll have someone take her then. Yes, God bless."

The nun hung up the phone, turned to me and said, "Mr. Torino will drive you to the Ping residence. Both your father and Mr. Ping called us this morning and apprised us of the recent tragedy. We will all be praying today. Christ be with you, Child."

As the nun, the doctor, and Alma vacated the room, I wondered if recent events made me exempt from any and all current and future homework. The idea brought a smile to my face as I passed out.

Closed Casket for the Living Impaired

The Ping residence was in Jesus-freak lockdown. Mr. Torino drove up the driveway in a maroon Buick, but I hadn't noticed we arrived because the whole way from school, all I could do was space out on the bobby pin that held down his white-man, Afro comb-over. There were a lot of people milling around, and I was reminded of the scene in *The Godfather* when the mafia goons were guarding the property, except here the gate was blocked by a crowd of Chinese people in black clothing.

Mr. Torino rolled down his window. He said, "I'm here to drop off Candace Ong."

A man gave a little nod. "Praise the Lord," he said. "Go up ahead."

I figured it was a wake for Ruby because I saw arrangements of carnations and chrysanthemums being unloaded from a truck. I spotted Mr. Ping standing between the two huge, ostentatious pillars on the portico. I wasn't sure how I expected him to look, but he didn't appear as devastated as I thought he should. His expression was serious, but with no tears in sight. Maybe he was all cried out, or maybe too old to cry, like he'd forgotten long ago how to do it or had trained himself to hold it back. Regardless, I briefly studied his face as he shook hands with the people who'd come, and I felt sorry for him even though I knew he was the same asshole who, a week ago, was about to raise the rent on us.

Mr. Torino got out and opened the door for me, then got some crutches out of the trunk. A few of the mourners trickling in offered to help me inside, and before I knew it, one big, fat guy in a dark suit grabbed me under the armpits and hoisted me over his shoulder like I was a rug. As he carried me up into the Pings' foyer, he groped my ass.

"Let me down," I screamed, disgusted by the pillowy feel of his man-boobs beneath the fabric of his suit. He sat me down in a Ming-style chair beneath the Jesus portrait, his hands copping a feel over my backside as he slid me into the chair. As he wiped perspiration from his glistening, porky forehead, I considered kicking him, but my ankle was still too messed up.

Meanwhile, Mr. Torino had brought in the crutches and set them down next to me.

"How come you're not at Safeway?" I asked.

"I don't work today," he said. "On my days off I buff the gym floor. Sister Eugenia asked me to give you a lift. " Looking around at all the mourners he seemed uneasy. A minute passed before he added, "Sorry about Ruby."

I had never talked about anything but basketball with Mr. Torino and neither of us seemed to know what to say. He veered back into sports talk and said, "She was a good player."

"Yeah."

"See you at graduation?"

"I guess," I replied, and he turned to leave.

He looked back and said, "Hey, Candace. Good game."
"Yeah."

He looked funny walking away in his coaching clothes, in contrast to the steady stream of people coming inside all dressed in their funeral duds. All the while, some churchy music was pumping through the speakers and I, still in a daze from being whumped by the Cadillac, sat and took it all in.

Waiting in the chair, my ankle swollen and lumpy, I thought back to Auntie Melaura's funeral when I waited on that pink upholstered settee with the figure-eight design. I never got to see Melaura's casket and I wondered if there was one for Ruby. Morbidly, I speculated what was physically left of either of them. Ruby really liked her tits. I wondered if they were in the casket along with the rest of her.

After a while, a woman with an austere bob clicked across the marble floor in ugly heels.

"Mr. Ping send me to help you upstairs," she said. "Service is starting soon, but your parents not here yet. Don't worry. You are never alone because He is always with you." She gazed up toward the Jesus portrait and smiled reassuringly at me.

With one crutch at my side and the lady on the other, I managed to climb the steps, counting them one by one. I hobbled to the second floor, and just as we reached the top, a bedroom door swung open. Mrs. Ping emerged in full dragon lady regalia. She was wearing a black jacket, a long skirt, and a scarf encrusted with jade bits the size of ladybugs. It looked like green beetles were devouring her neck. Plus, a hat with black netting sat like a nest on her head, and a veil decorated with pearls covered her face, giving her the appearance of a beekeeper in mourning.

The fat guy who felt me up and another skinnier guy came bounding up the stairs to help Mrs. Ping. They looked like a Chinese Laurel and Hardy. Mrs. Ping took mincing steps and collapsed melodramatically onto one of the hallway chairs. The Chinese Laurel and Hardy picked her up, chair and all, and slowly teetered down the stairs. Meanwhile, I hopped into Ruby's room with the help of the Chinese woman, whose perfume was strangely comforting. She helped me to the bed, took off my one remaining shoe, and pulled the covers over me. Before closing the bedroom door, she turned to me and said, "You are smart girl. Pray to Jesus and save yourself from the Beast. Remember, in the Book of Revelation, one thousand virgins will ascend to heaven in the Rapture."

She looked at me with fierce eyes, but with all I had been through that day, I just wanted her to go away.

"Got it," I said, then closed my eyes and pretended to fall asleep to avoid further conversation.

Alone at last, I burrowed under the blankets, being extra careful with my sprained ankle because it felt heavy, like a rock was strapped to my foot. The nurse had said to ice it, but all I wanted to do was sleep. Actually, a part of me wanted to locate a suitable stuffed animal to have a party in my underpants, but dang, I was just too tired.

Clinging to Ruby's pillow, I imagined that instead of a poly-fil cushion, I was clutching the ever-understanding, all-compassionate Adam Ant. If I had, in fact, found a stuffed animal to hold against my crotch, I would have pretended that it, too, was Mr. Ant. But the pillow was all I had.

Then I saw Snoopy. Grabbing it from the between the mattress and the headboard, I squeezed it with both hands, wondering if the little black pom-pom nose was firm enough to get me off. For a moment I lamented the loss of Mr. Ferretface, whose famililar snout always knew how to do the trick. I never really considered him one of my favorites, but having shoved him between my legs for the last two and a half years had to count for something. His snout was just perfect for my purposes, and I felt a pang of regret as I pressed in the nose of dead Ruby's Snoopy doll, or rather, my Snoopy doll.

Fondling the stuffed animal's stiff tail, I pulled it forward between its legs and it looked like a funny dog dick. I was amused by the look of the black tail between the white legs, and smiled at the idea of Snoopy with a beagle boner. I sank under the blankets, thinking I might test the limitations of my underpants' elasticity by maneuvering the dog around my zinger.

My head under the covers, I suddenly heard a voice.

"Don't you dare," said a voice. Uh-oh. I didn't want to hear any more doomsday talk from the jasmine-scented Jesus lady. Remaining motionless beneath the blanket, I hoped the lady would think I was asleep and just go away. For a second it seemed to work, but then I heard the voice again. It said, "Don't you dare even *think* of fucking my Snoopy."

The voice was so familiar and bitchy that I didn't consider being frightened. I pulled the blanket off my head, and saw Ruby.

Lo and behold, there she was. Gleaming like Obi-Wan Kenobi when Luke Skywalker spotted him on the Hoth landscape. Glimmering like Yoda beyond the grave at the end of *Return of the Jedi*, I could see through Ruby's body to the closet door behind, but the girl who liked her tits was definitely standing there. And her tits were there, too, still looking pert in an out-of-focus, magenta T-shirt.

It was Ruby, all right. She was leaning against the white sewing table with her heart-shaped butt stuffed into a too-small miniskirt with silver buttons down the back.

I was obviously hallucinating. I knew that mental illness

could be hereditary, and I wondered if this was how it started with Auntie Melaura. Had she seen ghosts, too? Maybe
Fozzie Bear had slipped me something other than aspirin back
at school.

Ruby said, "In case you're wondering, I'm not one of the
thousand virgins on the fast-track to heaven. Some dude in
white said I had to stay back and help you."

Gee, this hallucination seemed so real. I sat up and decided
to test how nuts I really was. I considered saying, "You mean,
you're like Clarence in *It's a Wonderful Life*?"

But before I said the words out loud, she answered me,
"Who the fuck is Clarence?"

See. It was all in my head. How else could she just read my
thoughts without me having to say them? So that's how it was
going to be. I was going crazy, just like Melaura. Great.

Ruby started meandering around the room, and I followed
her with my eyes. She tried to pick up a magazine with C.
Thomas Howell on the cover dressed as Ponyboy Curtis, and
said, "I'm not sure when I can catch the next plane to heaven.
I'm riding standby and I keep getting bumped."

I wasn't exactly convinced that acceptance into heaven
was so lenient as to let in someone like Ruby. But curiosity
got the better of me and I asked, "How are you supposed
to help me?"

Ruby said, "Think of me as your Mr. Wizard, Great Gazoo,
Glinda the Good Witch, and Jiminy Cricket all rolled into one.
Oh, shit, someone's coming."

There was a faint knock on the door and my mom poked
her head in.

"*Bi Bi?*"

My mom walked in and shut the door. Distracted by the
appearance of my mother, I couldn't tell if Ghost Ruby tem-

porarily evaporated or was just hiding in the closet. My mom said, "You okay, *Bi Bi?* Twist ankle?"

She approached the bed, but hesitated. She looked afraid to touch me.

"Apartment almost fix. You come home tomorrow, okay? Everyone nice here? Nice room." My mom tried for a smile, but her timidity suddenly struck me as supremely irritating.

"I just want to sleep," I said, and turned my face away from my mother. I wanted her to leave, but she didn't.

"You want anything?" she asked.

I didn't want to give my mom the satisfaction of crying in front of her. I didn't want to talk about how lonely I felt, or how Ruby was no longer my Best Friend Forever. In fact, nothing was the best, no one was my friend, and forever didn't mean anything. *Forever* was just the title of a Judy Blume book where some guy's dick was named "Ralph."

Dead Hair in White Underwear

The next day, my dad came to pick me up in Mrs. Lum's car. Mr. Ping was standing in the chandelier-lit foyer as my dad helped me down the stairs. I glanced around, half-expecting to see ghost-girl Ruby giving me the finger from behind a pillar, but I didn't see her. I had all my repossessed clothes and Snoopy in a bag, but Mr. Ping didn't notice or care that I was taking all this stuff. I would have explained that it was all mine in the first place, but neither Mr. Ping nor my dad seemed concerned with my girl-things.

As we left, my dad thanked Mr. Ping profusely for letting me stay. It bugged me that my dad had to kiss Mr. Ping's bony ass. As for me, I wanted to say, "Sorry Ruby's dead," but that seemed obvious and retarded so I just kept my big maw shut.

In Mrs. Lum's crusty Corolla, I inhaled the stale car smell. My ankle was a little less swollen than the day before, but it still ached.

"You can stay home rest of the week," my dad said. "School

says with all that happen, you can rest up and still graduate this weekend."

"Thank you, God, thank you, God, thank you, God," I said in my head. Although I was glad to be able to graduate, I was mostly relieved that I didn't have to see any of my classmates or Sister Mary, the human toad.

I asked, "So everyone at school, I guess, they know . . . everything?"

"Yeah. Said you could stay home. Is okay."

As we rode the rest of the way home in silence, I wondered how Bruce Fung's lip was, and if he was able to eat apples yet, or if he needed stitches. I thought about the little white spot on his front tooth. I thought of Ella, too, and how I humiliated her when I pulled down her underpants in front of everybody, and how Ella helped me anyway when that bird shat on my head. Maybe God made me get hit by the car to settle the score for Bruce's face and Ella's underwear. God was really into smiting people, and I felt deservedly smoted.

We finally arrived home, and I wobbled up the charred steps to our apartment. The restaurant was all boarded up, but a construction crew was already traipsing in and out, dragging out debris, and carrying lumber and new fixtures inside.

The apartment had a smoky smell, not unlike the time I burned the chocolate Pop Tart in the toaster and didn't clean it for three days, only much stronger. I limped past my parents' bedroom and was surprised to see that it looked okay, with all the furniture still there and everything. When I got to my room, though, I was shocked. All the walls were smudged, smoky and black. My old bed was gone, and now there was just a sleeping bag with a quilt on the floor. My room was right over where the fire had been and was the most damaged.

Great. Now when I lay awake at night I could ruminate on the fact that Ruby was incinerated right under me.

"We borrow extra blanket from Trudy Lum," my mom said, coming up behind my dad. Kenny was nowhere to be seen, and my parents hovered in the doorway, looking at me, worried.

"Some clothes still okay, just have burn smell. I could try wash again," my mom said with what passed as a smile for her, which meant she made her lips into a flat line. "I save few things, store in basement, but mostly, things too damage to save."

And then I noticed. The main house of the Habitrail city was gone, and only the small, plastic condo was left. A few pieces of yellow plastic tubing still connected to the penthouse poopdeck, but most of the outbuildings and the "gymnasium" were gone. Some of the pieces were blackened and misshapen, like the plastic had collapsed, cooled, and then rehardened.

I squinted. Upon closer inspection, I discovered that a real, *live* hamster was frolicking inside one of the misshapen tubes, skittering into the penthouse. But the furry rodent within the plastic walls was not peach-colored. It was white with red eyes, not brown ones. It wasn't Twinkiechubs. I mean, it wasn't Twinkiechubs Three. As I stood and watched the hamster run through the yellow tube and up to the penthouse, I realized my parents had done it again. They had resurrected the dead by switching hamsters for a third time, hoping I wouldn't notice.

"Oh, brave hamster is okay, see?" my mom said with unconvincing enthusiasm.

I lowered myself onto the sleeping bag and started to remove my jacket and socks.

"Same one, same one," my dad said, and received an elbow in the side from my mom.

"Of course, same one!" They both smiled at me eagerly.

"Yeah, same one," I repeated, for their sake. My mom sighed

and my dad smiled with relief, and they seemed satisfied that they'd saved me from the unpleasant reality of death.

"Where's Kenny?" I asked.

"Friend house," my dad said.

"Oh." I settled down on top of the sleeping bag and felt instantly sleepy.

"You hungry?" my mom asked.

"No. I just want to sleep."

But they didn't leave. They pulled two chairs inside my room, chairs salvaged from downstairs. The vinyl seats were blistered with shredded foam poking through.

"We got telephone call from your teacher," my dad said.

From behind his back, he pulled out my *Jesus and Me* book, and turned to a paper-clipped page. He showed it to me, and it was the page where I'd written ROCK'N'ROLL SUICIDE over and over in the margin.

"Yeah, so what?" I said, sleepy.

My dad said, "Sister Mary say you may be at risk for kill yourself."

"Yeah, she wishes," I scoffed, but then realized my parents were serious.

My mom said, "No do anything craze, okay?"

They shut the door, and I looked around the rest of the room. I saw that my tapes, records, and stereo were all gone, and I imagined that they fused into one plastic mess and had to be thrown out. All my stuffed animals were gone, too. Burned, along with my Barbie Corvette and all the money I'd saved for years, seven hundred dollars. There went my escape money. I suddenly longed to feel the pleasant heaviness of Big Mama's beanbag body on my face. I closed my eyes and imagined the calico cloth underside of my old froggie toy.

And then, a voice.

"You're way too old to be busted up about that frog. Get over it."

I opened my eyes. Ruby was sitting cross-legged on the floor, examining her cuticles.

"Auntie Melaura gave Big Mama to me." I wasn't sure if I said this out loud or just thought it, but Ruby seemed to hear it. She was shimmering and see-through like before, but this time was wearing her school uniform. I could even see white panties against her ghost crotch.

"Hey," Ruby said. "You could use this suicide thing to your advantage. You could say you need new clothes, lotsa spending cash, and a car. If they don't hand them over, say you'll blow your brains out. Or better yet, just eat Pop Rocks and drink Coke at the same time. Your stomach will explode just like Mikey from the Life cereal commercial."

And with that, Ruby vanished, and I fell asleep in my charred room on the floor, with no one watching over me except Twinkiechubs Four.

Curled-Up, Pink Piece of Shrimp

*E*ven though I had skipped the last week of school, I was still eligible to graduate since all I missed were desk-cleaning activities, special Masses, and field trips. The commencement ceremony was on the same Saturday as Eggroll Wonderland's grand reopening, so neither of my parents were coming to the graduation.

My ankle was still messed up, so instead of walking to school, I hobbled onto the bus. The ride was just a few blocks, and when I arrived, I went to the auditorium where I was supposed to pick up my cap and gown. I saw Christy and Gwen with the Greasy Bangs in the corner, pinning and cinching their slick acetate gowns this way and that. I grabbed one from the table where Alma the Admin Lady was checking names off a list, and I ripped open the plastic wrapping and pulled the gold gown over my head like it was a rain poncho. The cap didn't fit and I hadn't remembered to bring any bobby pins.

"I have extra, you want some?" said Ella Ng who stretched out her skinny arm to me.

"Okay, thanks." I took a couple of the black pins and even though I didn't ask for her help, Ella proceeded to scrape them into my scalp, affixing the bright gold mortarboard to my head.

"So wrinkle!" Ella said as she swept her hand over my gown, trying to smooth it out. I was taken aback by her fussing over me, but since I was still on crutches, I really did need the help. As Ella pulled at the hem, messed with the zipper, and fixed the pleats, I was grateful, and also ashamed. I didn't know why she was always so nice to me.

We all lined up in alphabetical order. Walking down the aisle in my yellow cap and gown as the fifth-grade choir sang "Eagles Wings," I noticed a huge framed picture of Ruby up near the altar, with flowers and a big sign that said, "Now in the arms of our Heavenly Father."

We filed into the pews and all listened to the priest's speech about two ships passing through the Puget Sound. It was supposed to be an allegory about life, or something stupid like that.

After the Mass, it was time for the awards. I got a ribbon for reading and a blue enamel pin with a crucifix on it for general academic excellence. When I heard my name and walked up to get my diploma, I heard clapping and spotted some Chinese people cheering for me. Standing there, I was confused for a moment and held up the line. For a second I thought maybe my parents closed the restaurant and had come after all. But then I saw who was clapping, and it was Bruce Fung's parents. He had already retrieved his diploma and was back in the pew next to them. I knew the lady was his mom because she had his same droopy eyes. My stomach turned as I recalled hurling Bruce into the schoolyard railing. I tried to see if his lip was still puffy, but I could't tell from where I was.

"Hurry up!"

The kid in line behind me gave me a little shove, and I moved on. I sat in a pew on the side by myself until the rest of the names were called, and soon enough, all of us graduating eighth-graders had our diplomas. When we finally got to throw our caps in the air, I forgot about the bobby pins and ended up ripping out several hairs on each side of my head at the triumphant moment. I didn't care, though, because it was over. Eighth grade was over forever and so was grammar school and wearing a uniform and having to kiss Sister Mary Toad's ass.

Everyone filed out of the church, and I left, too, genuflecting in front of the altar for perhaps the last time. With my ankle and crutches, it was no easy task, but I managed not to wipe out. As I walked outside, I scanned the crowd to see if anyone from Ruby's family was there, but I didn't see any of them.

"Hello, there, Candace." It was Bruce's mom with the droopy eyes. "Congratulations! Where are your mom and dad?"

"Oh, they had to work." I shifted my weight to my other crutch, and just then Bruce walked up. I could see that his lip was still a little swollen.

"I'm really sorry, Bruce," I blurted out.

His parents raised their eyebrows in unison as Bruce grabbed me by the yellow sleeve and pulled me away from them.

Making sure they were out of earshot, he said, "I told them I fell off the monkey bars."

"I feel really bad," I said. "I don't know why—"

"I've got hurt worse before."

I looked at Bruce's sad little eyes. "I don't know why I did that . . . to you," I said.

Bruce didn't seem to want to talk about it anymore. He

ignored my attempt at apology and said, "You missed the last math meeting. We had cookies, you know."

"Oh?"

"Yeah, too bad for you. There were sesame cookies, and chocolate chip. And that almond kind from Chinatown. Alvin's mom brought them."

Bruce's mom came over and said, "A shame your parents couldn't be here today." After a moment she added, "You do know they work very hard for you, right?"

I shifted uncomfortably and said, "Yeah, I know."

"Well, congratulations again."

Bruce and his parents started to walk off toward their car, but Bruce came running back and said, "To celebrate, we're going to Eggroll Wonderland. Do you want to come?"

"I'm going home anyway. I'll see you there," I said.

"We'll give you a ride," Bruce's dad called over, pointing to my crutches. They were insistent, and before I knew it, we were all smashing into the Fung Family Mercedes. Although they were hardly rich, Bruce's dad was all about his baby-blue 450SL. I had heard rumors that he was a bookie, but wasn't sure. At this point I was just glad to have a ride home, and they let me sit in front because of my ankle. Through the open window, the crutches just managed to fit inside.

We got to the restaurant fast. As we parked in front, I noted that the restaurant was only medium busy.

"*Ai-ya!*" my mom said, greeting the Fungs. She knew them because Mrs. Fung was a seamstress and had made some things for my mom.

"You take big table. Go 'head, go 'head!"

Then to Bruce, my mom said, "So smart boy! Graduate, eh? Destin for success!"

"Candace very smart, too," Mrs. Fung said. "You should be very proud of straight-A daughter!"

My mom smiled and nodded without saying yes, she was proud of me. Instead, she scrambled off to get menus and a pot of tea.

The restaurant smelled like new paint and onions. The whole front wall had been replaced, and the new window and front door looked exactly the same as the old ones, but less filthy. A new awning had yet to be put up, but the place had all the basic components to be open for business, including a new to-go counter, which now had a short line forming in front of it.

"Don't worry, you sit," my mom said, coming over with the menus and tea. I figured my mom was just trying to be nice in front of the Fungs, because ordinarily she'd tell me to get off my ass and run the to-go counter, crutches or no crutches.

"Is special day," my mom said in the best English she could muster. "Stay and keep company with Mr. and Mrs. Fung." She spoke slowly and carefully, and smiled in a way she never smiled at me.

Bruce and I compared our diplomas, but after about ten seconds, I felt weird just sitting there and not helping my mom. I watched her take orders and clear tables while I hung out with Bruce's family like I was just a regular customer. When two other groups ordered eggrolls and crab Rangoon, I instinctively began to get up, but my mother barked at me to sit back down, then went and fixed the appetizers herself.

Bruce's family ordered all the best stuff on the menu, things that I never got to eat because they were too expensive. They ordered sizzling cubed steak on an iron platter, prawns, seared scallops, and Peking duck, the last dish reminding me of my pet,

Op, who ended up as dinner so many years ago. At the end of the meal, my mom brought almond gelatin and said it was "on the house" because the Fungs had been so kind to me.

After the Fungs left, I wondered if I would ever see Bruce again, but then I remembered that he and I would be going to the same high school in the fall. For me, the idea that I would see at least one person from eighth grade gave me a sense of some things continuing, and that, for the time being, made me feel less alone as I sat there poking at the last curled-up, pink piece of shrimp.

Come on Like a Regular Superstar

*E*ighth grade and school as I'd known it had ended almost two weeks ago, and since then, I'd been cultivating mopey, suicide-risk behavior. I'd just lain in bed listening to the radio, and hadn't washed my hair in a couple of days. Kenny had gotten a television for cheap from some hood in Chinatown, and I had been watching it—afternoon movies like *The Initiation of Sarah*. Also, since school had been out, every day at 3 p.m., Channel 7 was showing reruns of Afterschool Specials featuring little white girls in every possible dilemma—anorexia, bulimia, kidnapping, drugs, prostitution, and posing for sick pictures orchestrated by a molest-o-rama basketball coach. The movies, one day after another, were like training films for how to get in trouble. That is, if that was the sort of trouble I was looking for.

More important, however, was that my Depresso Act was working. I thought people who were at risk for suicide were supposed to be watched carefully, but my parents had left me completely alone since Sister Mary narc'ed me out about the

Jesus and Me book. They seemed to think that displeasing me in any way was going to send me off the deep end, so now I could pretty much do whatever I wanted. I hadn't even helped once in the restaurant since I'd hurt my ankle.

I was no longer the eggroll girl. Not only that, but I ordered whichever dishes I wanted from the menu and my dad not only made them, but brought the food to me like I was a regular customer. He and my mom both acted scared to upset me, as if I was going to get all *Twilight Zone* on their asses and start blowing shit up with my magic powers.

I hadn't seen Ghost Ruby for a while now, so I figured maybe I had just been temporarily out of my head when I'd hallucinated her talking to me. Since my ankle felt better, I was spending a lot of time with Albert at his loft. One afternoon I was hanging out there when his friend, Fred, came to visit.

Fred was even better looking than his picture. Dressed exactly like the Thin White Duke in a crisp white shirt, black pants, and vest, he was the most elegant person I'd ever seen. His streaked blond hair was combed back, and as he said hello I noticed his deep voice was tinged with an accent—vaguely European, fake continental, hard to pinpoint exactly. I could easily picture him as the voice behind "Sorrow," "Sound & Vision," and all the other songs I had listened to so many times in the dark. Gazing into Fred's eyes, I knew he was the closest I'd ever get to the real Bowie.

He said, "Did you ever see *Gigi*? Or how about *Pollyanna*? I loved that movie because I lost my parents, too. Do you know the story? Her father was a missionary in the British West Indies, but she went to live with her rich Aunt Polly, played by the first Mrs. Reagan. Can you imagine? Boy, dontcha bet that stupid cunt was sorry when her fool, dumbfuck ex-husband became president? Well anyway, in the movie the dumb twat is faaaabulously wealthy, so of course the first thing she does is buy Pollyanna the most arch petticoats the town had to offer . . ."

As he went on about the movie, I wondered where on God's green earth did this guy come from? I had never heard so many cusswords from anyone, and in such colorful arrangement. His command of profanity far outshined any of the idiotic drolleries I'd culled from the schoolyard.

Fred suddenly turned to me and asked, "What kind of movies are you into?"

"*Godspell*, *The Rocky Horror Picture Show*, and *Foul Play*," I said.

I answered fast because I was excited, but I hoped my answers weren't too dippy.

Albert interjected, "I told Fred all about what you've been through."

Fred put his hand to my cheek and looked right through me. He brought his face close to mine and whispered, "*Just be still with me. You wouldn't believe what I've been through.*" A chill electrified my skin. I had been thinking of that line from "Cat People" all day. How could he have known that?

"Let me guess," he said. "Got your mama in a whirl? Don't cry, my sweet. You gotta get smart. Do you think I sprang from a clamshell like Venus, as fabulous as I am today? Of course not. Necessity is the mother of reinvention."

I listened with rapt attention.

He went on, "I was the favorite fuckdoll of Fire Island. But I knew, ultimately, it was an empty life."

He smiled charismatically and a honey-colored lock of hair fell down in a graceful wave across his forehead.

"I was Freddie Miller and my parents had a deli in Brooklyn. Miserable stuff—pickles in jars, cold cuts, headcheese. The lowest of the low vibration, my dear. When my parents died in a car wreck, my Aunt Agatha adopted me. Thank goodness she was rich as shit. She took me all over the world, and I became an international jetsetter. I got very good at being a fucking degenerate. So don't tell me I don't understand you. Singapore slings, or slinging chow mein, it's all the same. Life is so fucking gruesome. And you, such a willow."

A willow? Yeah, maybe I had gotten sort of skinny lately. But I didn't think about that. I had never heard anyone talk like this. His theatrical gestures, his *Bowieness,* and his strange selection of words peppered with expletives had instantly captivated me. I wanted to re-create myself, too. I wanted to talk fast and be as confident as he was. He drew me in and exploded a bomb of curiosity in my head.

"So," he said. "What do you want to be? What shall we make you into?" He shot Albert a wink from across the table.

Tongue-tied as usual, I couldn't think of what to say. In fact, I was so overwhelmed by someone actually paying attention to me and asking me questions about myself, I almost started to cry.

"Don't worry," he said reassuringly, touching my face again. "You're lost that's all."

Albert interjected, "Hey, we're having a party tonight. You should come."

I sniffled, and brightened. "Really?" I said. "What should I wear?"

"A Chinese dress, of course," said Fred. "Do you have one? One of those slinky kind with the long slit up the side?" He turned to Albert and said, "Won't that look faaabulous?"

Albert turned to me and said, "It's okay if you don't have one. Wear anything."

I thought immediately of Auntie Melaura's Miss Chinatown

dress hanging in my mother's closet. I wondered if it was still there and whether it had been damaged in the fire.

"I'll figure out something," I said, already eager to be what Fred wanted me to be.

He came over and sat down next to me. I was so flattered by his attention that all I could do was look at his shoes. They were expensive-looking, patent leather, and of all things, he had suspenders holding up his socks. The little bands of black elastic peeked out from under his pant cuffs as he crossed one leg over the other.

He gently lifted my chin with the tip of his index finger. Forcing me to meet his gaze, he said, "We're all in the gutter, but some of us are looking at the stars, *n'est-ce pas?*"

I didn't understand that last part, or what he meant at all. But that didn't stop me from being dazzled. I smiled, glad to be in the company of people who seemed excited about life. I was tired of moping around and wallowing in dead-girl guilt, and the way Fred looked at me and smiled made me feel special.

Around Fred and Albert I didn't feel like the fat, Jewish girl on *The Facts of Life*. I didn't feel like Jo or Tootie, either. Fred seemed interested in me, like I was Blair, even. I know that sounds stupid. But that, seriously, was what I was thinking.

I got up to leave and promised them I'd be back for the party. As I walked home, I felt alive in a way I never had before. It was different from the elation of winning a basketball game, or how happy I used to feel when everything was cool with Ruby, or even the thrill I felt when Andrew first poked his tongue in my mouth. This Fred person had sparked a different something in me. Was it true that I could be anything I wanted, starting now? If Albert could go from being a record-store clerk to a Mexican mime and this guy, Fred, could transform himself from a deli kid to a Fire Island fuckdoll, why couldn't I, Candace Ong, change, too?

Once I got back home I decided to take a nap. As I stretched out in my sleeping bag on the floor, I imagined that I could see right through the ceiling, through the upstairs apartment where Mrs. Lum lived, and straight through the tar-and-pebble roof, and up above the fog. I pictured a clear, bright night above the city and yes, I was looking at the stars.

Put Your Ray Gun to My Head

That evening, I went into my parents' room. I was mad at first, wondering why the fire had to damage my room but left theirs mostly unscathed. Their bed, furniture, and stuff were all okay, and I briefly wondered if my dad's nudie magazines were still under the bed, but then I remembered why I was there. I went to the closet and opened the door. All the clothes were hanging there just like before, and I reached in and pulled out the black garment bag. I unzipped it and took out Auntie Melaura's cheongsam. It was the same as before, but now death smelled like Rive Gauche, talcum powder, and barbecue. I gently folded the dress into a plastic sack.

Instead of going downstairs and running the risk of getting stopped by my mom, I slid the window up and crawled through. Climbing down the fire escape, I jumped down to the garbage area and walked quickly through the narrow alley that led to the sidewalk. Sniffing the air for the smell of cigarettes, I took a chance that my dad wasn't nearby, and dashed out to Polk Street.

Although it was nighttime, the summer sky was still fairly bright. The air was warm and some of the shops were still open. I decided to not take the bus, and as I walked to Albert's loft, on a whim, I ducked into Emerald Lily's, a vintage clothing store.

"Howdy," said a haggy lady behind the counter.

"Hi."

I perused the store filled with silver, glittery shirts, fake-leather miniskirts, and snakeskin-patterned leotards. In the jewelry case was a haphazard mixture of rhinestone earrings and necklaces, as well as antique stuff that looked like it came from dead people's houses.

"Anything I can show you?" said Haggis, her saggy, fleshy arm reaching inside the case to rearrange a few items.

I looked up at the display racks behind her which were filled with sparkling tiaras.

"Actually," I said, "Could I see that crown up there, the one with the stars?" I pointed to the most ornate one that was encrusted with rhinestones.

"That's the most princess-y one of the bunch, all right," said Haggis.

I watched as the lumpy lady grabbed a nearby stepladder and climbed up to retrieve the tiara. Balancing on the highest step, she held onto a curtain rod, trying with all her might not to fall back and crash into a pile of used Levi's.

"Here ya go," she said, placing the gleaming tiara on the counter for me to admire. I held it up, and instantly loved it. It was shiny and new, like how I wanted to feel. If I ever thought I could be a Chinese princess in a fairy tale, well, this was the crown to have. I was only sorry that there was no way to shoplift it since Haggis was watching my every move. And to boot, the price was steep.

Haggis seemed to sense my longing for the tiara, coupled with my lack of cash flow.

"I like the jade," she said, peering down her nose at my necklace. "Take it off the chain and let me see it."

I reached up and felt the cool, smooth stone. I moved my hands to the clasp at the back of my neck and undid the necklace. Loosening it from the gold chain, I plopped it in my hand. I was looking at the sweet profile of the jade rabbit when Haggis reached out and took it out of the palm of my hand and said, "You got yourself a deal."

Before I knew it, Haggis had stuck the jade inside the jewelry case and had begun wrapping the tiara in tissue paper. I hadn't been positive I wanted to trade, but she already had the tiara in a plastic bag and held it out to me.

"Come again," she said. The trade was already said and done, and I didn't know how to protest. The time to change my mind had passed, and now Haggis wasn't even looking at me, but was writing a little price tag for my jade rabbit, the Chinese lucky charm that Auntie Melaura gave me along with Big Mama the day she jumped off the Golden Gate Bridge.

It was about nine o'clock by the time I crossed Market onto 9th Street. The blocks were long and I didn't see any people, just forlorn, parked cars and traffic whizzing by. I passed the El Dorado Hotel and the Billboard Café, and finally arrived at Albert's place.

I ascended the dim stairwell and reached the top landing where a pink spotlight illuminated the area. Albert was wearing a shiny green spacesuit, and was flitting around greeting guests as *Pinky Blue* by Altered Images blasted from the speakers. When he spotted me, he threw up his arms and waved a ray gun made of tinfoil at me.

"Chinese princess!" he yelled. "Go upstairs and change."

I nodded and headed upstairs. People in costumes were dancing and grabbing each other. A disco ball rotated in the corner with a propped-up flashlight aimed at it, creating white bubbles of light that whirled around the space.

Suddenly, I found myself surrounded by a herd of men dressed as satyrs. They were all shirtless, wearing fur pants with stuffed, bulbous derrières and tails. I got jostled by one of the man-beasts who was having trouble walking in his platform hooves.

"Pardon me," he said, bumping against me with his furry haunches. Then he turned back around and said, "Hey, are you Fred's Chinese girl?"

"I guess," I said, figuring, yeah, I was Chinese, and a girl. I was about to ask him where Fred was, but he'd already galloped away.

Ducking under the curtain to the sleeping area, I went to a corner and started to undress. I kicked off the red jelly shoes I'd gotten from Ruby's closet, and pulled off my jeans and sweater. As I lifted the red cheongsam out of the bag, I realized I should've tried it on at home first. I stepped into it and slid it up my body. Zipping it slowly, I prayed it wouldn't be too tight. It wasn't. It fit perfectly.

Unwrapping the rhinestone tiara from its cocoon of tissue. I placed it onto my head, sliding the combs into my hair to keep it in place. It was fairly heavy, and required a balancing act to keep it from sliding into a lopsided position. I held my head still as I lifted the hem of the dress and slipped my feet back into the shoes.

When I emerged from behind the curtain, the specks of light from the disco ball caught every sequin on the dress and I suddenly became twinkliness personified. As people turned

and noticed me, I could see sprays of light on their faces reflected from the rhinestones on my tiara.

"Love your dress!" hollered a guy dressed up as the devil.

"You're a juvenile success!" yelled one of the satyrs, slapping the back of his fuzzy, prosthetic ass. He grabbed my
hand and pretend-galloped over to a makeshift stage under
the disco ball. He wanted to get onstage and dance, but just
as he was about to pull me onstage, a curly haired woman
wearing a black plastic garbage bag beat us to it. She jumped
up on a stool, pulled up her legs, and asked the crowd, "Am
I a tarantula?"

As the woman raised her legs in the air, the garbage bag
bunched up around her waist, and she wasn't wearing any underwear. At first I wasn't exactly sure what I was seeing, but I
was suddenly eye-level with her big, hairy vagina.

Someone screamed and pointed, and the crowd erupted in
squeals. People pushed their way up onto the small platform,
and suddenly I was hoisted up as the music continued to blare.
Everyone was dancing, and I was sandwiched between a Pills-
bury Doughboy and a Mad Hatter.

A few people stumbled and fell off the stage, and just then,
some guy dressed as the Jolly Green Giant twisted my skirt
around so the slit was in the back, bent me over, and started
dry-humping my ass. Someone grabbed the light and shone
it right on us as people started to cheer. I felt the Jolly Green
Giant's boner through his green tights pushing against my
butt, and I tried to struggle free. In the commotion, my tiara
flew off. I reached out my arm for it, but it tumbled to the
floor and got trampled under someone's hoof.

After a second I managed to break away, but only because
my jolly green assailant had suddenly dropped to the floor.

Clutching his balls, he was writing around. Someone had swiftly kneed him in the nuts, and that same someone was now gently but purposefully leading me offstage and out of the crowd.

"Does that fucking smurf think he can stub out his cigarette-sized dick in the most arch Chinese vessel?" It was Fred, wearing a silver halo made of pipe-cleaners.

They Forced China to Open Her Legs Even More

*F*red and I were sitting in the Billboard Café beneath a wall-mounted sculpture of a huge, white hand that held a strand of glowing lights. My crown was gone, and the silk dress was torn in some places. I knew I looked pathetic as Fred checked me over for any further damage.

He shook his head in dismay. "That audacious pervert. And after what you've been through."

Gently Fred wrapped his arm around my shoulder. "We haven't known each other long," he said, "but you think I don't know you? Your ageless heart . . . it can mend. I promise you. You think your tears can never dry, but they can. I know you, China girl. And the fear of losing you . . . enrages me."

Boy, did Fred have a way of paraphrasing Bowie. He stared at me with his eyes so bright they were like shattered blue and white porcelain. I sat in awe of him.

He went on, "When people see something beautiful, they just want to destroy it, you know? Just look at the fucking

English and what they did to the Summer Palace. What a fucking disgrace."

"What's the Summer Palace?" I asked.

Fred took a sip of his drink. "How do you not know what that is?"

I shrugged and he said, "How can you be a Chinese princess if you don't know your own Chinese history?"

I didn't say anything in my own defense, so he went on, "You mean you don't know about the real Empress, her shawl of a thousand pearls, and the imperial jade dildos?"

I had never heard this last word, but was pretty sure it was something I should at least pretend to understand.

I said, "I wasn't born in China. I'm from here." Then I added, "I don't know about history."

"Well, you should," he said matter-of-factly. "In this life, evil people will be coming out of the woodwork to absolutely fuck you up and you need to know more than they do. And like tonight, because you're such a beauty, people will always want something from you. You're as pretty as a Chinese Betty Bacall, my Oriental Brooke Shields. But you're not a persnickety little twat like them, you're faabuulous!"

He reached out and removed the mug of tea from my hands, then kissed my fingertips. He looked at me imploringly, and said, "My dear, you have no idea how lucky you are that I found you."

I wanted this much attention all the time, with all my heart. I loved being compared to Brooke Shields.

"You come from a land where golden Buddhas adorn every home, with lush courtyard gardens, and fields of pink and magenta peonies. The imperial hairdos of black lacquer are decorated with fistfuls of jewels—tourmalines in green and pink, rubies, and sapphires. Veils of coral branches cover the faces of brides. The Chinese princesses have koi ponds and giant cabinets of many drawers, each stuffed with tiny velvet bags of loose diamonds. As for the jade dildos for pleasuring themselves, well, of course!"

What planet was this guy from? I didn't care. He was the most amazing person I'd ever met.

He went on, "Centuries ago, China was tops in naval exploration. While Europeans were crawling around in their hairshirts on their way to Canterbury, Chinese explorers sailed all around the world in enormous boats, even to Antarctica. Then, one day, the emperor got pissed off at some crass Westerner—probably some fucking Jesuit priest who got all haughty on his bad self. His Highness, the emperor, ordered all the maps and boats destroyed. No longer would China explore the seas in search of twatty little twats. He said, 'We're the best. All the other countries can writhe like maggots without our tea and silver.' Eventually, all the navigation technology was lost, but who the fuck cared? They had their foo dogs to play with."

"Really?" was all I managed to say.

He went on, "Oh, yes. By the 1700s, the European countries were sailing to China and begging for an audience with the emperor, but he sent them away with nothing but their cocks in their hands. Those lily-white turkeys wanted China's tea, silks, and porcelain but were too bitchy to kowtow to the Son of Heaven. But you see, my dear, here's how it worked. Those fucking British made opium in the vast, brilliant-orange poppy fields of India, where they were already making the finest people of this earth into whores, and they got the Chinese addicted to this drug.

"These English schoolboys who, up till now, had spent all their time playing spunk on the biscuit, well, now they had the emperor's *huevos* in a vice, do you understand? The emperor was forced to allow the Westerners in, but at first only through the port of Canton. All the other cities and ports were off-limits. But eventually, the English got tired of paying for their tea in taels of silver, so they got together with the other European countries for the biggest gang bang of all time, and mercilessly fucked China until she was no longer the proud Pearl of the Orient, but just a wretched little ragdoll. She wasn't even a colony, so there was no Big Daddy to protect her, and everyone—the Dutch, the English, the Portuguese—they all had their way with her. They gang-raped that little bitch until she didn't know which way was up."

Fred stopped to take a sip of tea, and I knew I should interject something to show I'd been listening. I wanted to say something smart, but I was still trying to sort out all the cuss words I'd just heard. I sipped my own drink to give me time enough to think of something to say.

"But China was so much bigger than all those little countries," I said, conjuring a map in my head.

Fred didn't miss a beat. "Yes, of course! Don't you know it's always the littlest pricks who want to fuck the big, bad mama? And besides, by the mid 1800s, the emperors were all sex-addicted, syphillis-ridden weaklings. And that, my dear, was why the Empress had to take over.

"The Empress?"

"She ruled all of China. She was a second-rate concubine who reinvented herself as the most arch queen of all time. Of course, she stole Hsien Feng's thunder. He was a wishy-washy ruler and she was such a firecracker in the sack that she drained his *chi* completely. Their son, Tongzhi, was the next emperor and he was an oversexed degenerate, too, so the empress had to run things while he was cavorting with transvestite prostitutes on the absolute wrong side of the tracks.

"She has a bad rap and historians blame her for the Ching dynasty's downfall. But they just cannot accept that she had ovaries and balls of steel. And was it so wrong that she wanted faaabulous jewels?"

Frederick stopped to laugh, his blindingly white teeth making him look somewhat like a mannequin. "The empress was pissed that the British were running roughshod all over the Middle Kingdom so she allowed this group, the Boxers, to kill a bunch of whiteys living in a compound near Peking. That really incensed all the European countries who were squabbling over who could rape China best, so then they forced China to open her legs even more. China had no money and was weak, so eventually the Republic and Sun Yat Sen overthrew the Imperials. Then Chiang Kai Shek took over and he was overthrown by Mao, who unfortunately sucked to high heaven. The worst part, oh, I can hardly think of it. The antiques they destroyed during the Cultural Revolution. *Mon Dieu.*"

I had heard of Sun Yat Sen, and at Red Peppers, they sold earrings with Andy Warhol's Mao paintings on them.

Fred was rolling his eyes and shaking his head in disgust. Finally he said, "Let's get you home. It's past midnight and you'll be turning into a pumpkin soon. Back to the dungeon with you before the 'rents notice you've been out simulating copulation with a giant asparagus."

We said our goodbyes and he headed back to the party. As I watched him walk away, he stopped, came back, and held his cheek against mine. "Don't worry," he said. "Don't think life ain't taking you nowhere. Stick with me and what you like will be in the limo, for sure. Good night, Girl."

I smiled as he walked away. I boarded the 19 Polk in my ripped dress and red shoes, and as I sat there, I didn't think much of anything.

Actually, that's not true. I thought about a lot of things, but it was just garbled stuff, nothing that was a concrete idea about anything. I pictured Ruby's blank face while she screwed that W.P.O.D. in the forest. I thought about the time one of my hamsters scratched out its own eyeball and ate it. I imagined Ruby's body in the casket, and then Auntie Melaura's. I hadn't seen either of their corpses, and I visualized their blue-gray faces with pink makeup to make them look alive. I wondered if, in the coffin, Auntie Melaura still wore high heels, and if there was still a scar on Ruby's dead hand from where her wart used to be.

Satin Rules

A few days later, I saw the writing on the wall, and it was misspelled. Stenciled graffiti that was supposed to be an homage to Satan was sprayed on a stucco building, SATIN RULES.

After walking a couple of blocks, I passed Double Rainbow and sensed something familiar in the beef-breath category.

"Hooo-ooo," Ruby whispered behind me. Then louder and bitchier, she taunted, "Hey, Fatty!"

I thought I was done hallucinating her, but I'd guessed wrong.

"Fatty, fatty, fatface!"

It was Ruby's voice all right. I turned around and she was laughing, just like she would have done in real life. I was so annoyed, it didn't occur to me to be scared.

I scrutinized the slutty ghost who, even in the beyond, had cooler clothes than I ever would. She was wearing a tight black dress with satin lace straining against the transparent flesh of her phantom boobs.

"Where did you get those clothes?" I asked.

"There's a huge Lost & Found in purgatory."

"Oh," I said, considering this idea.

Ruby flipped her hair. "You know," she said, "I could be totally fucking you up, scaring the shit outta you at every turn. But I'm not. I'm a friendly ghost. Aren't you glad?"

"You were scary enough in real life."

"Man, the attitude on you."

I waited at the stoplight on the corner of Polk and Clay. Ruby stood with her hands on her hips and said, "You're not even scared of me, are you?"

"Nope." I was fairly certain I was still hallucinating. But then again, I wasn't talking out loud, she was just hearing me and I was answering in my head. I wasn't sure if that was proof or not that she wasn't really there.

"Okay, bitch, you want to see some real ghosts? You'll see how lucky you are to have me following your flab-ass around. You and I are getting on this bus."

Aside from not being scared of Ruby, I was curious to know if this spectral version of her could lead me to Auntie Melaura somehow. The 1 California pulled to the sidewalk and I got on. I walked down the aisle and took a middle seat with Ruby sliding in next to me. Looking around to the other passengers, I searched for any sign that other people might be able to see Ruby, but no one was even glancing my way.

I got off the bus at Stockton Street, and noticed a woman leaning up against the wall of the Celadon restaurant with an ear-to-ear slit across her throat, dried blood caked around the collar of her jacket.

"She hangs out all day," Ruby said.

"What happened to her?"

"Who knows? Gangs fucked her up or something. There are plenty of ghosts in Chinatown who never leave."

"I saw *Poltergeist*. Shouldn't you all be going into the light?"

"Do you want to see some trippy shit or not?"

I really didn't have anything better to do than walk around all day, and I was curious about what Ruby had to show me. I decided not to worry about whether she was real, or if I was going crazy. I clammed up and decided to follow her.

We walked up the block to the YWCA and Ruby pointed up to the brick tower.

"See that lady? She sits up there all day, waiting for her man. She looks out that way because that's the direction the ships came in."

I saw a dark figure, but was unimpressed. "So what?" I said.

"That's what happens if you just wait around your whole life for dipshit Prince Charming to rescue you, that's all."

"You're not doing a very good job of scaring me."

Ruby narrowed her eyes at me, and then said, "Come on."

I followed her up the street and down an alley until we reached another building, this one built with reused, charred bricks. The place was quiet, and after we entered, we tiptoed across a black tile floor and went through an unmarked door to the basement.

"See," Ruby said, "down that hall was a secret passageway. It led to a tunnel where Chinese slave girls could escape."

I peered down the pitch-black passageway and heard faint crying that sent a chill up my neck.

"It's boarded up down a ways, but if you want, I think we can sneak through here."

"No thanks," I said, chicken.

And then, right before my eyes, I saw something crazy. An old man in a rowboat materialized, hovering in the air of the room, boat and all. He was dressed pretty raggedy and held an oar in one hand as he and his ghostly vessel cruised through the space and into the opposite wall. He held out his other hand to me, as if asking for help.

"Stay away from him," Ruby said. "He looks like a nice old guy, but he'll trap you in his fishing net and pull you down."

"Down to where?"

"Hell, stupid. He's like all unhappy jerks. You try to help miserable people and it only makes them hate and envy you more. They'll drag you down. But it'll be your own fault for being so full of yourself that you think you can rescue people. You gotta take care of yourself first. Why do you think he's in that crappy rowboat? He gave all his good shit away to assholes and now he's in the same boat. Begging to be saved from his own stupid self."

Ruby led me back outside. The sun was shining and the air was warm, which seemed like strange weather for ghosts to be out, but deep down I was relieved because the sunshine and blue sky made everything less scary. I wasn't sure why I was suddenly able to see all these ghosts, especially when I'd walked through Chinatown a thousand times before and had never seen anything. Ruby seemed to read my mind and answered, "You were just never paying attention."

As I followed her down the sidewalk, I saw a woman in flowing robes standing precisely atop a streetlight overlooking the Chinese Playground. Her hair was in a topknot, and I noticed something around the woman's neck. Balanced like a ballerina on her tiptoes, she looked down to the sidewalk and fixed her gaze on me. She winked, and I stopped to watch this ghost who seemed to have taken an interest in me.

Just as she seemed to lose her footing, she jumped and dropped through the air. The rope around her neck snapped taut, catching her by her snowy white throat as her limp body swung above the playground against the powder-blue sky. I looked away instinctively, and when I looked back up to the streetlight, the ghost-woman was at the top again. Another few seconds passed before the scenario repeated. She winked again, and then fell upon the noose, her lifeless body twisting in the wind before a trick of the eye replaced her atop the lamppost. The children playing below noticed nothing.

"Don't look at her too long," Ruby said, nudging me down the street. "She'll drive you crazy, which is what she wants."

"Why?" I asked, confused. "What does it all mean?"

Ruby stopped and watched her, too. "It was the only way she could escape her family. She listened to everything they said, and did everything they wanted. She thought killing herself was the only way to defy them. But in the end, if you think about it, she really just fucked her own deal. She's the one who's dead, not them. Joke's on her, the idiot. The point is, you don't have to kill yourself. You can get back at your parents by—"

"—By being a slut?" I interjected.

Ruby smiled. "Well, it's better than being dead."

I wanted to point out the obvious, that she *was* dead. But she kept walking, and I followed. We passed under tiled awnings and painted balconies, zigzagging between tourists. "There used to be a lot of fires in Chinatown," Ruby explained, "and some people tried to escape the flames by jumping from roof to roof."

Across the street, over a narrow alley, I looked up to a flash of light about thirty feet overhead. A man, his clothes aflame, was leaping through the air. Hitting the side of a building, he scrambled for a foothold, but fell to the ground, his crumpled figure igniting a few swirling newspapers that curled black and orange, wisping away quickly.

"Was he a victim?" I asked.

"Him?" Ruby scoffed. "He was a guy who wanted to be so special, he convinced himself he had magic powers. He wanted to be as bright as the sun, so he set his clothes on fire and tried to leap into the air. See what he got for thinking he was better than everyone else?"

Ruby looked at me accusingly.

"I don't think I'm better than everyone," I said.

"Yes, you do. Or at least that your problems are bigger than other people's. And you think you're clever."

"That's not true."

"Yeah, you do. Even this little ghost tour makes you feel superior that you can see ghosts now and other people can't." Ruby smirked. "Why are fourteen-year-olds obsessed with dead people? By the way, are you still writing Jim Morrison's name in your pancake syrup?"

"I stopped that months ago," I said, shaking my head. "And what's wrong with being clever?"

"Nothing. As long as you can tell the difference between being clever and being full of shit."

We proceeded down Grant Avenue and stopped in front of the Sun Sing movie theater. There was no one at the ticket booth, so we walked inside, past the lobby, toward the seating area. Although a kung fu movie was playing, no one was in the theater watching.

Ruby and I sat in the front row and watched for a while.

Onscreen was a swordfight with men in robes flying through the air. The movie was dubbed in dopey, simple English, but even so, I couldn't pay attention because somewhere a woman was singing loudly in Chinese.

Ruby cupped her hand against my ear and said, "Before it showed movies, this place was a Chinese opera house. There was a poor actress who was really jealous of this other woman's money and clothes. They were both in love with the stage manager, and when the man went off with the richer girl, the poor actress cursed them both. Let me show you what happens when you obsess too much about someone having more than you."

Ruby got up out of her seat and ran onstage. To the side of the movie screen was a thick curtain, and she pulled it back a little bit so I could see behind it. A woman dressed in a red cloak with white and pink opera makeup and a gold headdress was hanging from the ceiling by a thick, white cord. Her legs, exposed below the robe and visible from below, appeared blue and stiff, the toes black. But she was singing. Somehow, loud and strong, from her broken neck the atonal sounds of Chinese opera filled the theater, suddenly so loud that my head was hurting. I got out of my chair and ran back up the ramp and through the lobby, bursting out into the Grant Avenue sunlight, which temporarily blinded me.

Ruby was out on the sidewalk, laughing her ass off.

"You should have seen your face!" she said. "I thought you were going to crap your pants!"

I squinted, waiting for my eyes to adjust to the light. "What's the point of all this?" I said out loud.

"Can't you at least figure that one out?"

I shook my head and wiped away my tears before she or anyone else noticed me crying.

"You and me," she said. "You always paid way more attention to me and my clothes. You should worry about yourself more, and stop distracting yourself by bitching about other people. No one watches over you, isn't that your big sob story? Well, why don't you watch over yourself?"

She went on, "By the way, didn't you see me at the Billboard Café last night? I was sitting in the palm of that hand sculpture above your head. Why were you letting a white person school you about Chinese history? What I'm showing you is real Chinese history right here. We've got one more place."

She headed off toward Pacific Avenue, and I followed. After a couple of blocks, I was feeling a little hungry and also had to pee. Ruby seemed to sense this, and as we stopped in front of the Great Star Theater, she suggested I go inside to use the bathroom.

"Just ask them at the front and they'll let you go inside," Ruby said. I nodded and went off in search of bladder relief.

At the ticket window, I said, "Is it okay if I just want to go to the ladies room?"

The old Chinese man looked up from his newspaper and gave me a weird look. His eyes sparkled. "Be my guest," he said in perfect English, then pointed a crooked finger in the direction I should go.

"Thanks," I said, then headed down a narrow, dimly lit hallway that suggested a filthy toilet-hole awaited me at the end.

I knew the Chinese character for "girl," which was drawn in black marker on the ladies' room door. I went inside and was pleasantly surprised to see that it was super clean, as if no one ever used it. I went into one of the two stalls, and as I sat down, I speculated that perhaps mostly men came to this theater, and maybe that's why the women's bathroom was so clean. The toilet paper roll was full with an unbroken seal, and the floor was the cleanest of any public bathroom I'd ever seen in Chinatown.

Just as I was pondering my good luck at finding a tidy bathroom, I heard crying from the next stall. I hadn't heard anyone else come in, so was taken a little off guard.

"Can you help me?" a tiny voice said.

After flushing the toilet, I unlocked my stall and pushed open the door to the adjacent one. There was no one inside, and I wondered if I was only hearing noises from the movie that was playing on the opposite side of the thin wall.

I went to the sink, and standing at the basin, I washed my hands, rubbing soap between my fingers. As I did so, I looked in the mirror and noticed dark circles under my eyes.

I felt a tap on my shoulder, but I was looking in the mirror and no one was behind me. No one. Grabbing paper towels from the dispenser, I dried my hands and was about to leave when I heard the crying again, coming from the same stall as before. Looking underneath the door, I saw petite satin shoes and legs with white stockings.

"Are you okay?" I said.

I heard more whimpering, and the same voice said, "Please help me."

I pushed open the door and jumped back. Although the bathroom was quiet a moment before, a chorus of screams now filled the air. I couldn't tell if the screams were coming from my own mouth or were within the confines of my own brain. A woman with no arms was gushing blood from her shoulders and laughing maniacally. I backed into the tile wall behind me as I watched the woman in a blood-smeared white dress. She stood up, rising higher and higher until she was over eight feet tall. Blood was dripping down her head like slow chocolate syrup. She cackled as blood spurted from her neck. Still stretching taller, her bloody hair hit the bathroom ceiling.

"Get out! Get out!" she screamed angrily at me. My plastic shoes seemed fused to the floor. Feeling my hands against the cool tile, I managed to move sideways a couple of feet, my eyes still locked on the terrifying ghost who was contained inside the stall, but towering over the top of the partition.

"I have lived for nine centuries . . ." the menacing specter howled, but just then I found my feet and lunged for the door. I pulled it open and ran out the way I came, up the low-ceilinged, carpeted hallway. I saw the sunlight up ahead beyond the glass entryway, and as I ran past, the man at the ticket booth was laughing.

"See something?" he said as I sprinted past him.

I ran as fast as I could, past restaurants, curio shops, and dress boutiques. I still heard the cackling in my head, and wondered if the nine-foot ghost could fly and was following me. I kept running, past the Cathay funeral parlor where my Auntie Melaura's funeral took place, until I took a wrong turn into a dead-end alley. Stopping to catch my breath, I bent over and placed my hands on my knees, heaving. I steadied my balance on a dumpster filled with decaying floral displays, the dying dahlias giving off a peculiar odor.

I felt a hand on my shoulder and flinched. It was Ruby.

"Did you make that happen? Are you trying to drive me crazy?" I yelled.

"Calm down, Fatty."

"I'm not fat! And why don't you leave me alone? So what if you liked your tits? You're fucking dead and there's nothing I can do about it. So why don't you just get lost?"

Ruby looked amused. "Well, it's about time you started to

stand up for yourself, dumbshit. And I know you're not fat. Look."

There was a broken mirror by the dumpster, and I saw my reflection in it. I took a hard look.

I certainly had lost a lot of weight. No longer were my cheeks chubby or my hands dimpled. My legs and waist were slender, and my hair fell past my shoulders. Despite the circles under my eyes and my tear-streaked face, I saw my face had changed, too. My skin was clear, and my lips had a natural color to them, like they were stained with pomegranate juice.

Sweaty from running, I saw the outline of my body beneath my thin T-shirt.

Ruby laughed. She whispered in my ear, "Hey, I really like your tits."

In the mirror, I didn't see Ruby's reflection. But I knew she was there. She said, "What else was through the looking-glass that you didn't know about? That nine-foot ghost is a thousand years old. She's formed from the combined souls of generations of Chinese women who've lived and died without getting what they wanted out of life. They died in China, but came over here on the ships, like ballast along with the export porcelain. Those thousands of souls weighed down the hulls of hundreds of sailing ships. When they got to San Francisco, they floated through the water, seeped into the soil, and gathered in the underground passages of Chinatown. They all came together to form that nine-foot tall ghost. She's so powerful now she terrorizes people here and overseas, moving back and forth between east and west, growing stronger with each Chinese woman who dies unhappy. Do you want to add to her weight, or are you going to change your life?"

"Leave me alone!" I screamed. I didn't know if it was out loud or in my head. "Why don't you just go away?"

"I'm never going away," she said. "I'm always going to be here, in San Francisco, with all the other dead Chinese girls."

Ruby pointed to the end of the alley, and I saw the ghost-corpses of dead prostitutes being loaded from stretchers into an old-fashioned wagon.

She said, "Do you know about the thousands of Chinese girls who were kidnapped and sold to be sex slaves here? China-town was lined with brothels, and girls our age lived in stalls and cages. Maybe the lucky girls were the ones who got sick or died on the ships before they got here. They just got tossed overboard. The ones who survived the trip, once they arrived here, they had to stand naked on an auction block. They were sold to brothels and had to fuck strangers for, like, a quarter. They got all sorts of diseases, and lost their teeth. Their skin would actually rot. When they weren't of any use to anybody anymore, they got sent to this holding tank to die. But look over there. That's where one of the escape tunnels came out."

Ruby gave me an eerie smile. "Fourteen *is* a cool, clammy wall, isn't it? These girls were our age, some even a little bit younger. I just wanted to let you know they were here."

I found myself alone all of a sudden. I looked in several narrow doorways, but didn't see Ruby anymore. Retracing my steps, I walked through Chinatown, but didn't see any of the ghosts she'd just shown me. Pretty soon, I realized there was nothing left to do there, so I bought a packet of Pop Rocks at a corner grocery, and headed back to Polk Street.

Duck, Duck, Goose

I hadn't liked my reflection in the broken mirror. I didn't want to be thin and pretty, because that probably meant I was on the road to being stupid. Pretty and stupid went hand in hand, didn't they? I was so used to being the Smart & Fat one to Ruby's Pretty & Stupid. And look what happened to her. Being pretty made it more likely to get followed by Jan Brady's pimp, more likely to "get rape," or blown to smithereens. As far as I was concerned, being pretty put a person on a one-way trajectory to getting dead. Dead like Auntie Melaura, second runner-up in Miss Chinatown USA, and dead like Ruby. Who else was dead? All those Chinatown prostitutes of the nineteenth century. Just girls, really. But dead just the same.

There was a time when I would've given anything to be dumb and pretty. But I didn't give a shit now. I went back to Eggroll Wonderland and ate a big plate of rice with roasted duck. Yes, I ate *op* and it was delicious. I hadn't eaten any when the Fungs had ordered it, and I had forgotten how delectable it was, with its succulent, fat and crispy skin. I hadn't had it since my mom had cooked my pet, *Op*, for dinner, but now that I was eating it I couldn't stop. One taste had reminded my tastebuds how scrumptious it was. I ate the whole platter, and asked my dad for more because I wanted to get fatter to insulate myself from the world. My dad obligingly brought over more glistening fowl and set it down gently in front of me.

The phone rang in the restaurant, but I just continued to scarf down a duck drumstick, stripping the meat clean down to the bone.

"For you," my mom called over to me.

Really? The restaurant phone never rang for me. It was mostly for to-go orders, and besides, who the hell would be calling me? I hoped it wasn't Ruby, playing a post-mortem prank on me. I wiped duck fat from my mouth and rubbed the grease off my fingers with a paper napkin, then went over to the phone.

"Hello?" I said, hesitantly.

"Empress? It's Fred, your fabulosity tutor."

I was relieved. "Oh, hi," I said. "How did you get this number?"

"Just looked it up," he said. "Listen for a sec, would you? Albert says things aren't so hot for you in your *chow mein* wonderland. Do you want to stay at my place for a few days? I'm going away and need a housesitter. And who knows? If things go okay, maybe you can stay a while longer. I'm always looking for, well let's see, shall we say, a caretaker? The boys are always stealing my most arch shit. So how about it?"

The succulent duck, a once-living creature that flew over ponds, was now beating its wings inside my chest. This was great news. More than anything I wanted to get the hell out of Eggroll Wonderland.

"Yeah," I said immediately. I lowered my voice so neither of my parents could hear. "Where do you live?"

He gave me the address and I memorized it. "I'll come tonight," I said.

Leaving the platter of duck to get cold, I ran up the stairs and dashed into my room to prepare for my great escape. How long had I been hoping for this chance? I knew it was just a house-sitting offer, but in my mind it was an offer of freedom. Yeah, I knew it was a spur of the moment decision, but if I didn't go fast, I'd lose my nerve. Besides, I'd heard somewhere that major decisions were something that you could just feel were right. And this felt right. It was my big, tragic, exhilarating "I'm running away from home" moment, just as I'd imagined and watched in so many dippy Afterschool Specials.

I looked around my room for things I wanted to take, but there wasn't a lot to choose from. I gazed at the sleeping bag where my regular mattress once was, and I felt the full severity of how lame it was that my Barbie Corvette had burned because I really needed that money now that I was leaving. I grabbed just a few articles of clothing, considered bringing the Snoopy doll, but then decided against it. If this was going to be my first foray into a new life, stuffed animals were not going to be part of the vision, as Albert might say. Twinkiechubs Four was sleeping, so I poured a heap of food pellets into the Habitrail and checked if the water bottle was full. It was. And now it was time to go.

But wait. What would I tell my parents?

They were supremely irritating, but still, I didn't want them to put my picture on the side of a milk carton, or worry that I was dead. Well, I did want them to worry that I was dead. But I didn't want them to send out the cops or anything, so I told myself to think fast. I decided to write a note.

Dear Mom and Dad,

Did I tell you that I'm going to CYO Basketball camp?
I got a scholarship so it's free. Will call you soon.

Candace

I dropped the note on the sleeping bag, slammed the door, and ran down the steps that led right to the sidewalk.

I was finally free.

I was going to start a new life. Bye-bye eighth grade, and dead Ruby and Auntie Melaura who jumped off the bridge. See ya later, Mom hitting me with the Hot Wheels tracks, and Dad watching naked ladies and drinking out of my Aquaman glass. Goodbye to Chinese restaurant boredom, hot-and-sour soup, pot stickers, and General Tso's chicken. Goodbye to shuffling around in an apron, looking and feeling dead. Adios, Twinkiechubs Four and burned-up stuffed animals forever.

Out on the sidewalk I took one last look through the window of Eggroll Wonderland. My tired-looking mom was wiping down tables. My dad's apron was so dirty with brown and red sauce that I could see its stained front from where I was standing as he dropped a tray of spareribs into the moat of the to-go counter. They both looked like zombies. They were so worn out and sad that I couldn't stand it. As I stepped away from them, I didn't feel sad or guilty, just separate.

J Robs a Bank

J looked up to the sky and then down at the charred exterior of our building. It reminded me of the crispy ends of *chasiu*, the barbecued pork that hung in the restaurant window. Well, so much for Chinese food. My new life was waiting.

I ambled away, past Paperback Traffic, the Royal Theater, and Double Rainbow. As I bid adieu to the familiar storefronts and headed down the street, I suddenly had a brainstorm. I crossed Broadway and arranged my face into what I thought was a mournful expression. Then I headed straight to Hibernia Bank.

It was right before six o'clock, and I slipped in just before closing time. Waiting in line, I was glad to see that the teller on duty was Mrs. Martin. Her son, Lorenzo, was in my class. Or was, since we'd just graduated. Either way, the important part was that Mrs. Martin knew me and had helped me with bank transactions ever since I became Commissioner of Finance back in sixth grade. I waited my turn and as I stepped up to the teller window, I affected as pathetic an expression as I could muster.

"Oh, Candace, how are you?" said Mrs. Martin. I didn't even have to say anything and already Mrs. Martin was full of motherly concern. "I heard all about the fire," she said. "Is there anything I can do?"

The woman sounded so full of pity that I almost burst spontaneously into tears. Up to this point I'd been planning on just acting pathetic, not realizing that I was, in fact, a total mess. Some tears pooled in the corners of my eyes and this spontaneous leakage worked to my advantage.

"The passbook burned in the fire," I said. "Can I take out some money even though I don't have the booklet?" I sniffled. "The student council is planning a memorial for Ruby Ping . . . the girl in my class who . . ."

"God bless!" Mrs. Martin reached across the counter and grabbed my arm. All weepy with emotion, she used her free hand to make the sign of the cross.

"Of course, of course," she said. Drying her eyes with a tissue, she reached down for a ledger and looked up the school record. She said, "The account has $392. How much do you need for the service, dear?" She was already pulling bills out of the drawer.

This scam was easier that I'd expected and I felt triumphant. But I didn't want to get ahead of myself, so I made sure not to show my utter glee that she was about to hand over the school's money right into my hot little hand.

I wanted to say I needed all of the money, but I didn't want to sound too eager or greedy. But then again, I did want as much as I could get, considering I probably wouldn't get a second chance to come back and nab the rest. A fizzle of panic started to rise from my stomach. Barfing was suddenly a very real possibility. But how would that look? Guilty as sin. I told myself to pull it together. I reminded myself that to the outside world, Chinese girls did not embezzle student council cupcake money. I was above reproach. I was here to get money for Ruby's memorial. In my head I gave myself a little pep talk:

Believe the lie or you'll never get away with it, Fuck-face. You are the Chink Commissioner of Finance, now and forevermore. Now show them how it's done.

"We're buying lots of flowers, and making special prayer-books," I said, my voice quavering a little. With more confidence, I added, "And the California Hall is expensive to rent."

Mrs. Martin listened intently, staring at me with a solemn expression. I was neither nodding my head nor uttering any sounds to give away even the slightest hint that I might just be a lying sack of shit.

A moment passed with Mrs. Martin saying nothing. I almost freaked out, but held myself together. I supposed she was waiting to hear how much money I needed. I knew I had to deliver the number with innocence and confidence. But against my better judgment, in a rash decision, I blurted out, "I need all of it. Three-hundred and ninety-two dollars."

As soon as the words popped out of my mouth, I regretted them. Stupid. I shouldn't have asked for it all. That was suspicious. Mrs. Martin looked at me with a blank stare. I imagined her reaching under the desk and buzzing for the security guard.

Mrs. Martin nodded her head. I was convinced that she was just humoring me, and the gesture was meant to stall for time until the cops came to take my embezzling ass away to the slammer. I'd be thrown into the clink, labeled *Prisoner, Cell Block H*, and then I'd be chained to a wall by a domineering bull-dyke who would make mincemeat outta me. Jesus, I'd really blown it. Maybe I should have just accepted my fate as the Eggroll Girl. A lifelong job frying eggrolls would certainly have been better than trading my ass for cigarettes in the Big House. I wondered what the food would be like in prison.

Mrs. Martin licked her index finger and started counting out the bills.

"Well," she said, "I do know how these things can add up. When my father passed . . ." She stopped counting to quickly make the sign of the cross again, then resumed talking. "When he passed, it was the same thing. The cost of services really took us by surprise. We had this beautiful, white silk bunting across the altar. But really, you'd think they'd give you a discount or something, but you know it was worth it . . ."

As Mrs. Martin rattled on, she lined up twenty-dollar bills in a neat row. She counted out the money with the expertise of a cashier at a racetrack window. I saw that in a movie once. But, hey. This wasn't a movie. Mrs. Martin was giving this money *to me.* Or was it a ploy to distract me until the cops got here? How could Mrs. Martin talk and count at the same time? I steadied myself and tried to appear calm.

Her hands finally stopped moving. The money lay there in a pile within my reach. I didn't say anything, but looked up at Mrs. Martin who said, "Now that's three hundred and ninety. I left two dollars in the account because we want to keep it open, right? By the way, who's taking your place as treasurer?"

"Elections have been postponed until after the service," I said, knowing this explanation was highly lame. But Mrs. Martin bought it.

"Well, of course, they would be wouldn't they? God bless you, Candace."

She slid the money across the counter and I calmly took it, folding it into my pocket.

"Would you like an envelope for that?" Mrs. Martin asked.

I couldn't look her in the eye. "No thanks," I said. Before I lost my nerve and confessed everything, I turned around and walked out the door.

There was no turning back now. Running away from home was such a cliché, but if Afterschool Specials had taught me anything, it was that I would need my own money or else I'd end up like Jan Brady, turning tricks in the rain to keep some crazy pimp happy. How fucking lame would that be? Lamer than frying eggrolls, that's for sure.

Really, I had no choice. It wasn't my fault that all the money I had saved burned to nothing within the molten wheel-well of my Barbie Corvette beneath my old bed. Who left me with nothing? God. Who made Mrs. Martin hand over the money so easily? God. Who made me the devious schemer that I was? God.

I began to walk. Up and over the hills, I had a lot of energy. I was leaving. Finally, finally. Good-bye, dork-ass! Hello, girl on the cover of Candy-O, or hello Miss Sakamoto, you're beautiful! I hiked up and over California Street and saw the big houses and the Mark Hopkins Hotel. The flags were flapping languidly in the wind, and San Francisco seemed glad I had made a decision. As I descended the steep street, passing a cable car with its friendly bell, I felt like I was doing a victory lap. The waving tourists hanging from the cable car handrails seemed to be cheering me on, wishing me a bon voyage from my old life. Smiling for the first time at tourists, I waved back.

Chinatown was cooling off after a hot afternoon. I had come here looking for my little brother, Kenny, or else someone who might know him. I figured if I told him I was going to basketball camp, he could corroborate my story when my parents found the note. What a sneaky little shit was I. That was Yoda-speak for "I was a sneaky little shit."

I stopped in at the McDonalds, borrowed a pen from one of the cashiers, and grabbed a paper napkin. On it I scrawled,

Hey Kenny,

*I'm going to CYO basketball camp. Will you feed the
    hamster?*
Tell Mom and Dad I'm not dead or anything.

                                        Candace

I left the fast-food joint and walked slowly down Grant Avenue, scanning the street corners. I knew that Kenny and his little hoodlum friends sometimes gathered around the Chinese Playground, so I headed up that way. Gazing up at the sky, my eyes traveled across the rooftops, and I saw the same ghost with the flowing robes standing on the light-post overlooking the playground.

Standing on her tippy toes, the ghost winked at me like she did the first time I saw her. I looked away before she jumped off from the lamppost, and as I turned my head, I saw Ruby, smoking a cigarette beneath the Hang Ah Alley sign. She was smiling a sly smile as she blew smoke out the side of her pretty mouth.

I approached her, but she disappeared. As I continued to walk, I kept catching glimpses of her here and there—a skinny leg, or the back of her head in a crowd of tourists. Her thick, black hair, even in ghostly form, was recognizable as it bobbed ahead, just out of reach. As I walked and searched for my brother and his friends, Ruby's ghost peeked out from behind brick walls, dumpsters, and grocery carts, but wouldn't let me catch her. In a way, it wasn't all that different from that day she was hiding from me at Pier 39. She was still playing tricks in the afterlife, which seemed fitting. I wanted to ask her if it was the right thing to do, leaving home. But she wouldn't stand still long enough. Nonetheless, she was still hanging around. Guess that meant she still hadn't boarded a standby flight to heaven.

Finally, I caught up with her near a pagoda-shaped phone booth. But her image immediately began to fade. Her face melted off first, and I could see the smudgy imprint of her skull with sunken eye sockets. I stopped, and from the short distance, I watched as her image washed away, like magnetic filings on an Etch-A-Sketch. Actually, as the outline of her body dissolved in the light wind, the effect was more like the swirling grains of white, black, and blue sand from my Magic Window toy by Wham-O!

Her spectral image disappeared in the phone booth. But as I turned and headed back down to Grant Avenue, I still continued to see other ghosts. There was a Chinese man with his long ponytail cut off, and he held the lock of hair in his fist. With his other hand, he held up his head that had a cleaver through it. I detoured up and through Waverly Place, where a row of babies lay in the gutter crying, some with blue, rotted faces.

Finally, I spotted Waylon, one of my brother's friends, in front of a magazine kiosk where they sold firecrackers.

"Hey," I said, glancing around. Thankfully, for just a second the ghosts had disappeared. Waylon shoved his hands inside his jacket pockets, then spat on the sidewalk.

"What you want?"

"You're Kenny's friend, right?"

"Yeah."

"I'm his sister. Give him this, will you?"

The kid nodded his head and slipped the napkin note into his jacket without taking his eyes off the street, like he was used to slipping things in his pocket without looking.

I started to walk away, and then turned around. "Don't forget, okay?"

He just scowled, so I figured that was all I could do.

Walking all the way down Grant again, at Columbus Avenue I cut over to Stockton Street. I ducked into the Dollar Store and decided to buy a few things with my new pile of money. Two T-shirts, two pairs of cotton pants, and a seven-pack of undies, socks, a toothbrush, and toothpaste. Deodorant, too. And Stayfree maxipads.

I brought my basket to the counter, and a middle-aged Chinese lady who smelled like mothballs rang up my stuff. The lady had a jade disc on a chain around her neck, and it reminded me of the jade pendant Auntie Melaura had given me, the one I had traded for that stupid tiara that got stepped on the first night I wore it. I was bummed out not to have my jade rabbit anymore, but I told myself that it was a part of my old life, and what's gone was gone.

Velvet Pelt

J looked at the city map affixed to the Muni shelter, and figured out which route would get me to Fred's place. After climbing onto the dreary bus, I stared out the window and sang the lyrics to "Golden Years" in my head.

It would've been great to start my new life in style, but I wasn't in a twenty-foot dream car. I was on the 15 Third. The ride rumbled downtown, and snaked through neighborhoods I'd never been to before. Even past the train tracks and the Esprit clothing outlet, the bus kept on going. After God knows how long, I almost fell asleep in my seat, but my head bobbed up before my chin hit my chest. It was just in time to see a street sign that told me I was near my stop.

I got off the bus, and the sky was dark blue with one last sliver of light illuminating the horizon. Wisps of clouds were outlined in orange from the sunken sun, and the streaks across the sky gleamed like red guppies. The sheen of a low moon spread across the bay, giving the water the appearance of a panther's dense, velvet pelt. Having never been too far from my Polk Street neighborhood, I wasn't sure what to expect as I walked along the dim road. There were no streetlights and the dusky, starless sky failed to light my path.

Walking along a quiet block of collapsing, one-story Victorians, up ahead I saw a house like no other. Surrounded by a high green hedge was a property of terraced stone with a tall rectangular tower. From behind metal grates, the windows glowed faintly. The miniature castle was the only welcoming sight on the entire block dotted with forlorn shacks, and when I saw the address on the metal sign, I was glad that this was the place I was looking for.

Behind the topiary wall was a garden hidden from the street. A low, cast-iron fence enclosed the perimeter of the courtyard that was lined with ochre bricks. A fountain in the shape of a lion's head spilled water into a terra cotta trough, and as I made my way toward the main entrance of the house, I passed under a lamp and walked through overgrown green grass and a swath of red and yellow poppies. I stopped when I finally reached a wide wooden door fitted with metal brackets. I wondered if I'd like it here, and I took a deep breath of straw-scented air before I knocked.

"You prissy little cunt!"

This was the first thing I heard when I pushed open the unlocked door. I stood in the foyer and peered around the corner. Fred was straddling a handsome young man, pounding his face into the shiny white tile.

"No, Fred, not my face!"

Upon closer inspection, the young man getting clobbered was younger that I thought, maybe my age. He had wavy dark hair, and pretty olive skin. I could tell this because he was practically nude, just in his underwear.

"You vain little fucker, don't you know you're beautiful

on the inside?" Fred grabbed the teen's hair and slammed his head repeatedly into the floor like a rubber punch ball. "Vanity kills!" he exclaimed.

He caught sight of me, and I felt like a dummy just standing there.

"Empress!" Fred dropped the young man's head and it hit the floor. Rushing over to me, Fred dropped to his knees and kissed the tops of my shoes. "Chinese princess, welcome to your castle!"

While Fred cooed over me, the black-haired boy picked himself up and rubbed his forehead.

"Empress of China, meet my Alexander the Great. I know you two piglets will get along."

"Pleased to meet you," said the boy, his black ringlets a little mussed. I smiled, trying to pretend it wasn't weird that I just saw him getting his face smashed into the floor.

"Hi," I said, a little nervous as I shook his hand. Then I turned to Fred.

"I thought you were going out of town?"

"Turns out I'm not. But don't worry, there's plenty for you to do here. I've got a little housekeeping list for you." He turned to both of us and said, "But piglets, I'm off for now. John, show Miss Empress around, would you? Papa bird will be back in a jiff."

Fred dashed around. He grabbed a jacket and keys, and eventually left John and me alone.

"I'll be right back," said John, clutching the side of his face. "Go ahead, have a look around."

I wasn't sure what to think—if John was his live-in loverboy or what. Where was I going to sleep? What kind of housekeeping chores did I have to do? Was Fred going to pay me, or was I going to clean to earn my room and board? I patted my pocket where I had my embezzled money from Mrs. Martin. I figured if things here were too screwy I could split.

Left alone, I relaxed a bit and took in my surroundings. The place was like nothing I'd ever seen before, not even in the movies.

Starting with the foyer where I was standing, the walls were painted in a high-gloss periwinkle lacquer, punctuated with gold-leafed angels' heads. An intricate painting of a Hindu goddess hovered over a Lucite altar that was covered with crystal lotuses, and flanking the painting on either side were turquoise-and-gold vases that looked as if they held the cremated remains of Prussian princes.

The wood floor was painted with the same lavender-blue lacquer, and a dark purple runner led me into the living room. All the furniture was made of the same clear prism-like Lucite, and it made the chairs, tables, and cabinets look like they were made of ice or cut from giant hunks of rock crystal. One wall was completely covered with flowers: cascading orchids, jasmine, lilacs, and bougainvillea. I reached out with a tentative hand and touched one petal, then several others. They weren't plastic like the shitty sprigs of carnations on the tables at Eggroll Wonderland. They were real.

To disorienting effect, all the other walls were mirrored from ceiling to floor. As I walked from room to room, the mirrors gave me the feeling of being in a fun house. As I tried to find my way back to the foyer from the living room, I almost bumped into my reflection several times. It was more like a movie set and not someone's home at all. There were no stains on rugs, crappy cabinetry, scuffs on the walls, or any other sign of regular life like stacks of bills, dirty laundry or dishes. Like the Pings' house, there was music piped over a speaker system, but instead of Chinese Musak, here it was space music, like the sound of strumming harps, Tibetan bells, and chimes.

I had practically forgotten that my first sight here was that of someone getting his face clobbered, but then I remembered John, and went off in search of him.

I heard water and followed the sound. I passed through another mirrored room with purple carpeting and gold, gilt furniture. Then to my surprise, I quickly found myself face-to-face with John who was standing stark naked in the bathroom.

Okay, no one ever said there were going to be naked people.

"Oh, sorry," I said, stepping back and looking for a door to shut, but there was none. I retreated into the den, and from where I stood I could see across the toilet and into the kitchen. The bathroom was open to both areas, which I thought was weird.

"Fred had the doors taken off," John said over the sound of the water. "It's okay. Hey, come in here and talk to me."

I hesitantly made my way toward his voice and noticed the empty hinges on the doorframe. Seeing me hovering in the doorway, he added, "Go ahead and sit down, I won't be long."

He pointed to the toilet, and I flipped the lid down and sat on it, averting my eyes. He continued to shower, standing just two feet from me, separated only by the completely see-through shower door. He soaped up his armpits and crotch, then shampooed his hair, and gently lathered up his face to shave.

When he was done, he turned off the water, got out, and grinned at me. I could see the droplets of water in his pubic hair and I couldn't help but see his penis, just hanging there. He didn't seem to notice or care that I was gawking at his private area. He pulled a towel off a hook, wrapped it around his waist and stared at himself in the mirror, checking the spot where Fred had banged his head into the floor.

"What was that about?" I asked softly, looking at him as he pressed his forehead.

He either didn't hear me or pretended not to, and said, "Do you want to take a shower?"

"No thanks," I said, squirming on the toilet seat.

I was feeling uncomfortable there, and was relieved when John said, "Come on. I'll show you where you'll sleep."

We went into the living room and he opened up one of the mirrored panels. It was a hidden closet filled with rolled-up foam pads and bedding.

"Here," he said, "Pick a mat. You can set yours out over by the sofa. I'll bring you some blankets."

The sky through the windows was darkening, and I had no idea what time it was, but sleep seemed like a good idea. As I set up my little bed in the corner, I knew my situation was strange, but I wasn't scared. I couldn't think of anything bad happening to me here in this periwinkle-lacquered place where John was now prancing around in his tighty-whiteys with Queen Marlene Mint Julep clay mask drying on his face. I had no idea where Fred was, but I figured I'd see him soon enough. Taking off my pants, I scooted under cool cotton sheets, and snuggled under the wool blankets. Pulling my arms inside my T-shirt, I wriggled out of my bra and placed it between the folds of my jeans, then tucked it all under my neck.

"We're civilized here," John said, tossing me a down pillow.

"And here." He popped the lid on a small plastic jar and proceeded to rub clay mask on my face. "This keeps your pores
tight and your face beautiful," he said.

I seriously didn't know what to think of all this, so I didn't
think, just fell asleep in seconds flat.

A Trickle of Strangers

When I woke up the next morning, the house was empty. Sitting up, I found a note attached with a clothespin to a bucket that contained rubber gloves, cleanser, and a scrub brush.

> *Little Bo Peep, Empress of China,*
> *Candace in Wonderland!*
>
> *Put away beds.*
> *Clean bathroom: scrub toilet, shower, and sink (bleach*
> * in cabinet).*
> *Floors: vacuum and mop.*
> *Empty all trash.*
> *Clean birdcage.*
> *You're home now.*
>
> *XXX Fred*

I studied the note for a minute. Well, if I was home, I must be Cinderella, cuz this list of chores sucked. What did I expect? I supposed I was living here for free, after all. But even still, I was disappointed to be left all by myself.

But I figured I was lucky because the place was empty and I could take a shower without fear of anyone walking in on me. I tried to remember which mirrored panel was also the closet door, and after clawing my fingernails across a few that wouldn't budge, I found the correct one and grabbed a few things from my designated cubbyhole. I headed to the bathroom, stood at the sink to scrub off the green mask that had hardened on my face, then waited for the shower to get warm. I pulled towels off the racks and lined the see-through door with them to create a modicum of privacy should anyone come in while I was naked. Out of my clothes in seconds, I jumped into the shower and managed a personal record by bathing in less than two minutes. I knew because I counted in my head the whole time, one hundred and eighteen seconds, terrified that someone might barge in.

After drying off, I was back in my clothes lickety-split. Although brief, this shower was the most luxurious I'd ever had. The towels were the fluffiest I'd ever used, and the soap and shampoo smelled and lathered so much better than the cheapo kind I used at home.

But eventually it was time to get to work. Having done a lot of cleaning at Eggroll Wonderland, I knew how to fill a bucket with soapy water and get cleaning. In a kitchen closet, I found a broom and a mop, and as I did my chores, I wondered what was happening back at the restaurant. I had no idea if my little brother got my note, or if my parents realized or cared that I was gone.

While cleaning the bathroom, kitchen, and the floors in the living room, foyer, and den, one weird thing I noticed was that there was a television and a Betamax video machine in every room. I hoped that there'd be cable so I'd get to watch lots of movies. But who needed a TV in every room? I guessed that's what you had when you were rich.

I finished cleaning all the rooms until all that was left to do was the birdcage in the kitchen. It was so gigantic that I could practically fit inside the wrought iron prison cell if I crouched down, and I wasn't eager to see what kind of creature required such a cage. Approaching it, I took a deep breath as I grabbed the corner of the coverlet, and gently pulled it off.

The heavy cloak was secured with Velcro tabs. When I finally got it undone, I removed it slowly and saw a majestic blue-and-gold macaw with its head cocked to one side, a white-rimmed eye staring right at me.

The room was quiet, but the bird made babbling noises as I studied it. After a minute, it spoke an intelligible sentence.

"Rape me," it said.

My head was stuffy with cleaning fumes so I figured I'd heard wrong.

"Rape me," it said again, as I was folding up the slipcover.

Looking at the creature, I wondered if it would lunge for my hand if I tried to reach inside and change the water or food trays. It turned its head and looked at me with its other eye now. The parrot was enormous, and I would have felt a lot better if it were just a hamster.

And then it said, "You stupid, fucking cunt."

I wondered if Fred or John had actually taught it to say these things, or if it had just picked up these handy phrases, and if so, how? I found some oven mitts and proceeded to clean the bottom of the cage with the protective gloves over my hands and forearms just in case the creature bit, which it eventually did. Its sharp black beak came down on my quilted wrist as I removed the gigantic water bottle.

"Easy there, Pigeon," I said.

It squawked and screeched, "Little bitches get fucked."

And then I got my period.

I could feel a hot blob in my undies and I knew exactly that that's what had happened. I pulled off the oven mitts, ran to the bathroom, and jumped on the toilet. Peeling down my under-pants, I saw the familiar red spot and tried to cram some tissue paper against my crotch for damage control. And then I heard some clicking noises from the front door. Jesus Christ, someone had just come home. And there was no bathroom door.

"Bo Peep!"

Fred breezed through the hall, past the kitchen and was now standing in the doorway of the bathroom.

"I'll just be a minute," I said, but he didn't move.

I pulled my underwear back up over my knees and waited for him to stop watching me, but he just stared at me curi-ously. I didn't want to be rude and tell him to go away since, after all, it was his place.

"Do you have much pubic hair?" he asked.

I didn't know how to answer. "Uh . . ."

"Eve's curse!" he laughed, then noticed his bird. "Parusha! See what human girls go through!" He walked away and opened the door of the cage and held out his arm. The bright creature climbed onto his shoulder, and the two exchanged kisses. I took the opportunity to wad up some toilet paper, and shoved it into my panties. Then I pulled up my pants and scurried to the closet where clean underwear awaited me in my cubby.

A moment later Fred called out, "Empress, do you need pussy plugs?"

"No," I yelled back. "I've got pads."

I ran back into the bathroom, put on clean underwear, stuck a pad onto the crotch part of it, and pulled my pants back up. As I rinsed my stained undies in the sink, Fred came up behind me.

"Don't forget to dust in the master bedroom," he said. "And by the way, you do know how to cook Chinese food, don't you?"

"Yeah, I guess."

"Good," he said, holding out a feather duster for me to take.

Drying my hands, I took it from him. He didn't hang around long enough to talk and I wanted to ask him so many questions, like, what was up with all the TVs, and why was that macaw so well-versed in cuss words? What happened here all day, and how was it that he was so rich? Why had he pounded John's face into the floor, and why did John just let him?

I told myself to keep my eyes and ears open, and in a way, actually hoped that Ghost Ruby might show up to tell me what was going on. I looked into the bathroom mirror and hoped she might be hiding in the reflection, like Ozma of Oz or something, but all I saw were towel racks, a shelf full of skincare products, and, of course, stupid old me.

After cleaning up my personal stuff and putting it away, I went down the hallway and found Fred's bedroom at the very end.

Inside, only one of the walls was mirrored, and the other three were covered in yellow silk. All the furniture was Chinese: a massive table with carved dragons slithering up the heavy wooden legs, lacquered chairs with gold-leafed carvings of herons and cranes, and in the corner of the room, a canopied Chinese wedding bed like the one I'd seen at Cissy's antique store. The bedposts were decorated with bits of colored glass and inlaid mother-of-pearl. Panels of turquoise silk hung from the frame, and the sheets and pillowcases were white satin.

As I stood there looking at all the pretty things, I heard a whisper behind my ear, "Boo!"

Startled, I flinched and turned around, expecting my ghostly friend. But it wasn't Ruby, it was Fred.

"Have you seen the cave?" he said, and from my puzzled expression I guess he figured I hadn't.

"C'mon," he said, and beckoned for me to follow. Back in the kitchen he walked over to what I figured was a pantry door. But when he opened it, I saw that it was a stairwell. The steps were polished stone, and steep, with no railing and not much light to illuminate the way.

"Watch yourself, Empress," he said, and I followed behind him, my hand against the wall for balance as I stepped carefully down the walkway. We spiraled down about ten steps, and I was grateful to see a little sunlight shining through a small square opening. It was more like an open porthole than a window, and it let air in from the outside. I could see San Francisco Bay, and stopping to admire the view, I thought I could hear the sound of water.

Fred continued down the steps and called back, "Are you coming?"

I caught up with him on the landing below. Inhaling the damp cellar smell, I inched out onto the platform. Despite the dim light, my eyes soon adjusted.

We were standing on a short sandstone bridge over a channel of water about twenty feet wide. An arched ceiling extended about thirty feet and beyond into the darkness. The echo of the water made it sound like the cave continued much farther, but I couldn't see. The cavern and water gave me the sensation of being inside a gigantic hollowed-out clamshell. The water was a pretty bottle green, and the ripples made it look like whittled glass.

"What is it?" I asked.

"It's an underground spring. This cave was hand-carved in the 1870s, and the building used to be a brewery, I think. The water leads all the way down to the field behind the house. Do you want to go swimming?"

The water was mesmerizing. When I finally did look up at Fred, he was hard to read. "Forget it," he said. "You still have your chores to finish."

I followed him back up the stairs, through the kitchen, and down the hall. Back in his bedroom, feather duster in hand, I got to work. I dusted the whole room, which was no easy task because he had a lot of vases and knickknacks. When I was done, I found a note on the door instructing me to clean all the mirrors in the front room.

By mid-afternoon I was thinking of the *Karate Kid*. I had a stack of newspapers and several squirt bottles of Windex, and I had been cleaning all the glass surfaces for a couple of hours. This was some serious *wax-on, wax-off, Daniel-san* bullshit. I was waiting for Mr. Miyagi to materialize and teach me martial arts, or maybe Fred would come out dressed in a kimono.

I didn't know what to think. I hadn't come here to clean all day. But I didn't utter a peep. I went on with my housekeeping duties throughout the afternoon and into the evening. Fred and John had gone out somewhere, the castle was quiet, and I was beginning to think that coming here was a pretty bad idea.

By the time it got dark outside, the house started coming alive. Fred and John returned from grocery shopping, and some new people came over, too. Although Fred had claimed he'd needed a housesitter, there were suddenly a lot of people who seemed to know their way around the place. I didn't know what he needed me around for.

"Hi," said a tall Aryan specimen with white-blond hair. "I'm Jack."

"But we all call him Snow White," interjected a creamy-skinned Mexican girl. "I'm Flor, and this is Monica."

"Hiya," said a pretty Indian girl wearing a pink sari over jeans.

Fred swept into the room. "Ah," he said. "The United Colors of Benetton, *n'est-ce pas?* Empress, I see you've met Snow White, and Flor, my Mexican conchita Lolita, and Monica, my Punjabi princess. And of course, you already know John, my perfect Alexander the Great."

As he mentioned their names, he went over and touched everyone's faces tenderly, like he was the owner of pedigreed Persian cats making sure each pet received equal attention. As they all stood around smiling blankly, I thought of *House of Wax* and how Vincent Price showed off all the corpses he had embalmed into mannequins.

"And all of you, this is my little Empress of China. Isn't she a beauty?" He came over and patted my cheek.

"Yeah," said Snow White. "We're the perfect mix for our multicultural gang bang."

Fred shot him an evil eye, then said, "John, take the little Empress into the kitchen, would you?"

I followed John into the kitchen as everyone else seemed to instantly know how to busy themselves—dusting, straightening furniture, and picking imaginary lint off their clothes. I wanted to know what was going on, but John diverted my attention.

He said, "Fred insists you're a great Chinese cook. We went

to the store and bought all this stuff for you to make soup."

I looked at the kitchen counter filled with vegetables, meat, tofu, and all sorts of Chinese sauces in bottles.

"You must know what to do, right?"

I shrugged. "Um, yeah, I guess."

"Great," he said, then left to rejoin the others in the living room.

Standing there alone in the kitchen, I figured there wasn't much else to do except start cooking. Eyeballing the ingredients, I figured it would be fairly easy to make a vinegared-chicken stew with Chinese wine. But as I took the produce out of the bags, I was miffed. My New Wave, Candy-O fantasy was hardly unfolding. All afternoon I'd been a maid, and now I pretty much was back to being a soup-and-eggroll girl, except in somebody's house instead of a restaurant. Was I, like every Chinese person, doomed to be perceived forever as "the help"? I was pissed, but started cooking nonetheless.

I rinsed a bunch of carrots and turnips, and looked inside the drawers for a peeler. I squatted down in front of the garbage pail and began the familiar task of vegetable preparation that I'd been doing as long as I could remember. The whole routine was so freaking automatic to me that in no time I had pots of water boiling on the stove, a stack of perfectly julienned veggies in a pile, and a deboned chicken ready to go. I worked quickly and effortlessly as I wondered what everyone else was doing in the next room.

I guess I got fairly carried away with cooking because by the time I was done, I didn't hear any noise from the other room. I went out to tell everyone that dinner was ready, but only Fred was left, polishing a smudge on one of the mirror panels.

"Where'd everybody go?" I asked.

"I sent them all away, the twatty little twats."

Looking around the empty room, I said, "Oh, well, dinner's ready."

He came over and put his arm around me. "Since I wasn't here last night, I thought maybe we could dine together, just you and me."

"All right," I said.

We went into the kitchen and I helped him pull out some plates.

"We can eat in here," he said, fanning a linen cloth over the small table.

As I ladled the stew into bowls, the quiet kitchen sounds were interrupted when the giant parrot suddenly screeched, "I like it in the ass!"

"Parusha!" Fred scolded the bird, then threw the black cloak over the cage. "Go to sleep!"

He returned to the table. "Sorry about that."

"Where'd he learn to talk like that?" I said.

"Oh, you know, the movies." He took a sip of soup. "This is delicious!"

There were so many things I wanted to ask, but I stayed silent. My eyes drifted to a tabloid magazine on one of the chairs, and seeming to sense we needed an ice breaker, Fred grabbed it and started flipping through the pages.

"Ugh," he said, "Look at these twatty, old twats. They're all just spiritually bankrupt hags."

"Oh, but I like her," I said, pointing to an actress from TV.

"Her? Don't be impressed. She's tricked everyone with her Kansas City pussy and now everyone thinks she's the next Princess Grace, but everyone knows that Grace Kelly, too, was just a slut social climber from Philly."

He got up to place his bowl in the sink, and began to rinse

a papaya. Grabbing a knife, he sat back down and cut the fruit in half, a few of the slimy seeds popping out.

"Sorry to speak in such crass terms, darling. But I just want to show you how they're just all trash, and not half as lovely as you, my little Quan Yin."

He resumed flipping through the pages of the magazine, and paused at one of Richard Gere posing with an Asian guy in robes.

"I hate the Dalai Lama," Fred said. "If he's so holy, why is he hanging out with the *American Gigolo*? And if he's so powerful, don't you think he could at least wear cuter eyeglasses?"

Having scooped out the seeds of the tropical fruit, Fred handed me half.

"I'm really glad you decided to come," he said, handing me a spoon.

I took a bite of papaya and it tasted like barf, but I just smiled.

That night, I had a dream that went on forever. I dreamed I was frying eggrolls for the rest of my life. I saw myself at fifteen, then at twenty, thirty, forty, and so on, standing there at the deep fryer. From Eggroll Wonderland, the setting of the dream changed and I was suddenly Ruby, lying inside a locked casket lined with white satin. I was alive, and I wanted to shout for someone to come get me, but I didn't yell. Instead, I lay quietly on the tufted, enclosed mattress, ashamed for liking my tits.

Then Ruby and I were walking around the Mission District. I said I wanted to go to La Cumbre for a tongue burrito, but instead we went to a vegetarian restaurant called Amazing Grace. It was closed, so we walked to another place called Real

Good Karma. The whole time in the dream, we didn't talk, but communicated through ESP. Ruby reached across the table and held my hands. In real life, Auntie Melaura had the softest hands I had ever felt, and in the dream Ruby's hands were Auntie Melaura's hands.

Funky Thigh Collector

W hat should we do about her?"

Snow White was lying right next to me, and John was on the other side of him. I pretended to be asleep and affected a soft snore, which seemed to convince them I was really in dreamland.

"Fred said he read some book on how geisha houses prepare girls for sex." John was saying. "He said the first night they spread egg-white between the girl's thighs, and that's it. The second night they do the same thing, but move their fingers up and rub the slime closer near her pussy. I guess the next night, they put their fingers inside. I'm not sure. But for some reason, he wants me to find a vegetarian alternative. Is Egg Beaters veggie?"

"No, but her pussy will have low cholesterol."

They stifled their laughs, got up quietly, and retreated to the kitchen. I realized I had to get the hell out of there.

Sitting up, I felt the stillness of the house. The low hum of the air purifiers seemed to keep out all sounds of the outside world. Flopping back down on my sleeping pad, I stared at the ceiling.

Unsure of how I'd gotten myself into this situation, I guess I still hoped for the best. I wasn't exactly sure how to leave. I'd read somewhere that people lost in the woods, instead of calling out for help, would hide in caves. I guess I was cowering in a cave in my head. Not that any emergency crew was coming for me either. No one was around to help me make any kind of decision, and I was disoriented from plopping myself into such weird surroundings where nothing was familiar. I knew things weren't looking good, but I felt compelled to stick around. A part of me was still deluded into thinking things could turn out okay.

So for the next three days, I was a cleaning fool. Dishes, dusting, sweeping, and mopping were my middle names. I played the role of nincompoop housekeeper by day, and in the evening I made Chinese food for everybody. *Wax on, wax off,* chop, mince, stir, clean up. When my Cinderella duties were finished, I went to the mirrored panel at midnight, rolled out my little mat, and tried to rest. But I couldn't sleep. I didn't sleep. I lay awake all night, afraid someone was going to peel off my covers and rub egg substitute on my clam.

Over the rest of the week, no one ever came right out and said, "We make X-rated movies," but I got the picture. And it wasn't as weird as it sounded. Funny thing, the longer I stayed at Fred's, the more that weird shit seemed normal. Flor, Monica, Snow White, John, and Fred all walked around butt-naked or in various states of undress at all times, in and out of the shower, or would go into the bathroom and start flossing their teeth even if someone else was in there taking a shit.

And I found out why there were TVs and Betamax machines in every room. Fred studied his homemade "tantric sex" movies like a graduate student getting a PhD in porno film criticism. As I dusted around him, he'd call Jack over for an opinion. "Do you think there should be more vanilla milkshake dripping off the balls right here?" he'd say. He used a chopstick to point out things onscreen that he thought were problematic.

As I cleaned, I always snuck peeks at the TV screens. I began to recognize my "housemates" as the stars of the films. One afternoon as I was trying to replicate my dad's General Tso's Eggplant, Fred was in the kitchen rewinding a video over and over, scrutinizing a particular scene. As I chopped, I watched Fred work, and as a result, had seen Snow White jizz on Monica's boobs in fast forward, slow motion, and freeze frame. I finally got up the gumption to ask Fred a question.

"What do you do with all these, um, movies?"

"Sell them," he said, taking his eyes off the screen to scribble in his notepad.

"Is there really a . . . I mean . . . do you make a lot of money?"

He looked up and made a sweeping gesture with his arm. "You think this place is cheap?"

Putting down his notebook, he came over and helped me crush some garlic. "There's a huge demand for multicultural videos in the, let's say, erotic market. People love to see other culture's twats. I have this great idea that I'm saving up for, too." He stood up and fanned out his hands. "Picture this," he said. "World history, told in porn. Remember our Chinese history lesson? There's the English fucking over India, and we'll have Monica, my Punjabi princess all dolled up. And the Spanish invading Mexico . . . I'll have to find a Spaniard, but that'll be no problem . . . the whole tableau, I'm thinking it can be a package set of ten videos, with lavish costumes. I know it sounds ambitious, but if we could do it right, it could be faaabulous."

I almost sliced off my finger when Fred said, "Remember our Chinese history lesson" because, as I recalled, he'd talked about a multitude of European nations screwing over China. Something told me he wasn't going to take, "Um, no thanks," for an answer. Ruby was right. Someday my prince would come. On my face. On video.

I felt a lump in my throat, and reached up to my neck only to be reminded that my jade rabbit was gone. Auntie Melaura always said I was a diamond in the rough and could be anything I wanted. Why did the world tell me my only choices as a Chinese girl were servant, waitress, and some kind of sex doll? I thought Fred was my friend, but it was turning out that he was like everybody else. He had the same fucked-up notions about who and what I could be, and none of those things was what *I* wanted to be.

Here I was, though, locked in a castle on the edge of my hometown, led here by my own bullshit, stupid fantasies, and inability to speak up for what I wanted. What would Ruby have done if she were in my shoes? Were these ruby slippers hers or mine, anyway? I didn't know, and didn't have the time to wonder about it.

I wanted her to appear to me like the Great Gazoo or Glinda the Good Witch and tell me what to do. But as I sat there staring at Fred, she didn't materialize. I guess that meant for sure that she was dead and I was the one who was here.

I wanted to get the hell out of there. I screwed up my courage and quietly said, "Fred, I don't want to be in your movie."

"Why not?" he said with a blank stare.

In my head, I pictured spirits swirling around me. In the silence I listened for Ruby, Auntie Melaura, Op, and the dead

Twinkiechubses rooting for me. I imagined them yelling, *"Run quick, now! Quick like a bunny!"*

Fred turned off the video and sighed. "Don't worry, Empress," he said. "I've got it all planned out, and it'll be easy for you. It's not like you're going to be like Brooke in *Pretty Baby*. You're not going to be carried out on the backs of Nubian slaves and have your virginity auctioned off on a silver platter. You're the *Empress*, remember? Don't you trust me? You'll be sitting on this fabulous throne behind a yellow screen, just overseeing the destruction of your vast empire. You won't even be nude, but in a very sensational, gossamer something. How's that sound?"

Oh, Jesus. How many Afterschool Specials had I seen where the pervert tells the teenage girl that she can leave her bra and panties on while he takes her picture? I wasn't *that* stupid.

"Hello!" he said with a winning smile. "Miss Sakamoto, you're beautiful! Don't you want to be fabulous, Miss Candy O?"

Boy, was he clever . . . and full of shit.

I showed no reaction, and he must have sensed that I wasn't falling for it because a second later he was suddenly really pissed off. He paused to rub his chin, and said, "We can't really stay our twatty waitress-self forever, can we now, Miss Candace Ong of Eggroll Wonderland?"

Up until this point I'd considered Fred my friend, but I hadn't lived through three years of middle school without learning to detect when someone was messing with my mind. The way he exalted me and then shamed me all in one fell swoop, frankly, was reminiscent of the talents of Miss Ruby Ping. Yeah, I did want to be beautiful, and no, I didn't want to be a waitress forever. But there were better things than being pretty, and worse things than working in a Chinese restaurant. Like having shitty, backstabbing friends who only wanted you around to do the crap they wanted you to do.

I put down my paring knife and washed my hands. Maybe I looked mad, or he didn't know what else to say to me because he patted me on the head and said, "You think about it." Then he breezed out of the kitchen like we'd settled everything.

I could hear voices in the living room. The foyer was packed with the gang. I still didn't know why Monica, Flor, Jack, or John chose to stay and make Fred's movies. They were all just a little older than me, and seemed to like it here. I hadn't been around long enough to figure out if they lived with Fred all the time, or lived at home, or in their own apartments. I didn't know if they were students, runaways, or what.

Although they came and went throughout the day, I wondered if I was trapped here. Since the first day I'd arrived, I hadn't stepped outside once, even into the courtyard or garden. No one actually physically stopped me or said I couldn't walk out. It just didn't occur to me to leave. Even though I had left home and thought I said goodbye to some old kind of me, I was still waiting around for someone to tell me what I could or couldn't do, or where I could go. I didn't want to wait anymore.

I was going to get the hell out of there and figured there was no time like the present. I didn't want to walk out the same way Fred had gone because I could hear them all right outside the kitchen door and I didn't want to talk to anybody. But my stuff was all still in my cubbyhole behind the mirrored panel and I had to get it. Were it not for the cash from the student council fund rolled up in a pink sock, I probably would have left everything else. But I had to get the money so I could return it to Mrs. Martin. I checked to make sure no one was taking a shower or a crap, and I slipped through the bathroom and down the hallway.

Luckily, they were all standing around one of the TVs, watching and critiquing a porno.

"Eew, my ass looks like a Thanksgiving ham," one of the girls said.

"Forget about the size, what you need is a wax job."

"Fuck you!"

I silently opened the closet panel and grabbed the canvas bag that held all my worldly possessions. I couldn't head out the front door without any of them seeing me, so I crouched down and scuttled back through the bathroom and into the kitchen.

I stood by the stove for a while, not quite knowing what to do. Spontaneously, I picked up the phone and dialed the restaurant, and after one ring I heard my mother's familiar, *"Eggwoe WunLand, Mayhepyou?"*

I hung up fast, and wanted to cry.

Shit. I could see Fred's arm stretched across the kitchen doorjamb through the frosted glass door. There was no way I was going to get past them there, and I was too chicken to bust through and tell them all that I was leaving. Maybe they wouldn't care and would just watch as I tore out the door. But there was a possibility, at least in my imagination, that they'd link arms, catch me, and make me join their side, like we were playing porno Red Rover or something. I couldn't chance it.

And that's when I remembered the cave. I unlatched the door that I'd originally thought led to the pantry but was actually a stairwell down to the bridge that overlooked the spring. I snuck out onto the cool landing, treading down the stone steps with my hand against the wall so I wouldn't slip. After a few twists and turns of the staircase, I came to the bottom landing and walked out onto the stone bridge. I peered over the ledge and took a breath as I stared out to the trembling, green water.

Along the arched ceiling was a cable that held a dim lamp over the water. I could see about twenty feet ahead. Beyond that, I wasn't sure if I'd be able to find my way in the dark, but I did remember Fred saying that the spring led out beyond the main house.

It was my hope that if I followed the channel I'd eventually discover some opening that led outside. Hesitating for a moment, I placed my bag on the ledge. I climbed up and sat on the stone wall, trying to guess how far the drop was down to the water. I figured it was only about ten or fifteen feet, but I was still scared. I wondered how cold the water was, and how deep.

Dangling my legs over the gently rippling spring, my mind suddenly flashed to Auntie Melaura jumping from the Golden Gate Bridge. I looked at my shoes and thought of her shoes. I saw my shaking hands and thought of her hands. My skin was cold, and for a split second, my skin became her skin.

Winding the strap of my canvas bag around my wrist, I told myself that jumping would be just like hopping into the pool at North Beach Playground. I also reminded myself that the high divers at Pier 39 jumped way farther than this, and they managed to smile and wave as they dropped through the air.

I took a breath and pushed off the ledge. I fell faster and harder than I expected, but before I could think too much about it, I plunged into the cold, clear water.

Regardless of what the real temperature of the water was,

it felt freezing. My lungs were momentarily paralyzed and all my joints went stiff with shock. With tense limbs, I sank like a stone. In a panic, I flashed on the very real possibility that I might drown.

Out of sheer fright, I forced myself to start kicking my legs. After the initial wave of panic washed over me, my feet found the bottom. I was relieved to discover that the water wasn't that deep. It only came up to my collarbone. I realized I'd be able to walk and not have to swim through, which was a relief because I wasn't a great swimmer. Sloshing over to one side of the cave, I held my arm against the cold, clammy wall. After catching my breath, I wiped my hair off my face, and followed the length of the cavern, swooshing my legs through the bracing spring.

I held my bag to my chest and plowed through the water. Fairly quickly, I reached the distance of the dim lamp overhead, then I continued farther until it got difficult to see ahead. Keeping my hand against the slippery wall, I kept going until I came to an opening on the side of the cavern, a sort of ramp leading to a wide slot. At the end of it I could see the dusky sky. It was still a little bit light out, and I was grateful as I threw my bag up and attempted to hoist myself from the water and onto the ramp.

I was considerably heavier because my clothes and shoes were saturated, dragging me down. But I managed to push the top part of my body up. While I slithered onto the slanted slab, the surface was slick, and I couldn't get a foothold. I tried to scramble up with my feet, and in the process lost both of my stupid red jelly shoes.

I dared not look back to watch them drift away in the water because the act of twisting my neck would have caused me to slip back down. My wet nylon socks provided the small bit of traction I needed, and I crawled up completely out of the water, pretending I was *The Very Hungry Caterpillar* as I inched forward. I pushed my duffel bag in front of me, summoning the energy to boost it out of the slot. Poking out my head, I saw that I was in a field behind the stone house. I shimmied out off the ramp and through the opening, and soon was lying flat on the grass, looking up at the cornflower sky.

I took deep breaths, and felt my lungs open up little by little. I was sopping wet and freezing, but free. As I lay still, I felt like a small animal in the woods, a raccoon or badger, maybe. Sitting up, I shivered as I reached up to wring the water out of my hair and shirt. I wished I'd been able to hold my canvas bag above my shoulders so now my extra clothes might be dry, but I hadn't thought ahead. My hands shaking, I reached in to retrieve the sneakers. At least I had a spare pair of shoes, my red slippers having ended up God knows where.

Drenched to the skin, I stood up and headed down an embankment that led to a sidewalk out of sight from the house. I knew I looked like a miserable, drowned rat, but I didn't care because I'd escaped the melting pot of porn with my wits intact. I wondered where Ruby was. She was probably watching me from the Other Side, laughing her ass off.

I headed to the bus stop to wait for the 15 Third, figuring I'd get on and decide what to do from there. As I sat at the shelter, I dripped a large puddle of water onto the cement. But I did feel a little proud of myself. I didn't realize that my screwed up evening was about to get worse.

In Dreams I Smiled in Slow Motion

*E*ven though the bus was practically empty, it was warm inside. As darkness spread over the night sky, I watched the changing light through the bus windows and was glad to be headed back to parts of town I knew better. Beyond the silhouettes of garages and liquor stores, the sky had turned quickly from periwinkle to black, and I could no longer see where the bus was going.

Starting to thaw out even though my clothes were still wet, I began to relax. I told myself I just had to look out for Market Street because that's where I'd get off and catch the 19 Polk back home.

I knew I looked a mess and was glad that the bus driver didn't turn my way when I boarded. He was listening to a transistor radio, trying to tune in to a station, cursing at the dial. As I found a seat and sat down, instead of thinking of my adventure as a failed escape, I was just glad to be heading home. I hugged my wet canvas bag on my lap, watching for my stop.

Eventually, I recognized Market Street. I held the door open for someone behind me who was also getting off, and I walked to the corner to see if the 19 Polk was coming. It wasn't, which was typical. Wet, a little cold, and making a sloshing noise with each step, I walked up Larkin Street, wondering what might be in the refrigerator when I got home.

I was thinking about boys, but not in the way one might expect. Did boys' moms tell them not to talk to strangers, accept rides in cars, or walk in dark places? I recalled all the paranoid things my mom had told me so often over the years, like beware of *hom sup loes*, stay in groups, and to not bring attention to myself. Did all girls have it drilled into them to scan doorways up ahead for possible muggers? My mom had told me that a zillion times. I never walked too close to parked cars, and if I found myself walking behind someone, in particular other girls or old people, I made a point of making a small sound with the sole of my shoe so they might know someone was behind them and not get startled.

I was so looking forward to getting home that I was focusing several blocks ahead, glad to see the familiar neon signs that lit up my neighborhood. When I had just about reached the corner with the taqueria and the candy store, I noticed the sound of footsteps behind me and glanced quickly over my shoulder. It was a suburban-looking white guy with a doughy face wearing light-colored pants and a windbreaker. He was about half a block away, but still I felt a little nervous, so I crossed the street.

He crossed the street, too, and I could hear his steps quicken. I picked up the pace, but pretty soon, he was so close behind me I could feel the fronts of his shoes hitting the backs of mine. My heart started to race, and a second later, I actually tripped as his shoe caught my heel and pulled off my shoe a little.

"Oh, excuse me," he said.

"It's okay," I said, not looking at him but quickly slipping my finger into my shoe and fitting my heel back in.

I resumed speed-walking, and he followed.

"Say," he said casually, coming right up beside me, his hands in his jacket pockets. "You don't know where there's a movie theater around here, do you?"

"Um, the Royal. It's up there a ways." I hugged my bag to my chest. I didn't have a good feeling about this.

"Really, where?" He reached out and tried to grab my arm, but I twisted away.

"Oh, I'm sorry. I didn't mean to scare you. Slow down a minute, would ya?"

I didn't stop walking, but turned and looked at him. He had blond hair in a side part, and looked like one of the Beach Boys. Also, I noticed he was wearing Topsiders.

The street was completely deserted. There was just him and me, and a countless number of doorways, dumpsters, and dark places. I could feel my brain trying to think fast, telling myself that I knew what to do, but my mind couldn't conjure a thing.

But I did know this: This was different from the pitbulls at Pier 39 who wanted to bust my chink fucking face. This was different from the girls at St. Michael's who wanted to hurt me. He smiled and looked at me so nice I knew something Humbert-esque was unfolding.

I never really thought about it, you know. All the times my mom had said all her usual things to me, it never actually occurred to me that anything would really ever happen. Even when I was in the juggler's apartment, I didn't feel this way. I couldn't explain it, but this was different.

It was the feeling of dread. The way he'd grabbed for my

arm, the way his fingernails scratched across my skin told me he wasn't kidding. I knew he wasn't going to just go away and leave me alone.

I passed the candy store where I used to buy Cadbury eggs, and I was afraid.

"Do you want to go to the movies?" he asked. "C'mon, I'll pay." He nodded up to the adult theater in the middle of the block that sold sex stuff and dirty videos.

"No, thanks," I said, stuck in my politeness mode.

My mind was sludge. And as my thoughts slowed down to nothing, I simultaneously felt panic rising up my throat. What were you supposed to do if a bear attacked you? Could rabid dogs smell fear? Were you supposed to look them in the eye or curl up on the floor in a ball? I was still seven blocks from home and not a single pedestrian or car was in sight.

"Saw you on the bus. Looking good," he said, but by this time I was so paralyzed with fear that I didn't even answer.

I thought of my mother, and how she would say she told me so. She had been right. She'd been right all along and I never listened to her, and now my stupidity was going to make her worst nightmare come true. She would get to say, "I told you so, stupid, bad girl!"

My mother would say I got what I deserved for acting crazy. "Don't act craze" was one of her constant sayings. "Don't act craze." Had I been? Acting crazy, that is.

Wait. Wait, wait, wait, wait wait. Act crazy. My mom said there was one time when you *should* act crazy. She said if someone tried to rape you, to act crazy. Do disgusting things. Do sickening things. Make them not want you. They want you to be scared, but if you act crazy, you will scare them. Try it. Pick your nose. Wipe your boogers on them. Make noises.

So I did. I turned to Mr. Nice Guy and started to pick my

nose. He chuckled at first, but I didn't stop. I pretended to flick a booger his way and he made a bad face.

"Woomp, woomp, woomp," I said. "Boosh, plop, plop." I made all the Space Invaders noises.

"What are you doing?" he smiled, but I could tell he was confused.

"What are you doing?" he repeated, then he grabbed me by the shoulders and threw me against a parked car.

I wanted to cry. I wanted to cry. I wanted to cry.

"You want to get in the car?" He tried the handle, but the door was locked.

"We'll find another car," he said, shoving me. "There's gonna be some balling tonight."

When he'd pushed me, my canvas bag fell from my grasp, but the strap was wound around my hand. An ambulance down the street threw its siren, and when Mr. Beach Boy in his Topsiders reacted by jerking his head to the side, I threw my bag at him, and ran.

I'd like to say I threw the bag as hard as I could, but it ended up just being a toss, really. But it was enough to startle him, and even though he blocked it with his arm, it was enough for me to get away. He made a start to go after me, and even got a hold of my shirt for a second. But I was a good sprinter from all those baselines we'd run in basketball practice, and after just a quarter of a block, I could tell he wasn't following me. I didn't look back, but felt the air and the sidewalk beneath my feet.

Once I knew I had gotten away, I wanted to scream. But the scream wasn't something I wanted to release into the night. It was a scream that I wanted to use to crumble the pain I felt inside. The pain that came from wondering why anyone would want to hurt me. Why did being a girl mean having to dodge perverted bullshit?

I ran past H. Dumpty, Emerald Lily's, and Empress Wu's Antiques. Even though I'd only been gone a week, when I saw Eggroll Wonderland it looked different to me. And it wasn't just because of the fresh paint and new awning. For once, it didn't look depressing. The restaurant looked friendly with its yellow lettering and squeaky clean window that reflected the car lights. Either way, I was glad to be there. I got in using the key I kept at the very top of the doorsill for emergencies.

After sneaking into my room, I peeled off my wet clothes and got into my sleeping bag. I burrowed inside, zipping it all the way shut. I didn't even want to have my head poking out, so I pulled my flat pillow over the opening and I stayed huddled within, curled up tight and shivering, imagining I was the meat inside a pot sticker. No one could see me, smell me, or hear me. I was a cold, greasy dumpling sealed off from the world. And I would never come out.

Twinkie the Kid Rides Again

I stayed in bed for three days. I told my parents I was home early from basketball camp because I had sprained my ankle again. They believed me, and brought food to my room.

Outside my window it was sunny, but the bright blue sky and fierce sunlight only made me feel more afraid. It was like I could see the particles in the air, reverberating, and the liquid colors of the cars, people, trees, and buildings were trembling ever so slightly. I didn't open the window even a crack. The idea of breathing fresh air frightened me. The world was dangerous, and by breathing its air I feared it would somehow get in my lungs and scare me from the inside out. And if the tiniest air pocket could get inside me, I'd burst like a thin-membraned bubble.

At some point, my little brother came into my room. Holding up a cookie, he said, "Almost Home? It's a new brand. Soft and chewy."

"No thanks."

"On the rag?" he smirked.

I threw a shoe at him and he left.

That same afternoon, my dad came upstairs and asked me what I wanted to eat. I asked for an order of eggrolls.

He came back about ten minutes later and put the plate down on a little makeshift table they'd set up for me. At the sight of the little fried logs, my mouth watered, but I waited for my dad to leave before digging in.

Taking the plate and placing it on my lap, I examined the eggrolls. They were piping hot, and I could tell the cooking oil had been clean and fresh, without the slightly rancid smell that sometimes happened with old oil. Whoever had put them together did a good job of rolling them tight, too. The *pei* looked translucent and golden brown, with tiny blisters that made for crispiness.

I took a bite, and the first crunch was pure heaven. The cabbage was finely chopped, and the watercress added a delicious hint of spicy bitterness. I dipped the next bite into the red sauce, and the sweet syrup was oh-so-right. The eggroll skin crackled in my mouth as I savored the grease, the crunch, and the sugary dipping sauce, gnashing it all together between my molars.

I remembered when I was younger, I used to pretend to run away from home. I would yell at my mom, "I'll run away and you'll never see me again," but really I'd just go to Ruby's mom's antique shop, or to one of the other stores on Polk Street. Here in my room now, I felt quite the same as I had after my less elaborate runaway attempts, but only I knew that this time I'd meant it for real, and it just hadn't turned out like anything I'd imagined.

Who was a runaway, just like in the Afterschool Specials? Not a Chinese girl.

Who was a fairy princess? Not me.

Who was a virgin for sale, just like Brooke Shields in *Pretty Baby*? Pas moi.

I was Candace Ong from San Francisco, a waitress from Eggroll Wonderland, niece to Auntie Melaura who jumped off the Golden Gate Bridge, and friend to a dead girl named Ruby. I was the *Say, Say, Oh Playmate* schoolyard champ from fifth to eighth grades, a CYO basketball player, honor roll student, and the Commissioner of Finance.

Maybe I was Chinky the Fuckface, too. But I was o.k.

Eating the eggrolls made me feel like everything was going to be all right. I didn't feel so much like a throbbing, raw nerve, and I spent the rest of the afternoon playing with Twinkiechubs Four. She liked being petted and only bit me once. Although she drew blood, I didn't get mad, but just kept petting her the way I wished someone would pet me. Softly, tenderly, and reassuringly.

To Sing a Song of When I Loved the Prettiest Star

The next morning around ten, I finally decided I was ready to venture outside. Polk Street was fairly empty and the sky was overcast, the damp smell of night faintly lingering in the air. As I made my way down the sidewalk, the other odors of the street hit me like the familiar notes of a song. By Swan's Oyster Depot, the bleach and fish scents wafted by, as did the aroma of roasted coffee beans from the nearby café. Donuts, pizza, and urine were also in the air as I kept walking until I found myself staring in the window of Emerald Lily's.

I was going to get my jade necklace back. The haggy lady was inside, the one who'd tricked me into trading Auntie Melaura's jade for that shitty tiara that got trampled by the furry, gay satyrs. Stepping inside, I saw the same leopard-print leotards, faded jeans, feather boas, and silver gloves that were the store's mainstays. I walked right up to the jewelry case and began scanning for the gracefully carved rabbit that used to adorn my neck.

"Looking for something?" said Haggis.

"Yeah, do you remember me?"

She looked at me for a second. "No, sorry."

I didn't know if she was playing me, or was just a space cadet.

"I was here a couple of weeks ago," I said. "Traded a piece of jade for a tiara."

She looked at me from behind the counter and I could smell the booze and cigarettes. Her eyes were tired and her skin had that look of mushy, old oranges with big pores. I said, "I want it back. Where is it?"

She raised her strangely plucked eyebrows, as if surprised by my direct questioning.

"Oh," she said, "Now I remember you. You look a little different."

She fiddled with her bracelets, and peered through the case. "Hmm . . . let's see," she said. "I think, yeah. Afraid I sold it."

I must have looked pretty disappointed because she added, "Sorry. This Chinese lady said it was nice, and I said I don't usually carry that sort of thing, but she seemed pleased enough and scooped it right up."

I left the store, totally bummed out. I should have never taken that necklace off. Now it was gone and I would never get it back, and this really depressed me. Furthermore, even if it had been still at Emerald Lily's, it's not like I had any money. The cash I took out of the student council fund was in my canvas bag that I tossed at the Brian Wilson look-alike, would-be rapist. Now I was not only broke, but I was a thief. Or *feef,* as my brother would say. I had planned on putting that money back into the school's account. I really did. But now I couldn't.

Fear in check, with stupid optimism, I walked down by the candy store and taqueria where the guy had thrown me against the car. I thought there might be a tiny possibility that my canvas bag might've rolled under a bumper or might still be lying around somewhere, but of course I was wrong. I searched up and down the block, and even on the other side of the street, but there was no sign of my bag or any of the stuff that was in it. The bastard was probably holed up somewhere counting my cash and sniffing my panties at that very moment. Fucker.

So I went back home. I was planning on an afternoon of watching TV when my mom came upstairs and found me lying on my sleeping bag staring at the ceiling.

She said, "If you well enough go shop Poke Street, you well enough clean basement."

"What?" I said.

"You heard me."

I guessed she was no longer worried about my mopey suicide act. She was back to ordering me around, which was sort of all right with me.

"What's in the basement?" I asked.

"Some stuff from fire I save, not burn too bad. Bring all down there, but just in big pile. Need sort out. Throw away things that no good, see what can be save."

"Okay," I said.

She seemed pleased that I wasn't being too bratty, and I was glad she wasn't asking me about basketball camp, or anything at all that would require me to think over my file cabinet's worth of lies from the previous week, year, or even farther back than that. When she walked away, as usual she left my door open, which always really bugged me, but I was too lazy to get up and kick it shut. Instead, I drifted off to sleep.

I dreamed about Ruby. She was sitting on the floor at the foot of my sleeping bag, wearing the jade necklace Auntie Melaura had given me.

She said, "I want to tell you something. About me."

"Okay."

"It happened last summer. I was hanging out in my dad's club. You know, in San Jose? Well, I was kind of bored, and went into one of the storage rooms to take a nap. This guy who'd been watching me all night followed me in. We found some A&W cream soda, a bottle of whiskey, and some Styrofoam cups. After drinking for a while, I enjoyed being in that kind of tipsy state, you know, when you can pretend you're not responsible for whatever happens?"

I was about to tell her that I wouldn't know, having never been drunk myself. She went on.

"He was so in awe of my tits, poking them like a little kid. I giggled along with him, pretending to be more wasted than I was. But after a while, I guess I was pretty out of it. I mean, if I absolutely had to get up and run, like if the place had been on fire, I could've probably gotten up. I remember wiggling my toes, and for some reason that cracked us both up.

"There was a knock on the door and a couple of his friends came in. The next thing I knew, guys were unbuttoning my top and pinching me. They laughed nervously, daring each other to sniff my armpit or touch my pubic hair. I wasn't sure how far I wanted to go, but I just went with what was happening."

Ruby told her story nonchalantly, as detached as a reporter. Just listening to her, I was terrified. I thought about how cool Ruby always was in real life. She'd never shown me she was frightened, even if she was.

"The first guy that Did It to me, I watched his face, but he wouldn't look at me. Of all things, I thought about this one time when I was trying to pull off a wet, too-small swimsuit. It got twisted up and clung to my waist, and got all bunched up as I tried to pull my elbows out of the armholes. Doing It reminded me of that, mixed with the feeling of an Indian burn. They took turns, and I counted rows of Pepsi cans and waited for that tight swimsuit feeling to go away."

I was in a half-asleep state, and in the dream I could tell I was crying in real life because my half-awake self could feel the tears streaking down the side of my head, dripping into my ears.

"Why didn't you tell me?" I asked.

She chewed her lip. "Isn't there stuff you never told anyone?"

Her question echoed in my head. Was there stuff I never told anyone? Yeah, of course. Shit happened to me every day that I didn't tell anybody. A few months ago, an obese black guy on the bus wagged his pink tongue at me and then whipped out his crawling king snake. Jonny Killroy in sixth grade reached up my skirt once and tried to stick his finger in my butt when we were in the church pew singing about seraphims. I never told anybody about seeing Andrew's pinky rat, or the pitbull girls wanting to break my chink fucking face. I never talked about watching Ruby screw that W.P.O.D. in the forest, or putting Band-Aids in pot stickers when the restaurant was slow. It was my own secret that I was proud of making those free throws at the St. Michael's game. I didn't tell anybody any of that stuff. Not to mention my history of humping my stuffed animals at night.

"I don't want to be scared," I said to Ruby.

She was about to say something when a voice came over an imaginary loudspeaker.

"Ruby Ping, white courtesy telephone," it said. "Flight 69 leaving from gate 14."

"I have to go," she said.

I watched as she pulled on a powder-blue jacket. As I watched her gather up her matching luggage, I wasn't mad at her anymore.

"Will we always be friends?" I asked.

She adjusted her belt. "Of course not. I'm dead, stupid."

"Say 'hi' to Auntie Melaura for me."

"Promise," she said, and I woke up.

Lady from Another Grinning Soul

I sat up in bed and turned the dream over in my head. I got on my feet, grabbed a jacket, and headed out the door. Walking down the steps and into the cool air of Polk Street, I made my way down the block until I reached the familiar storefront of Empress Wu's Antiques. Cissy was standing behind the jewelry case staring into space like a pretty zombie. She looked at me as I came in and sat down in the chair by the door like I'd done a thousand times. When she used to see me, she would always say, "Ruby will be down in a sec." But this time she didn't say it. We just both stared straight ahead and kept each other company without talking.

We stayed that way for about twenty minutes. Then Cissy went into the back hallway and came back a few moments later. She had two 8 by 10 pictures in her hand. I stood up and walked over to her and she handed me one over the counter.

"Do you think that looks like Ruby?" she said.

I looked at the photo and saw a pretty Chinese girl in a

cheongsam and tiara. She wore a satin sash that read, "Miss Chinatown, USA."

"Is this you?" I asked, knowing it was. She did look like Ruby. Or rather, Ruby looked like her.

"Yeah," she said. "That was me. Later that same year . . . my best friend died."

She handed me the other photo. It showed her and three other girls all dressed in similar Chinese dresses, tiaras, and sashes. She pointed to the girl on her left.

"Second place," she said.

I felt a tingle run down the length of my spine. I knew who it was before Cissy even pointed her out. It was Auntie Melaura.

"She was my best friend," Cissy said quietly.

I digested this information, wondering why no one ever told me they had been friends. But I knew why. I didn't have to ask.

Don't ask questions. Mind your own business. Go to your room. Who wants to know? It was a long time ago. What difference does it make? None of my beeswax. Finish your homework and go to bed. That's why.

No one ever talked about anything, and no one ever would.

Cissy's face brightened and she shrugged off her melancholy. Like her old, chatty self she said, "Shoot, you know, your auntie was always much prettier than me. She always treated me like I was the good-looking one, but everyone knew she was the real beauty. No confidence, you know? And shit, she really should have won Miss Chinatown. But when the judges asked, 'What do you want to accomplish in life?' she went blank and stood up there and everyone stared at her.

Finally, she just said, 'I don't know. Nothing.' I shot her this look, like, 'Are you crazy, Melaura?' She blew it right there. You know those judges, so conservative, right? When it was my turn, I said I wanted to be a secretary. Pathetic, huh? But that's why I won."

I opened my mouth and started to say, "I miss . . ."

I wasn't sure if I was going to say Auntie Melaura or Ruby, but Cissy cut me off and said, "I know, I know. Me, too." She grabbed my hand and I could tell she didn't want us to say any more about either of them. We both missed both of them. As we squeezed each other's hands I knew neither of us could say anything more without turning into blubbering idiots. We stood there and held each other's hands for a long time. My eyes drifted down and through my tears I stared into the jewelry case, my eyes lingering on different things: a cinnabar brooch, a kingfisher feather-and-tourmaline hairpin, a gold coin, and . . .

My jade rabbit from Auntie Melaura. It was a deep green and there was a vein of smoky white along the left edge. I had worn it around my neck for six years. I knew it very well. I could practically feel it around my neck now, as if it had never left its place against my throat since the day Auntie Melaura gave it to me. As if I'd never traded it for that stupid rhinestone crown.

Cissy had been staring at me, watching me with curiosity. She reached inside the case, picked up the pendant with her delicate fingers and placed it on a satin pad.

"I picked this up down the street for practically nothing," she said. "Don't usually shop in those used places, but something told me to go in that day."

I touched it, and the rabbit felt like an old friend. The cold stone turned immediately warm in my hand. Did Cissy know? And if she did, I wondered how. Did she dream of Melaura the way I dreamed of Ruby?

"Go ahead and take it," she said.

I'd been wearing the empty chain by itself, and I undid the clasp, slipped the pendant through the gold loop, and fastened it on. Feeling its weight at my throat, I was about to say thanks, but Cissy waved me away. Her mascara started to run and I could tell she'd begun to cry.

As for me, I was tired of crying. I walked out the door, and as the Quan Yin statue gave me a lotus-pout smile, I smiled back.

Before You Start Professing that You're Knocking Me Dead

*B*ack at home, my mom was screaming like her usual, pre-menopausal self.

"Didn't I tell you to clean out basement?"

"Yes, *Mother*." I smiled at my own sarcastic tone. I was having a laugh, playing the only role anyone expected me to play—that of the surly, disgruntled teen. But I didn't care. It was all a stupid game, and I felt, at least, I was ahead for once.

I walked through Eggroll Wonderland, out to the back by the garbage cans, and down another flight of stairs that led to the old basement. There was a slight smoky smell still, and as I unlocked the door, the odor was even more pronounced. My mom had thrown a lot of stuff in there and it was heaped in haphazard piles: chairs that were damaged but not completely ruined, boxes full of extra napkin dispensers, salt and pepper shakers, burned-out woks, stainless steel trays, and 5-gallon tubs filled with ladles, spatulas, and other oversized utensils with burned and bent handles.

There was stuff from our apartment, too. Boxes full of old towels and sheets that she'd saved from the closet, some ugly clothes from ten years ago that she refused to get rid of, an old blender, a toaster, and storage bins from the inside of the refrigerator. She'd even saved the scorched and warped remains of our burlwood coffee table. I saw the metal frame of my old twin bed, some toy golf clubs of Kenny's, even a couple of orange tracks from the Hot Wheels set, except the plastic had melted. Maybe my mom was saving them for future whippings of my ass. I scoffed at the thought. I wasn't going to let anybody hit me again.

I started sorting boxes, separating them into restaurant stuff and house stuff. Digging through, I was hoping to find some of my old cassettes and records, but there were none. I did, however, find my Etch-A-Sketch, Wham-O Magic Window, and my old copy of *Where the Wild Things Are* with its pages warped and singed at the edges.

And then I saw it.

Pink spoiler. Magenta racing stripes. White-wall tires and a melted front fender. Googly-eyed flamingoes on the sides from when I was in my sticker phase. Yes, yes, YES.

Barbie Corvette you are mine. You are right there, and were here all along.

I reached into the box, beneath the rusty, busted desk fan. As I lifted the Corvette out I didn't dare think the money was still there, in a roll in the back wheel-well. Bracing myself, I flipped the car over.

Yes! Stuck in there, crammed in there, rolled up in tinfoil and tied with a rubber band that was twisted, dirty, and crusty.

I yanked the axle out of its plastic clip, and pulled out the wad of cash. I peeled back the foil and knew it was all there, all $736. I could go to Hibernia Bank and pay back Mrs. Martin now. I wasn't a *feef*. Are you there, God? It's me Candace. Thanks, Man!

Still Tougher than Diamonds

Sitting at the kitchen table, I was watching the butter pool in its dish, the yellow fat glistening after hours in the bright sun. It was six o'clock and still sunny out, and although it was hot and stuffy inside, I didn't bother to open the window. My father's reading glasses, smudged and greasy with fingerprints, were lying face down on the table, but I didn't flip them over. The Roman Meal bread was steamed up in the plastic bag, but I didn't care if it got rotten.

I had swiped some Pop Rocks from Kenny's room and poured half the packet in my mouth. The intense sizzling and crackling of the carbonated candy was making my whole face tingle. I found a wayward chopstick on the table and stuck it inside the foil pouch to retrieve every last speck until I cleaned out the whole pack. Then I was bored again.

I decided to get some fresh air, and ducked out the door. Out on the street, an awning was being repaired. Pink and black, in pretty cursive it read, *Still Tougher than Diamonds.* I stopped to watch a guy squeegeeing dirt off of it, and just then a Vespa putt-putted down the street. I watched the driver's hair blowing, dirty and sleek.

It was Andrew Fink. He scowled as he made his way through traffic, not seeing me. I pretended that I didn't see him either, my would-be boyfriend and designated molester had Ruby not lured him away. It didn't matter now, anyway.

It seemed really far away, that day he and I had made out. As his scooter sputtered down the street I didn't care to stop him or ask if he knew about Ruby. I didn't want to talk to that asshole about her. I didn't want his diddly piddliness staining the pictures I had in my head.

I kept walking. Ducking into Rooks and Becords, I made my way to the children's section and flipped through some old picture books that used to be my favorites. I picked up an old heavy one and turned to a double-page illustration of village youngsters following the pied piper. The piper was on the left side with the mountains and twilight sky, and on the right side of the book were the scampering children. The space between them disappeared into the middle of the bookbinding.

Staring at the double-page image, I bent back the book's front and back covers, putting strain on the spine. I wanted to see where the picture disappeared into the crevice of the binding. There was a girl I couldn't see in there, hidden where the book came together.

Holding the book this way and that, I needed to see the girl's face. All I could make out was one sad eye and the hem of her Swiss Miss outfit. I could also see the corner of her puckered cherry mouth. The other kids on the right were youngsters but she seemed on the edge of something older. As I scrutinized the picture, I was convinced that if I could only see down into that book's spine I'd find out something, something about the border where kid life and pubescent gore started to blur.

The book was so thick, I couldn't see the girl without tearing it apart. It was an old book and I didn't want to damage it, so I stopped short of ripping the pages. Meanwhile, a clerk peered down the aisle, making sure I saw him in case I was thinking of shoplifting something.

I put the book back and headed into the record section, pausing to look at the album cover for *The Soft Parade*. I thought of the line, "The men don't know, but the little girls understand." Could Jim Morrison possibly have been talking about me? I wondered just what it was I was supposed to understand by now.

I left the store and decided to walk into Chinatown. I hiked over the hill into North Beach, then crossed over Columbus Avenue into the land of the black-haired people who all looked like me.

I knew that both Ruby and the spectral version of her were gone for good because I didn't see any Chinatown ghosts. I walked by the Chinese Playground, Cameron House, and several pagoda-shaped telephone booths. No ghosts. Something told me to keep walking, and eventually I ended up in the alley where Ruby had showed me the ghost-corpses of the slave girls.

I remembered her pointing out a munchkin-sized doorway, and how she said it was the exit from which a few lucky slavegirls escaped. I looked down and saw a rotted plank of wood. I leaned over and gave it a little tug, but the rusty, square-headed nails were unyielding.

When Ghost Ruby and I had come here, she'd said that the brick tunnel led from that building where we'd seen the ghost in the rowboat. I imagined that the passage was really narrow, and the girls had to turn sideways to shimmy their way out. Maybe some girls had to stay lodged in there for days, until it was safe to go out into the street. I wondered if they had to stay in there with the rats and the drippy rainwater, with the stench and the sweat.

I spoke too soon when I said I didn't see any ghosts that day. As I stood there staring into space, I jumped back when I saw a little girl-ghost crawl out from behind the wooden plank. She was wearing a silk band around her forehead and a dirty cotton outfit. Another taller girl followed behind her, and soon another girl, then another followed. The whole alley was filled with transparent Chinese girls, shimmying out from the passageway, running off on skinny legs, and disappearing halfway up the alley. They giggled and shouted to each other in Chinese, and their high voices drifted up to the sky. I watched them as they delighted in their new freedom, and for the first time in a long while, I felt a little happy.

Give Us a Smile
Before You Vanish Out of View

There was only one week left of summer and I had to admit, by now I didn't think too much about Ruby Ping or all the stuff that had happened over the last couple of months. The one other time I went to Chinatown, all I saw were shopkeepers, tourists, and people going about their daily business of buying *bok choy* and bitter melons. I even went to the alley where all the ghost-girls had breezed past me, but I didn't see them anymore. I only heard the laughter of real girls who were playing Chinese jump-rope on the sidewalk.

Ruby the Ghost had gone, having finally caught her flight. I didn't feel her presence, smell her beef-breath, or feel her watching me. Strangely enough, when I saw Cissy or Mr. Ping, we hardly looked at each other long enough to get sad about her being dead. In a weird way, maybe we all had to act like she never existed at all in order to get on with our lives. It was like a pact. If one of us acknowledged her, we'd all lose our stupid little heads.

If I stopped in Empress Wu's Antiques to visit, Cissy and I talked about the weather or her new merchandise. I acted like I hadn't walked behind that beaded curtain, upstairs and across the lumpy runner and over the dead ferns a thousand times before to go visit Ruby in her messy room that smelled like corn chip socks. I wondered if Cissy finally cleaned Ruby's room and turned it into something else, like a library, or maybe she left it the way it was. I didn't ask and didn't want to ever go back there again.

Likewise, when Mr. Ping came to collect rent, I never mentioned the two creepy nights I spent at his house with him and his spooky old mother. He never acknowledged with even a sad glance that he had had an only daughter who was my best friend. He said hello and I said hello back, and that was all.

And just like how my parents never mentioned Auntie Melaura, they never mentioned Ruby either. She never existed, and quicker than even I would have expected, I buried my memories and feelings of her.

It was easy because there was a lot to do. My parents were happy because they were in negotiations to buy Eggroll Wonderland from Mr. Ping, who was going to put his time into his properties in San Jose. And I was preparing for the new school year, buying textbooks and getting a head start on my reading list.

There was a time when I wanted to be dumb and pretty, and a period when I thought it would be safer to be smart and ugly. Now I figured I didn't want to be a total dogface, but I decided to concentrate on being a brainiac. It was a lot easier to decipher integers than to think of my summer of one-eyed pinky rats and would-be molesters. I stopped going to Pier 39, and put the whole summer behind me.

The day of my fifteenth birthday was also freshman orientation at my new school. Arriving at Lowell, I walked through the door and the black dot that was my head joined a sea of other black dots. There were lots of other Chinese kids there, and even though they looked normal and happy to me, I wondered which of them had had weird summers, too. Kids with Hello Kitty and Gobots backpacks, Rubik's Cube keychains, and Trapper Keepers clamored through the halls. I didn't look any different from them so I figured, yeah, at least some of them had been through freaky shit, too. I felt a twinge of envy for the clueless-looking ones, the skinny mole-voles with thick glasses and violin cases. But the more I looked at them, I noticed that even they had darting, tortured-rabbit eyes.

I saw Bruce Fung in line and we compared schedules.

"Hey, we both have Spanish third period," he said. "Let's try to sit together."

"Okay," I said, glad for at least one friend in this new place.

As I made my way to my homeroom, I nervously touched my jade necklace. Looking at the other kids standing around, I wondered what the coming year would bring. When I reached the end of the hall, I thought I heard someone call my name, and the voice sounded like Ruby's, but I didn't turn around as I walked through the door.

Ruby was dead and I was here. I hugged my Pee-Chee to my chest and took a deep breath. I was in high school and it was a brand new year. I was gonna never look back, walk tall, and act fine.

Kim Wong Keltner

When **KIM WONG KELTNER** isn't writing, she collects Chinese porcelain and plays Whack-a-Mole. She lives in San Francisco with her husband and daughter, whose first words were "capybara" and "museum quality."